2

SHARES
AND OTHER FICTIONS

BOOKS BY
RICHARD STERN

GOLK

EUROPE, OR UP AND DOWN
WITH BAGGISH AND SCHREIBER

IN ANY CASE
(reissued as THE CHALEUR NETWORK)

TEETH, DYING AND OTHER MATTERS

STITCH

HONEY AND WAX

1968: A SHORT NOVEL,
AN URBAN IDYLL,
FIVE STORIES
AND TWO TRADE NOTES

THE BOOKS IN
FRED HAMPTON'S APARTMENT

OTHER MEN'S DAUGHTERS

NATURAL SHOCKS

PACKAGES

THE INVENTION OF THE REAL

A FATHER'S WORDS

THE POSITION OF THE BODY

NOBLE ROT. STORIES 1949–1988

SHARES AND OTHER FICTIONS

SHARES
AND OTHER FICTIONS

RICHARD STERN

delphinium books

harrison, new york

encino, california

For Alexander Baron, in hopes that in ten or fifteen years, he'll be able to read, perhaps even enjoy, this book of his loving grandfather.

Library of Congress Cataloging-in-Publication Data
Stern, Richard G., 1928–
    Shares and other fictions / by Richard Stern.
        p.   cm.
        ISBN 0–671–78040–9 : $20.00
        I. Title.
    PS3569.T39S53   1992
    813'.54—dc20   91-48140
                                                    CIP

First Edition   All rights reserved
10 9 8 7 6 5 4 3 2 1

Published by delphinium books, inc.
P.O. Box 703
Harrison, N.Y. 10528

Distributed by Simon & Schuster
Printed in the United States of America

Jacket Design by Milton Charles
Text design by Milton Charles
Production services by Blaze International Productions, Inc.

Some parts of this book appeared in more or less different form in the following publications:
"The Illegibility of This World" in *Commentary*, February 1992. Reprinted by permission.
"The Degradation of Tenderness" in *Bostonia*, Summer 1992.
"Veni, Vidi . . . Wendt" first appeared in *1968: A Short Novel, an Urban Idyll, Five Stories and Two Trade Notes* from Holt, Rinehart and Winston © 1968, 1970. Reprinted by permission.
"A Share of Nowheresville" in the *Chicago Tribune Magazine* May 5, 1991. Reprinted by permission.
"Obie and Jocko" in *The Antioch Review*, Volume 49, Number 4, Fall 1991 copyright © 1991. Reprinted by permission.
"Del Plunko Performs" in *Paris Review* 129, January 1992. Reprinted by permission.
"The Beautiful Widow and the Bakery Girl" in *Literary Out-Takes*, ed. by Larry Dark, Ballantine Books, © 1990. Reprinted by permission of Ballantine Books, a Division of Random House, Inc.
"In a Word, Trowbridge" in *The Antioch Review*, Volume 48, Number 2, Spring 1990, copyright © 1990. Reprinted by permission.
The author remains grateful to Easley Blackwood for composing the tune now on page 88, and the two bars of music on page 88.

CONTENTS

I·TWO STORIES
THE ILLEGIBILITY OF THIS WORLD   3
THE DEGRADATION OF TENDERNESS   23

II·A SHORT NOVEL
VENI, VIDI . . . WENDT   43

III·SHARES: A NOVEL IN TEN PIECES
A SHARE OF
NOWHERESVILLE   111
OBIE AND JOCKO   118
A SHARE OF
GEORGETOWN   128
GEORGE FINDS BUG   134
THE WALL   140
VENICE   143
THE DEPUTY'S VISITORS   160
REG IN VENICE   168
VENICE BY AIR   172
A SHARE OF THE PACIFIC   179

IV·TWO STORIES
THE ANAXIMANDER FRAGMENT   185
IN A WORD, TROWBRIDGE   196

PART·I

TWO
STORIES

THE ILLEGIBILITY OF THIS WORLD

Tugged by sunlight and the phone from a dream about populating the universe with sperm; a spaceship stocked with fertile cells unloading on empty planets with the blueprints of civilization; the humanization of the universe. "Yes?"

"Mista Biel. Deejay."

"Jeesus. What time is it?"

"Comin on nine, cep you put the clock back. Joo member to do that?"

Did I? "Yes." On the table, the knowing pine face of the clock, gold fingers at VII and X. "It's ten of seven."

"Rilly eight."

"How many times, Deejay?"

"Was finkin you wanted those leaves up."

"The leaves, yes, me, no."

"You doan want me to come over?"

"I should say 'No'."

"No?"

"No, come on over."

"I be over haf'n hour." This could mean three hours or the next day, depending on whom he ran into or what; what bottle, that is.

"You don't need to ring. You've got the garage key."

"I need mawr bags."

Ellen wanted me to get rid of him. "Never darken our door again." I can't. We're the last people on the block for whom he can work. He botches most tool jobs. Still he can fetch, lift, carry, mow the lawn, pick up leaves, he's not stupid, he's honest, he's not always drunk; I like him. "I'll put some on the porch."

This weekend, between the World Series and Halloween, I'm alone. Ellen's in Buffalo for our daughter Annie's thirty-sixth birthday. Friday, I drove her to Midway, then went downtown to my one-room office on Adams, checked the markets, bought a Kansas City municipal, faxed a letter to our insurance agent, sent copies of our living wills to our granddaughter—old enough now to be in on it, who knows, she might be the one to unplug the tubes—and walked five blocks to the Pub Club for the best hour of the day, lunch at the Round Table on the eleventh floor looking over the silver river and the blue bulge of the State of Illinois Building.

I've been a club member thirty-five years. It's more important than ever now that I've retired. I used to ridicule my Uncle Bert's life, a shuttle between the City Athletic Club and his rooms at the Hotel Warwick across the street. I thought that twenty-five yard shuttle the icon of his narrowness and ignorance. Now my life resembles his. I arrive early enough— 11:45—to insure a seat at the Round Table. (It's gauche to turn up earlier, but if you come as late as 11:50, the table's full and you take your chances with less congenial company.) The table doesn't have the best view, but I've had enough scenic views in my life. I hunger for the day's stories, for jokes, for the latest aches, grandkids, market tips, slants on the news.

We usually start with stories in the *Wall Street Journal*, the *Trib* and *The New York Times*. Royko's column gets big play from us. International, national, local news, the latest this or that. We've got fellows who follow science, books, the arts, we're all readers and TV watchers. Mondays we go over the Bears' game. We cover restaurants, travel, we're a worldly bunch. We know each other's formsheet, we have roles: I'm the left-winger; three or four of us are political neanderthals basically unhappy that Gorbachev has changed the old game. Two regulars have been Assistant Secretaries (one of State, one of Commerce) and one of us was on Reagan's Economic Council; we feel we're privy to inside dope. Anecdotes about politics in Washington and Chicago are one of our stocks-in-trade.

The talk I prefer is personal. Friday, we talked about fathers: time has cleared mine of wrong, translating his naiveté into honesty, his timidity into modesty. I told how he read the morning *Times*, so lost in it he flicked cigarette ash into his coffee and drank without blinking. No one laughed. I described his going down the elevator in his pyjamas, forgetting his address in a taxi. I drew another blank: the Round Tablers know what's around our own corners. We've all had operations. Bill Trask's back curls with osteoporosis, Harlan Schneirman's lip from last year's stroke. Death bulletins are a regular, if unstressed, feature of our talk.

Of his father, Harry Binswanger says, "I shcarcely knew him." Though he's been in America more than forty years, German phonemes pass in and out of his speech. Till he retired, he was my dentist, a good one, though Dr. Werner, my dentist since, says my mouth was in poor shape when I came to him. Harry—it used to be Heinz—is large, clumsy, thick-fingered. I felt secure with the heft of his fingers around my jaw, though they may have handicapped the delicacy of his bridge and canal work. I've heard something of his history for twenty-five years, but there's always more to know. Nor do I mind listening to what's familiar. (I'd have to leave the Round Table if I did.) Harry's parents divorced when he was eight. He visited his father in Mainz every Christmas. "Muzzer sent him my presentss. He unwrappd zem, showed me vat they vur, zen mailed zem back." Harry shook his head, a semaphore of passed anger. "He vass eggcentric, eggcitable, unshtable, couldn't make a liffing. Muzzer's fazzer said she deserfed vat she got, marrying 'a *hergelaufenen Juden*,' 'a Jew from God knows vere.' Fazzer had a farm near zuh Neckar Riffer. He bought turkeyss; zey drowned; he bought marigoldss—he luffed flowerss; zuh riffer flooded zem; he bought pigss; zey broke out of zuh penss. Grandpa said, 'Not even pigss vill stay viz him.' He became a portrait photographer, but vass no good viz children. He vanted a picture uff me on zuh riffer, crying. I vouldn't sit on zuh raft. He tied me zere, slapped my face: 'Now cry.' He put his photographss in—vat-do-you-say?—a cabinet viz a glass front. *Vitrine*.

Tough kidss—Nazi toughss—broke it. He said, 'It's time to get out.' He vanted to go to Brassil. He'd been born in Bufovina, zuh Rumanianss lost his paperss. At zuh Emigration Office zey said, *'Für uns, bestehen sie gar nicht.'* 'For us, you don't exist.' He vuss schtuck. Somehow he made it srough zuh var. I saw him after, vonce. He lived in a basement room, zuh rest of zuh block vuss wrecked. Outside his vindow vur a few inches of dirt viz sree zinnias.''

Driving back home along the lake by the Museum of Natural History, it struck me that Harry's in-and-out German accent was his mind's way of preserving that *hergelaufener* father of his, even as his stories turned him into comic relief.

Ellen called at eight o'clock. "How're you doing?"

"Fine. I warmed up the chicken. Delicious. How's Annie?"

She was fine, so were Chuck and little Anne, the Buffalo weather was being its notorious self; the plane was an hour late. "Take care, dear," she said. "I'll see you Monday."

"You'd better."

Though it was nice to be alone, a hue of freedom I hadn't noticed that I hadn't noticed. At the same time, the house felt loose around me, slightly spooky.

In my leather armchair, I read a new book about an escaped prisoner and stopped at a German phrase I didn't understand. (The second time today.) *"Die Unlesbarkeit dieser Welt."* *The illegibility of this world.* The German pleased me, and I repeated the words till they felt at home on my tongue. Their author, a poet named Celan, was born—another coincidence—in Rumania. His mother was killed in a death camp—the phrase suddenly made sense—and, decades later, he drowned himself in the Seine.

There's a quiver in my pleasant self-sufficiency; but I am comfortable, snug, taken care of. (Because I've taken care?) Who knows, maybe Harry's father, in his basement, looking out at his zinnias, felt the same; having survived what so few had might have been his comfort. Harry himself had been sent to Amsterdam, and, like Anne Frank, hidden. After the war, unlike Anne, he'd gone to a Dutch school. Had I forgotten, or never known, how he'd gotten to America, this man with whom I'd spent five or six hours a week for twenty-five years, whose hands had been in my mouth, to whom I'd paid thousands of dollars?

Saturday morning, I drove up to see my son, Peter. He'd moved again, the third time in five years. He gets bored with a neighborhood, seeks what he calls "action." A large, rangy boy—I shouldn't say boy, he's thirty-two—with lots of energy, he's chosen to be a salesman because he can't sit still. He sells polyvinyl traffic cones and is on the road three weeks a month. He doesn't much like the job, or any other he's had. The routines of money-making, the hierarchy of business authority, the cheerleading and critiques of salesmanship, the ups and downs of sales, go against his grain. And grain he has. As a boy, he was exceptionally gentle; in adolescence, he assumed a roughness which I felt contradicted his nature. He's still rough, argumentative, sarcastic, but now he mocks the roughness and regards it as a comic scurf he can remove at will. Deep down—whatever this means—is the gentle boy he was at five and six; very lovable.

A year after he graduated from the University of Illinois in Champaign he married a girl he met in a singles bar; a year later they divorced. He asked his mother and me why we hadn't stopped him from marrying. "Couldn't you see it was a mistake?"

His mother said she'd suspected it, but what could she do? I said, "I liked Louise."

Ten years and many girls later he's still unsettled. I ask him, "How long can you go on being Casanova?"

"Envious?"

"A little. Mostly worried. Not just about disease. This is a critical decade of your life. Squander it courting, you'll end up like the queen in *Alice in Wonderland*, just where you are."

"What's wrong with that?"

"I don't mind, but I think you do."

His new apartment is on the first floor of a redbrick six-flat on one of the thousand tree-lined, quiet streets which root Chicago in a domestic independence which gets it through bad times better than the other industrial cities around the Lakes: Cleveland, Detriot, Erie.

The front door is open, he's been watching for me. I follow

him into a bright room with an old couch, an armchair, a stack of pictures leaning against the wall, boxes of books and dishes. There's a stereo, no TV. "I don't want to get addicted." His addiction is bars, music, girls, cigarettes. There are four rooms, all in more or less the same tumbled shape, though the kitchen has a built-in orderliness. "Nice," I say. "It's light, the rooms are a good size, it's a pretty street. How much're you paying, may I ask?"

"Five hundred."

"I should move down here myself."

"Too much action for you."

"Not that I can see. Except for the hurricane that hit your place."

"Come back in two weeks, it'll be immaculate. Ready to play?"

Now and then he consents to play tennis with me. I've been playing over half a century, and still get around pretty well. I know where the ball's coming and get it back. Peter has speed and power, and when he's playing well, doesn't give me any points, but I can frustrate him with tenacity and junk shots. Then he starts slamming balls out, or laughs so hard he misses them altogether. Now and then he gets angry—"*Hit* the goddamn ball"—but rarely, and I enjoy playing with him. Since I had a hernia operation a couple of years ago, the old sweetness of his boyhood comes through, and he's been easy on me. There's also some—I suppose classic—resentment. As we drive a few blocks to public courts on Montrose, he tells me what a lucky life I've led. "You retired early, you've had a good marriage, you've got a granddaughter, and except for that hernia, you haven't been sick; you still play tennis, you liked your job, you've got some dough, you haven't been hassled—"

"The demographics were in my favor. No baby boom."

"Right. I'm one of too many."

"I wasn't much of a boomer."

"Two's more than enough."

There's some sibling resentment, though he and Annie are good friends.

It's a bit chilly. I keep my windbreaker on, but play well, serve hard and hit good backhands. I run Peter around the court, which he needs. He sets up the game so he has to chase around. Life cramps him. He spends too much time in cars, writing reports, closed up in his apartment, in bars. On vacations he goes to national parks where he climbs or paddles white water. A few times he's gone to the Alps and the Pyrenees. But it's not enough for him.

Sometimes I feel that I stand in his way, a wordless—usually wordless—rebuke to his life. Then too I was off a lot on sales trips—neckwear, accessories—when he grew up; he missed me and I think he thinks I sacrificed him. The travel seemed more romantic to him than the chore it was. He thinks I've seen much more than I have, know much more than I do. I feel that he hardly knows me at all, which I don't mind. Should fathers and sons know each other? Or love each other? Well, I love him, though there are gaps of cold in all affection. Yet if the love isn't constant, it is recurrent. That should be enough for security, shouldn't it?

I win the set, 6–3. A rarity. We play another, and I don't win a game. I'm delighted. I always either try hard or appear to try hard, but it's been years since I've wanted to do better than Peter at anything. I want him to have what I've had and more. Above all, I want him to have—to want to have, and have—a child.

Back at his place, I clean up in the bathroom, he washes himself at the kitchen sink. He comes into the living room, the towel working over his wet body. I haven't seen him naked for years, and I'm a little shocked. He's very hairy, has a bit of a belly. This man, who as a boy looked like an angel, is into middle age. I look away. I don't want to see him this way. There's a book open on the beaten couch, I move it and sit down. "What's this?" I ask. He's got on his jockey shorts. His legs are enormous, they should be running up and down basketball courts or hills.

"Kafka," he says.

"Never really read him. Good stuff?"

"Not exactly." He's buttoning a blue shirt. "You ought to read that one."

" 'Ought to'?"

"You'd understand me better."

"Maybe that's not a good idea. What's it about?"

"Read it. Take it home. But return it. I need it for my sessions."

"Your doctor's paid to understand you. All I have to do is love you."

He's put on blue jeans. "What's to love?"

"I'd better read it."

He's putting on white socks and sneakers. "How do you know it's me you love if you don't understand me?"

"That's too complicated. Do you have to understand *me* to love *me*?" As soon as I say this, I feel the discomfort of presumption. Maybe he doesn't love me. Love's too big a word anyway. It's used much too often. Morons in front of microphones hold out their arms to millions they never met and cry, "I love you." All they mean is, "How wonderful to be shining up here." I never talked about love with my wife or children, my parents didn't with me, and I'm grateful. Love was assumed. A million feelings were bunched up in it.

I'm against all domestic analysis, I'm against understanding. That word also means too much. You understand a request, a situation, but how do you understand a person? You reduce him, that's how. Do I understand myself? Does Harry Binswanger understand his father? In a way, yes, because he hardly knew him. That is, he turned his father into a little vaudeville act, a comic handle that lets him carry the hot pan around. Why did he remember "For us you don't exist"? Because of his own fright that his father didn't exist for him, except as some snapshots of intimidation and pathos. Not enough, he knows it's not enough. Peter and I have had thousands and thousands of moments with each other, many of them, maybe most of them, charged with something you can call love. But the word itself is just a convenience, a pigeonhole that can't really hold the complexity of it all.

His blue-shirted arms lie on the seamed, brown arms of the chair; he looks as big as Lincoln in the Memorial. He says, "I'm paying through the nose to find out if I'm capable of loving anyone."

That night, back in my armchair, I read the book. Had to force myself through it, though it's short, sixty or seventy pages, a story about a salesman, the support of his parents and sister, who wakes up one morning transformed into a huge bug. He can't go to work, they pound on his door, the chief clerk of the office comes to fetch him. (It's rather ridiculous.) Naturally he astounds, terrifies and disgusts his parents and the young sister who for a while takes care of him, bringing him the rancid leftovers he prefers to fresh food. In time he annoys them so much, they want him to die; when he does, they're released and happy.

Now what in God's name makes Peter think that this *Metamorphosis* story has anything to do with him? In the kitchen, I open a bottle of red wine, pour a third of it into a water glass, clip and light a cigar, and go back to my chair to think it out.

In the first place, Peter's never supported us. *Au contraire*, though in the last three years he's made a point of not taking money from me at Christmas and his birthday. Still, he knows I'm there, ready to help him. "I helped your sister when she and Chuck bought the house, and I want to help you when you're ready to buy." I wouldn't dream of his sharing, let alone taking, a check in a restaurant. All right, then, what's the similarity? Does he feel like a bug? Have his mother and I made him feel like a bug? Does he disgust us? Do we want him dead? Absurd. I sit puffing, sipping. Beyond this lamplit circle, it's dark. Here, it's warm, comfortable, charged with the warm pleasure of the wine, the special, bittersweet fullness of the smoke; yet my heart's hammering away. Clearly, Peter feels that he's inadequate, repulsive. What's askew in this boy of mine?

Or is he putting it on, dramatizing himself, using the author's own self-dramatics as his crutch? (But the author invented these things, and, I think, thought they were funny. There is something funny about it.)

I went to the desk and wrote a note.

Dear Peter,

You're no bug, and I hope I'm not a bit like that pompous, cringing, bullying, self-righteous father. I don't see this story as a key to you. Maybe you can explain it to me. You can do it over the best lunch in Chicago, or in one of your bars. You choose.

Love—if that's still a permissible word,
Dad

I'm on my way upstairs to draw a bath when I wonder what the word actually means. *Metamorphosis*. I go down again, lift out the heavy—eight pounds, I once weighed it on the bathroom scale—first volume of the Compact Edition of the OED, for which we joined the Book of the Month Club about twenty years ago. I polish the big magnifying glass on my pants and read *Change of form*, from the Greek.

Upstairs, as I unbutton my shirt, I feel restless. I need a walk. I button up, put on a sweater, exchange my moccasins for the springy walking shoes Annie gave me last Christmas, and, downstairs, put on the black leather jacket young people on the street or in stores look at in surprised approval. (Sometimes they say something like "Niice.") I pat my pocket to make sure the key's there—I don't want to be stuck outside with Ellen in Buffalo. I hope she doesn't call when I'm out, getting the answering machine, worrying that I'm looped around a lamppost on the Outer Drive.

The relief of the air, the dark. There's moonlight after the early evening shower, the oak tree on the lawn has shed its last leaves, they're thick on the lawn, a sea of shapes. The branches are transformed by bareness, a predeath bareness. Lucky, in a great city, to live on a street that registers the seasons so clearly.

The cold air feels wonderful. The small lights of the small houses, the interrogative iron curl of the lampposts, the pools of moonlight on the metal skin of the cars; beautiful. I don't want to leave this. After my operation, I was so fatigued I didn't care about living or dying. Only the idea of leaving Ellen kept me going. Now I understand what I'd laughed at in the obit column this week, the eighty-nine year old mogul, William Paley, asking people why he had to die. I know life usually wears you down and you're ready to go. Not with him. Not with me.

A *Trib* piece said Paley was a rat, sold out everyone who loved or helped him, took credit for everything; in short, a perfect dead horse for newspaper whips. Is egomania what keeps you alive? Maybe for tycoons. I don't need an empire. Leaves are enough, the moon, the air.

I walk through the bank parking lot, I turn left on Dorchester. The maples are half-full of pumpkin-colored leaves. (Are the ones still there the Paleys?) Pumpkins are lit on porches. The confidence in these houses. Chairs, lamps, bookshelves, the purple flair of TVs.

I'm the only one on the street. No, up ahead, someone coming. Should I turn? No. Courage. A black man in a raincoat, eyeglassed; a fellow burgher. We should say "Good evening," the way they do in small towns, but we don't. We just pass each other, relieved. I round the brick six-flat on the corner. Back on my block a couple I know stands on their porch, white man, black woman. I don't know their names. I wave, she waves.

My block.

In the bath, my body looks heavy, fattish, knees big, dingus floating in soapy foam. God, man's ugly. No wonder people write about metamorphosis. My body. Peter's. My body forming his, my mind—whatever that is—his. Chromosomes, genes, strings of sugar and protein generating versions of themselves which somehow become others. There's some of Uncle Bert in me. Is it why I live as he did? Transmission. This floating dingus rose to Ellen's innards and generated Annie, and later Peter. Annie's Anne has my stuff in her, and when she signals doctors to turn off my life, she turns her own spigot. Thought. Ghosts. Spooks. The world, so clear and snug, isn't. Metamorphosis. A rational man turns verminous. A rational country declares some citizens verminous and kills them.

I soap arms, armpits, the side where my scar begins, the left leg, the right, the crack, the ankles, the toes. Lovely. The mind lolls. What is a thought? Form without bulk. "For us, you don't exist." How could he not exist? He was there. But existence meant a paper, a name, a class. Citizen, father, uncle, niece, son, president. Tuesday's Election Day. Men and women run *to be*, to be entitled. I'll push a stylus through numbers on a card to make a governor, a senator. (Later, they could make or unmake me.) The father in *Metamorphosis* becomes a bank messenger, has a uniform with brass buttons and, like the doorman in that old film *The Last Laugh*, swells with pride. Fired, uniform taken away, the doorman shrivelled.

If I died here in the tub, Ellen would be a widow. She wouldn't know it till she came home. Knowing changed things. That's why you had to remember, especially those who did nothing memorable, had no children, planted no trees, wrote no books, carved no stones, left nothing but lines in old telephone directories, on stones in suburban cemeteries. Where is Bert buried?

What's the sense of remembering the unmemorable? Can't be helped, it's involuntary. Why hasn't evolution weeded it out? What does it have to do with survival? On our bedroom calendar, the November quotation (in blue letters beside the ironic, ethereal face of Albert Einstein) is: "What I value in life is quality rather than quantity, just as in Nature the overall principles represent a higher reality than does the single object." But isn't quality in the single object? What's worth more, the singular jerk, or the genetic dictionary which formed him?

"Don't foul your own nest." Uncle Bert.

That was what he told me forty-odd years ago. My parents and sister had taken off for a month, to Banff, Lake Louise, the Rockies, California. I was left in our apartment alone, very happy. I worked in the Paramount Films Sales Trainee Program on 43rd and Broadway. Weekends I went up with my cousin Andy—who had a car—to Quakerridge, my sister's club. I played tennis, swam, ate hamburgers and signed her name to the chits. One Saturday I saw Lynette Cloudaway lying by the pool. Two months before there'd been a feature spread about her in *Life*, an Arkansas girl who'd come to New York to be an actress. A photographer followed her around snapping pictures, at work, shopping, taking a bath, kissing her boyfriend goodnight. I'd fallen for her in *Life*, and here she was, in the flesh, by the pool. I could hardly speak. "May I sit here?"

"Sure." The smile I recognized, the throaty voice was new, devastating.

"I recognize you."

"It's me."

"What are you doing here?"

"I'm with Willy." The guy she kissed goodnight. "Not exactly 'with,' he's playing golf."

"Good. You can marry me."

"What name will I have?"

"Mrs. Larry Biel."

"Set the date."

We talked schools, jobs, where we lived, siblings, boy and girlfriends, movies, books, songs, the works. How confident Willy must be to leave this perfection by herself; he didn't deserve her. "Leave him."

"I haven't had my swim yet."

From the diving board, she jumped into the water. I paddled after her, dodging kids and dowagers. Beyond the flagstones, cigar smokers played bridge. On umbrellaed lounges, bodies toasted. Lawns, blue sky, the rich, Lynette; a Jewish Fitzgerald scene (the madness and cruelty evaporated).

Andy showed up. "Time to go."

To Lynette: "I better not miss my ride."

"You coming to the dance?"

"I will now. If I have to walk."

But I talked Andy into driving up again, white jacket and all.

Bare shouldered, breasts under lace, Lynette was in another gear of beauty. On the dance floor, I kissed her ear, her cheek, her mouth.

"We shouldn't do that."

"Why not?"

"I like it. And Willy would see."

"Let him," I mouthed. Tough guy, who'd melt at a leer.

"Let's not dance for a half hour or so."

"If you think so." Snootily. But before she went back to Willy I got her phone numbers.

Monday I called her office from mine. "Lunch?"

"Tomorrow."

We met at Toffenetti's, the glittery restaurant a block from the Paramount. I brought her the Viking Portable Fitzgerald, told her to read *Tender is the Night*, and asked her to go out with me Saturday.

"I spend weekends with Willy."

Thursday night she called me at home where I was working off my passion for her by myself. "Willy's going fishing in the Adirondacks. I've got to get my shoes fixed on 82nd and Amsterdam. I could come by your place after if you like."

Would I like. I bought the first bottle of wine in my life, got whitefish and rye bread from Barney Greengrass, stacked records on the phonograph, and by noon was lathered out of my mind. When the bell rang, I nearly fainted. Again, she looked different, playful, subtle. How many selves was she? I trembled too much to kiss her, could hardly talk. I managed to unscrew the bottle and trot out the sandwiches. We listened to Bing Crosby sing "Moonlight becomes you, it goes with your hair, you certainly know the right thing to wear." I had to go to the bathroom. The phone rang.

"Shall I get it?"

"Yes." Proud to show whoever called what I had going here.

"It's your Uncle Bert. He wants you to call him back. He sounded funny."

"A laugh a minute. What's he want?"

"He didn't say. Better call'm."

I did.

"Larry," he said, "Don't foul your own nest."

Old sap. *Foul.* Even then I felt its comic pathos. Yet also sensed the stupid debris of something brought down in stone. "She's my friend Al's wife," I said. "We're just going out."

"All right, but you don't foul your own nest."

The condom I'd gotten from the bathroom was ready, and I was getting there when the phone rang again. I didn't answer but thought, "The bastard'll probably come up here." It was nervousness talking. Despite my reading, despite six months' fornicating with my first girl between rows of boxwood near the stadium at Chapel Hill, I knew nothing. (Six years after Lynette, a week before Annie's birth, I still believed children were born through the—enlarged—navel.)

Don't foul your own nest. You fouled it for me, you old jerk.

Wednesday, Lynette called my office. "I have something to show you." At lunch, she held out her hand with the diamond ring.

I never saw her again. In person.

Two years ago, *Life* published an anniversary issue, and there was Lynette as she'd been, mouth open, gawking at a Broadway street scene on her way to work. Ravishing, perfect, the girl of my life. Under the forty-year-old photograph was one of a crinkled granny: Lynette today. I tried to see the young Lynette in the old face; couldn't, not a molecule. A caption said that she and Will lived in Seattle near their grandchildren. I thought of writing her. But why? I didn't want this grandmother. I wanted, *still*, the girl who'd come to the apartment.

Remembering acts on you, not you on it.

Why remember Bert? That sterile neatness, that concupiscent propriety. Immaculate in his blue suit, white silk handkerchief in the lapel pocket, gold tie and collar pins tucking him into himself, black silk socks taut in black garters, black shoes and hair gleaming with different fluids. So clean. My mother, another acolyte of cleanliness, was, in womanliness, beyond that. You wouldn't say she was immaculate. There was flow to her, dress over breasts and rear.

Arms hooked, she and Bert strolled Fifth Avenue, mirrored paragons, proud to be with each other, going into Saks and Sulka's, Bert commandeering the service that was the chief source of his self-satisfaction. That and his Packard, his annuities, his neckties, his opinions, the blondes whose signed portraits—"To Bert with love, Jocelyn"—stood on his chiffereau.

I'm unfair. I'm repaying the resentment he felt for me as mother's baby. There was decency and generosity in him. I needed five thousand dollars to put down on a house—it would be fifty thousand today—and he gave it to me. Every winter, he sent Ellen and me a crate of grapefruit and oranges from Boca Raton. Isn't he in that generous gold fruit as much as in the Sulka ties and antique injunctions? (The last crate of it arrived a week after he keeled over in a Florida pool.)

After Deejay's call, I try and fail to crawl back into the dream, then put cold water on my face, pee, brush my teeth, and go down the L of carpeted staircase to the kitchen for my branflakes and muesli mix. I get out a pack of two-ply, thirty gallon refuse bags, put them against a post on the porch, and bring in the Sunday *Tribune*.

Taking in the news with these flakes of dried grain is as close as I get to a sacrament. Today, election predictions and polls; Edgar and Hartigan in a dead heat, Simon ahead of

Lynn Martin. Then Hussein, Bush and Desert Shield, features on the wives, mothers and children of reservists yanked from their cereal and *Tribunes*. Then the usual montage of misery, the shot, the burned, the flooded, the starved, the planet's daily moil served up as *digestif*. Even the prick of conscience about this serves my wellbeing.

I wash my blue breakfast bowl—always the same—go upstairs with the Entertainment and Book sections and, sitting on the john, shave with my Norelco's trinity of rotor blades. Then another sacrament: a television show I've watched for years, stories about small towns in crisis, the courage of the handicapped, musicians, photographers, all introduced fluently, over fluently, by a benign, wise roly-poly. The program's critics are literate and scornful, their taste is mine (or becomes mine). Is this the equivalent of a Victorian gentleman's hundred lines of Tennyson?

The doorbell. Deejay, holding the bags, leans against the porch post. He wears stiff black pants, a porkpie hat, a stained brown windbreaker. His small mahogany face is, as usual, intense. There's always something pressing him. "Mawnin." A lace of booze on his breath, a flash of gold molar.

"Morning, Deejay. What can I do for you?"

"That downspout near the back porch's rotted out. You gotta get you a new one, for winter. You member that ice piled up there last year."

"Is that the reason?"

"Sure it is. What you think it was?"

I go around with him to the back porch, he taps the spout, breaks off a rusted section. "Take a look a that."

"Doesn't look good."

"I can go git one, put it on tomorrow."

Ellen doesn't want him doing any more jobs that require tools—he puts hinges on upside down, he broke our mailbox, he screwed up a toilet, he painted windows shut—but she won't be home till late afternoon. "Fine. How much do you need?"

"Ten bucks, maybe twelve. I git you the receipt."

"I know." If there's a gene for honesty, he has it. "I'm gonna do some raking with you."

"You calls it." He's of two minds about this: it cuts down his work time, but he likes company. He lives alone, somewhere in the neighborhood, has a schoolteacher brother who looks down on him. I don't think he's ever been out of Chicago. Occasionally he takes the El looking for jobs. They've never worked out. A couple of months ago, he took a Quality Control course which "guaranteed a full-time job." He came by dressed in a grim tie, his windbreaker and porkpie, to borrow bus fare to the North Side. Two days later, he came by again asking if he could mow the lawn.

"What happened to the job?"

"I took that bus a hour, walked bout two miles, and this man at the plant says they doan have nothin' for me."

"I thought he told the school to send someone up."

"He said I should be bilinguial for the job."

"But you're not."

"I got a brother knows Russian, I can learn Spanish."

"It's not easy to learn a language. I've been trying to learn German since high school. Almost fifty years."

"My God, man, you old."

"And I still don't know it."

"I know some Nippon. Least I can unnerstan it, I can't talk it."

Sure, Greek and Hittite, too. Still, I was angry for him. "He should've given you the job. You went through the school."

"Maybe it's this secession."

That took me a second, but one language I've learned is Deejay. "A job's a job. He told the school he had one for a graduate."

Deejay made the old shrugging motions of human acceptance, but I was upset. That job was his, bilingual or not. Unless of course he'd started popping off about how he'd rearrange the plant, or what he'd told Mayor Daley or Brother Farrakhan about running Chicago. Anything could come out of him when he got going.

"I'll do the flower beds," I said. Ellen doesn't like him working there, claims he pulls out what she plants.

We rake away within yards of each other. I pick up a refuse bag to fill it. He says, "Lemme do that." I hold, he fills.

We rake in a sort of harmony. I like it, but wonder if he feels awkward. After all, I'm doing what he's paid to do, cutting into his space, his authority. Even his habits; if I hadn't been there, he'd've smoked a cigarette.

He calls over, "What you fink bout this Ayrab war?"

"Not a war yet."

"Boosh gonna get us in?"

"What do you think?"

"Somepin mean bout his mouf."

"I guess that means war." He doesn't answer that. "You been in the army, Deejay?"

"They wouldn't let me."

"Who wouldn't?"

"The army, who you fink?"

"Why not?"

"What they gonna do wiv me? Rakin' bullets? How bout you, you a vet?"

"Too young for World War II, married by Korea, too old for Vietnam."

"We bof lucky. Doan haveta shoot nobody. What you fink bout dis Hussein?"

"A tough guy. He's shot people."

"He sure has nice suits. A nice moostache too."

"You like that?"

"I like a good moostache."

"Hitler had a hell of a mustache."

Deejay breaks up at this. "You a card, Mista Biel. You oughta grow *you* a moostache. A nice white one. Look like a million dollars on you."

"I'm not old enough."

He breaks up again.

Enough. I go in the front door, then think of something. "All these years you've been coming by here, and it just struck me, I don't know your full name. Is Deejay a nickname?"

He leans on the rake and laughs, showing the gold molar and eight or nine discolored teeth. "Deejay's mah nishes. Daron James. That's the name."

"Your whole name, first and last?"

"First and last. Like Lawrence Biel. 'at's your name, ain't it?"

"That's it." For some reason, I come down the stairs and

shake hands, as if, after all these years, we've finally been introduced.

Driving downtown Tuesday, I recover from the small dislocation of Ellen's return. Spend so many years with a person, seeing her again after even a brief absence is like seeing her in closeup. Many unnoticed things are noticed, lines in the face, white in the hair, a rawness in the voice, dents and discolorations in the body. The least strange person in the world is, for an hour or two, a stranger. Perplexing, a little frightening.

Then the indispensability of the familiar returns, feelings of reliance, confidence, the identity and accepted disparity of views. There are habits of self-restraint as well as self-expression. It's one package.

I enjoy the grace and ease with which Ellen unpacks; her reports on the trip. At supper it's mostly about Annie, Chuck and Anne. New problems, the resolution of old ones; the death of the big oak across the street; Chuck's worry about the recession—though a pharmacist should be almost recession-proof—the new Medicare regulations. "Are things better with Bostorf?" This is Chuck's assistant, who Annie thinks is swindling him.

"He's still trouble. At least, Annie's worry about him is troublesome."

We've been worried about Chuck and Annie. They express their difficulties with each other obliquely; Bostorf is one of the targets of this indirection. "And Anne?" We worry a lot about the dangers to which so decent, open and, we believe, innocent a girl can fall into in an American high school. For someone as much concerned as I am about the future of my seed, my fear about Anne's fall into womanhood—the antique phrase that comes to me—is puzzling.

I tell her about Peter, omitting *Metamorphosis*.

While we're stacking the plates in the dishwasher, the phone rings. "Mista Biel?"

"Deejay. Didn't you get the money?"

"I got it, but I need another twenny."

It's the second time this month that he's called up to ask for more than we'd agreed. Ellen doesn't like this at all. "It's a bad month for me. Lots of bills."

"How bout ten?"

"You really need it?"

"Would I be askin?"

"Sorry."

"Spose I come roun now."

"How about tomorrow?"

"Tomorrow I doan need it."

He must be buying all the liquor tonight. "I'll leave it under the mat."

"Twenny?"

"Ten."

"You a hard man."

"That's right."

"Least you stick wimme."

And you wimme, you poor bastard.

Some afternoons are hard. After the Round Table, I play cards, or billiards, or read the magazines, then walk back to the office and check the market close. I get going at 3:30, before the rush hour, and am home by 4:15. We eat at 6:00 in front of the MacNeil-Lehrer Report, then watch one of the scandal programs, people abusing, deceiving, molesting, kidnapping, killing; the human works. Then we read, watch programs, occasionally go out, or have friends in for bridge; then bath and bed. Beside Ellen's familiar warmth and fragrance, I go to sleep. Sometimes feelings bunch and we're active; afterwards, we express gratitude to each other.

I don't sleep as I used to, and often go to the guest room to read till my eyes tire. I'm conscious of aches in the balls of my hands, my feet, my chest. Sometimes I fear these aches. After all, how much longer is there?

I've been a bystander, done nothing memorable. I've had no real trouble, have lasted six-and-a-half decades, raised— whatever that means—what will live after me, and live in my paid-up house with someone I love. I'm lucky. Still, now and then, it comes to me that I don't understand anything. As if the world's speaking a language I can't follow. Fear gets so loud, I can't sleep. Once in a while, I go back to our room and hold on to Ellen. Sometimes this helps—like finding a dictionary—but sometimes it doesn't.

THE DEGRADATION OF TENDERNESS

—— 1 ——

Infantile, hysteric, passive, regressive, masochistic, narcissistic, frigid. A sample of what, over the years, I've heard and overheard from male colleagues.

It's changed some since I made my slow way into professional security, but attend any psychiatric meeting, you'll hear a hundred new versions. Lou Andreas-Salomé probably heard it from the Master himself. (She knew the score. "The vagina is 'rented' from the rectum." *"Anal" and "Sexual," Imago.* 1916.)

Our professional meetings are like medieval tournaments, "fights to the utterance." ("Utterance" in its medieval meaning of "death" and our—professional and non-professional—meaning, "words.") Behind our own doors, the patient prostrate before us, we're all masters. (Young sisters-in-arms can work out a feminine for this.) All of us know what it's like: we've been on the couch, have had our *ripostes* riposted, our ploys employed against us. Now, faces hidden from recumbent patients, we riposte, we counter, we review.

At professional meetings, on our own, in armor, we try to unhorse each other. (What can outsiders make of it?)

Still, as I say, in the last twenty years, we women have done better. We've been elected, chosen by the chosen. I myself have been nominated. (Lost—to another woman.)

—— 2 ——

Charlie's gone now. He chose to go. (Choice!) And I? Angry, resentful, bereft. The anger's like a madman's gun, aimed at Charlie, at Patricia, at Alfred, at myself, the spectator of this family mess.

Thirty-five years ago, Charlie's first article scuttled the "death-instinct." ("Freud's Incomprehension of Aggression," *Journal of Psychopathology*. XLVIII, 2, pp. 117–124.) It analyzed the Master's attachment to biochemistry and elementary physics, his discovery of the ego's need to abolish chemical tension, his contempt for the Adlerian power drive, his refusal to accept aggression as a component of creativity.

Charlie's last articles, "The Father as Clinical Observer I, II," instead of dismantling the Master-father, dismantled his children. If Freud analyzing Freud or Freud analyzing his daughter—my namesake, Anna—was brave, so, thought Charlie, was Charlie. At least until his children's responses blew him out of the water (that psychic Mediterranean on whose deceptive blue the world's Charlies sail).

—— 3 ——

Charlie gone, Alfred gone, Porphyria Ostreiker gone, Patricia in Amman, as good as gone.

—— 4 ——

Zennor, Cornwall
Dec.1, 1989
Dear Annuschka,

I'm thinking of those Hopper pictures of people stranded in the corners of restaurants, theaters, towns, staring into nothing while people closer to the center are going about their own business. That's the way it is with me now. Growing up, at least the way we all did, is like Renaissance painting. You're always center stage. Here I don't count, at least not much, and it's fine with me.

What's the theme of Upstairs, Downstairs *but "If you don't know your place, you get in trouble"?*

Isn't that what Daddy did to us? We thought we were the apple of his eye. It turned out we were only its worm.

Too clever?
It seems I wasn't clever enough.

Still, at least partially, yours,
Patricia

—— 5 ——

"The Father as Clinical Observer." Charlie's bid to be as masterful as the Master, trying to make the subjective objective. "Am I that far off, Annuschka?"

"Freud exposed Freud, Charlie. You expose Patricia and Alfred."

"But that exposes me."

"More than you think."

"*You* think."

The sidetrack. I refused it. "You understand how the children have taken it, Charlie. Are they so wrong?"

"How did Einstein's children take the Special Relativity paper? That's how I expect them to take it. Did Jean Renoir fold under his father's portraits of him? Look how beautifully he writes about him."

"He wrote! He handled the handler. Patricia and Alfred aren't as—" I said "lively" instead of "gifted." "I'm sure he gives his resentment away every other page."

"It's the risk I took. I must have known I was taking it."

—— 6 ——

We become what we're accused of being. Anti-Semites—as Sartre said—define the Jew. We define our patients by redefining their self-definitions. What I'm getting at is that despite three decades of "being on top of other people" (face hidden, God-like), I'm still the weak-kneed prisoner in the male dock. Which means that I can feel with victims, with Alfred and Patricia and with Charlie too.

—— 7 ——

I mothered them. (Real motherhood would have been unendurable for me.) In part, they used me to punish their mother. (Francine died when they were ten and twelve.) I didn't *love* Patricia and Alfred, but for much of their lives, they stirred me.

"The child is an erotic plaything." "Cuteness," "innocence," then, later, "charm" and "sweetness."

My emotional life is—largely—agapean, that is, like Charlie, I'm an obsessional, psychically invested in Truth.

—— 8 ——

Patricia was Charlie's pal, his angel. When Francine died and Annette came on the scene, she faced down her rage, wrote understanding notes: Dear Dad, I'm happy for you. She acted as she looked, the good, dear girl with clear eyes of the softest brown, small-boned but not fragile. Healthy, as if she'd just come in from a three-mile tramp in the snow. She looked beautiful in winter. Summers were tough. Too fair, she didn't tan well. (Couldn't take the heat?)

After Francine's death, she was sent to boarding school in Poughkeepsie; then Holyoke, graduating *cum laude*. She got on a Virginia newspaper, and became political: the country was a machine running on the flesh of its poor. She became briefly famous for a newspaper column about William Buckley, "the classic American exemplar of selfishness," with "his facial tics and verbal tricks, his baroque vocabulary of concealment, cloud-chamber smiles and frantic energy. The Reichian armor against Oedipal terror and natural tenderness." Buckley's lawyers made noise, Patricia's newspaper mounted the First Amendment high horse, but then its business office threw in the hat. The hat was Patricia. She was fired, then spent a year helping the Lakota Sioux hold on to a radio station, their only non-Patrician link to the outside world. The next year she passed out soup and sandwiches to the homeless in Cleveland.

Then came Charlie's case.

—— 9 ——

Charlie had been sued for malpractice. Not extraordinary. Of 19,000 therapists in Cook County, 9,800 have been sued. I probably spend forty hours a year in court. Everybody digs up everybody else's business. (The shovels are lawyers.) Charlie's litigation hit the papers.

What happened was this. For fifteen years, the daughter of a well-known actress shuttled from doctor to doctor. The actress was shooting a film in Lake Forest, someone told her about Charlie, and she went to see him about the daughter. The actress was—is—charming, beautiful. Charlie made space for the daughter, three hours a week. The daughter was theatrical, self-dramatizing, moderately ill, a powerful manipulator. Charlie was good with young women, sympathetic, firm, charming, unfoolable. The daughter wanted more time, a quicker cure. An old boyfriend was coming to live with her, she wanted to be better for him. Charlie took her seriously, but resisted her pressure and kept his cool. Daughter persuaded mother to bring in her doctor to pressure Charlie. This idiot bypassed Charlie and made direct calls to the daughter. He even prescribed for her, Mellaril. Mother brought it to her; daughter went into a spin, tried to get hold of Charlie. It was Sunday, he was in Wisconsin. Daughter threw herself off the roof. The fall was broken by a first floor cornice, she lived, but horribly, a paraplegic. Mom's lawyers took it to court. The newspapers played it up: the iconography was powerful: Crippled Beauty, Ogre Doctor.

Enter Patricia. She investigated, dug up dirt; stood by her dad. She sat beside him every day of the trial.

He won the case, Patricia wrote a book about it, maybe you know it. Several thousand Chicagoans read it, and twenty thousand other people. Actress, daughter and doctor were the villains: Charlie and Patricia, the father-daughter team, took all the marbles.

—— 10 ——

Appear on television or in the newspapers, and you become the lightning rod of ten thousand idling haters. In the eight week course of the trial, Charlie had to change his telephone number three times. He came close to moving from the house in which he'd lived since his marriage to Annette. You can forgive what you understand, but when anonymous haters intrude with regularity, forgiveness and understanding collapse. You never know when you'll be struck. In those eight weeks, Charlie lost his celebrated cool (the cool in which overheated patients, friends and children, too, took dips). I think his experience with the maddened, maddening crowd spawned a desire in him to master it, like an entrepreneur who sees a waterfall or some other source of natural, free power he can exploit.

Then there was Patricia's book, which gave Charlie not just a new sense of her, but a reminder of the power of words. He'd read the pieces she'd published in weekend supplements (he'd given her a few tips for the Buckley column), but newspapers were disposable, so degraded, *trayf*. Books were meant for eons. Patricia's book was not a work of high culture, but it was a responsible, careful work. Charlie was particularly taken by the footnoted allusions to psychoanalytic literature. Scholarship was both deferential and authoritative. Patricia's scholarly seriousness altered his familiar, dismissively tender paternal view of her, and—in my view—opened the way to his clinical portrait.

By the time it was published in the *Journal of Psychopathology*, Patricia was living in Cornwall with a Cornish fisherman, making ends meet preparing meat pies in a Cornish pub ("the one"—she wrote me—"in Zennor where Lawrence wrote *Women in Love*"). I sent her the article.

—— 11 ——

Charlie's aim, his boast, was candor.

NO TIME FOR VANITY OR SHAME, THAT FEAR OF SELF-EXPOSURE, WHICH MANNERS MASK . . . FREUD DESCRIBES THE WAR BETWEEN TENDERNESS AND SENSUALITY, THE NECESSARY DEGRADATION OF THE SENSUAL OBJECT. IN THE OEDIPAL GRIP, THIS WAR CAN BRING THE DEATH OF EROS. TO TRIUMPH OVER IT, AS MY DAUGHTER DID, RESULTED IN AN ACT OF PARRICIDE, A BOOK ABOUT HER FATHER'S INDICTMENT AND HUMILIATION. WHO RESCUED HIM FROM THAT PIT? THE FILIAL AUTHOR. THE CHILD PARENTS THE PARENT. DEVOTION AND REVENGE ARE FUSED. EROS IS SAVED.

—— 12 ——

Every portrait reduces, simplifies, diminishes. I was uneasy. Thirty years before, I'd been in therapy with Charlie. Our collaboration and friendship, our erotic refusal of each other, my mothering, or *aunting*, of his children, all make up so large a part of my life that I was not up to analyzing them. They were part of my bedrock. If an earthquake occurred, I wasn't going to shake myself to see if I were in one piece. Better to be still. So for a while I didn't say anything to Charlie.

He asked, "Your silence means disapproval?"

"I'm not sure."

"Nothing withers like silence."

"I'd thought it was golden."

"Midas-gold. Death. Unfriendly."

"Unfriendly, hah. Unpaternal. Unfilial. We're not all brave enough to risk what counts for us."

"If it didn't count, it wouldn't be worth risking. Since when have you thought analysis destructive?"

"Always. Destructive of illusion."

"Well?"

"Well yourself, Charlie. These illusions kept us warm."

"What's this 'us,' Anna? I don't believe there are ten words about you in the piece. Have you seen something I haven't?"

"I'll have to reread it before I say anything."

"Several times. And perhaps you'd better say nothing then. I had no idea your skin wrapped Patricia's bones as well as your own."

"I'm sorry I can't respond better. I don't want to hurt you."

"Of course not."

—— 13 ——

Every few years I get out my old Greek textbooks and spend a few hours convincing myself that I'm in touch with the great minds of antiquity. The other day, I went through *Oedipus Turannos* and read the great scene of revelation in which the messengers (the *angeloi*) tell Oedipus "*Smikra palaia somat' unaze hropo.*" "A small touch on the scale sends the old to their rest." Wising up, Oedipus responds to Iocasta's telling him it's best not to keep prying: "The *best*! *That's* what always made me suffer." "*Ta Iosta! Toi nun tauta m'algune palai.*"

Charlie had the best and ruined it. (It takes so little to tip the scale and ruin a good life.)

—— 14 ——

The portrait of Alfred was to the one of Patricia as Grüne-wald is to Van Dyck. Alfred's defenses, crutches, props and poses were exhibited not only in the name of truth, but love! Charlie didn't miss an Alfredan trick.

—— 15 ——

The day he got Alfred's letter, he'd come home early. "I had a cancelled appointment," he told me. "I wrote *that* up, then looked out and noticed how beautiful the lake was, all green and silver. The trees too, decked out in those November colors. I decided to go home early. I walked very slowly. I suppose it's an ugly walk, but it's mine, the Del Prado, the brick six-flats, the bakery with the coconut cakes and sugar rolls, the IC tunnel with the murals and Jim's Tobacco Shop, Harper Court with the truants and dope peddlers on the grass. Like the Grande Jatte."

Charlie's street is a hundred-yard block of wood and brick houses behind the bank. His house is a brown-shingled cottage built during the Columbian Exposition. There are ten square yards of lawn with a young oak tree bent at the top, woodbine hedges and two cottonwood elms which steal sunlight from the oak.

A middle-aged black man in faded green workshirt and pants was raking leaves there. "I'd never seen him." There were eight glascine sacks of leaves "tied up like carcasses on the curb."

"Does my wife know you're doing this?" Charlie asked him.

"Wouldn't be doing it otherwise."

"I was a little embarrassed," he told me. "He spoke so clearly, so intelligently. I went upstairs. Annette told me she'd paid him fifteen dollars for two-and-a-half hours work. It was too late to catch him and give him fifteen more, and I was angry about it, punishing her for expressing my anality, then punishing myself for letting her. I'd been so happy on the walk, then here was this decent man, my age, walking the streets to make a few dollars, doing my work. I thought of him going home to his children with the fifteen bucks. I thought, 'Why is he he, I I?' The unfairness of it. After cocktails, Annette brought in Alfred's letter. She'd been saving it, guessing it needed an alcoholic cushion."

Dear Dad,

You win again.
Congratulations.
Understanding?
No.
Brilliance of insight? Yes, but not into what you're sighting.
Brilliance of style? I guess so. So what?
Down here, where it counts, in me, bad as I am, dumb as I am, nothing. No light, no help, no justice and—of course—no mercy.
I suppose I'd mistake anything, but could I mistake such a mistake?

Your repellent clown of a son,
Alfred

—— **16** ——

Between four and five A.M. of the sleepless night, Charlie wrote his answer.

Dear Alfred,

Three California researchers have invented a mathematical way of making sense of the random. They take off from a famous quote of Laplace, "If I know where every particle in the universe is, and what forces are generated there, from then on I can predict everything." They imagine an ideal billiard game in which friction plays no part. If, however, there's a single electron on the edge of the universe, which isn't figured into the Laplacean equations, the randomness it introduces will reach the billiard table in less than a minute and cancel the ability to predict the position of the balls.

A family is a bit more complicated than billiards. Life's randomness is infinitely greater than an unpredicted electron. My professional life has been dedi-

*cated to making some predictable sense out of it. My
hope was that my children had enough confidence in
themselves, in me and in our relationship to understand and sympathize with this goal.*

*I printed what you call "portraits" and I call "case
studies" not in the* Reader's Digest *or* The New York
Times, *but in a technical journal with a circulation of a
thousand and a readership—judging from my own
habits—half that.*

*Your indictment, your anger, focuses on the fact that
I used you and your sister as the subject of these case
histories. Who else could I use? The whole point was
that this was a father as well as an analyst examining,
as honestly as he could, the parental relationship.
Freud analyzed his children's dreams and experiences, and much of the civilized world is in his debt
for it. If I am egregiously comparing myself to Freud, I
respond, "What better model?"*

*Have I violated "the confidentiality" of the parent-
child relationship? I have. And I haven't escaped the
pain of it. Your letter sees to that.*

*There is something odd about the act of interpret-
ing, the act of writing. The interpreter, the writer, has a
sense of not being there. This feeling is one of the
defenses of the ego. Freud called it the* Entfremdungs-
gefühl, *the "feeling of estrangement." It's the opposite
of that other defense mechanism of the ego, déjà vu,
in which the ego masks its panic at a new place by
imagining it's been there before.*

*My point is that I did insulate myself from your and
Patricia's feelings while I analyzed and wrote about
our relationship. An apology for that is inadequate. Try
and understand how much of my self-worth is bound
up with this effort to uncover another inch of Truth.*

*Human beings are composed of dark impulses as
well as tenderness, affection, duty, high-mindedness
and love of every sort. Everything is mixed up. Illness
and health inhabit the same system. The family is the
source of nurture and also the deadliest carcinogen.*

I am praying—I have my version of prayer—for your
understanding, your forgiveness, your love.

> *Always, no matter what happens,*
> *Your Father*

—— 17 ——

Let me try seeing Alfred without the powerful lens of his
father's portrait. (Or without my anger at it.)

A Saul Bellow character counters Feuerbach's, "You are
what you eat," with "You are what you see." After years in the
emotion racket, I was tempted to opt for, "You are whom you
desire," although in our professional deconstruction, this
emerges as "You are the opposite of those you desire."

What I come down to now, my own rule of thumb, is "You
are what you are." (The thumb is the least sensitive finger.)

Outside his technical analysis, Charlie pitied and griped
about Alfred. "How can a reasonably intelligent boy be so
geschmoggled by the world?" By "the world," Charlie usually
meant "women." "He's just like those bowling pins which
reset themselves after each knock-down." Charlie thought
Alfred unprepared for women. "It was Francine's death. Then
Annette's coldness and fear of the children." Alfred had gone
out with a particularly wild bunch of girls.

—— 18 ——

The one that Charlie couldn't get out of his head was
Porphyria Ostreiker.

Her appearance first. An hourglass punk. Voluptuousness
in Nazi deco. This daughter of Abraham wore T-shirts embla-
zoned with swastikas. Her breasts nuzzled those logos of
hatred. Her hair, whatever its original color, changed overnight from orange nails to purple snakes; her eyes were
triangled with gold paint. I never saw her wearing a nose ring,
but almost any part of her could be spiked with bangles,
crosses, crescents, an anthology of devotional horror.

Alfred defended her à la de Tocqueville: "It's democracy.
Everybody can look the way he wants, king of his own appearance."

Porphyria's deeds didn't quite match her looks. That is, she wasn't on the streets machine-gunning children. Nonetheless, from what I heard, twice read and once saw on television, she was a minor public menace. She bared parts of herself on planes or in department stores; she stowed herself in a bin of tomatoes in the supermarket, she made scenes at concerts, movies, plays. During an Elliot Carter quartet, she rose from her seat and tucked wads of cotton in her ears. In theaters, she opened a laugh box during romantic scenes. She sprayed wolf urine during a Peter Sellars *Così fan tutte*. "A chauvinist work which should have been shelved a hundred years ago," she told news cameras when she got out of jail. At pro-life rallies, she carried posters of starving children inscribed "Fruit of the Womb" or pictures of Charles Manson, Hitler, Stalin and Ronald Reagan reading "These Are Your Children."

Why this mistress of surprise attached herself to repressed, studious Alfred is as surprising as anything else. Tall, stooped, mild, thoughtful, Alfred was, in Charlie's phrase, "a gull in the garbage wake of that filthy putt-putt."

—— **19** ——

Freud told Lou Andreas-Salomé that he wished he had five or six disciples like Otto Rank. "He disposes of the negative aspects of his filial love by interesting himself in the psychology of regicide."

Alfred was doing research on Oliver and Richard Cromwell at Washington University in St. Louis. To support himself he repaired typewriters. (This was a year or two before typewriters disappeared from American campuses.) It was here that he met Porphyria, who brought him her Remington Correcto and, as Alfred said she told him, took him back to repair her.

The next spring after the second article appeared, their mad little campaign aganist Charlie began. Dressed in storm trooper outfits—boots, knickers, leather belts, swastikaed caps and armbands, not black, though, but pink—they walked the block outside his office on South Shore carrying pickets. Alfred's read, "If you're Dr. Grasmuck's patient, get your head examined." Porphyria's read, "Beware! We were Dr. Grasmuck's patients."

It's a quiet block, little traffic, tennis players going to and from the clay courts, children in the playground, mothers, strollers, cars which turn off the small Outer Drive exit. A few people gathered, and more looked out at them from the apartment windows. Charlie was alerted when his second patient, a woman who'd driven down from Evanston, called him from the Del Prado lobby and asked him what was going on; she was afraid to enter the building. He looked out his seventh floor window and saw the small crowd around the two odd picketers. He only recognized them when he went downstairs.

"Alfred! You gone outta your mind?"

Alfred and Porphyria took off round the corner, pursued briefly by Charlie, who, feeling himself part of an eager crowd, stopped, shrugged his shoulders, raised his eyes to the sky, and walked back with as much dignity as possible to his building. He was extremely upset, and spent the rest of the emptied hour brooding.

His next patient, a local painter, asked him off the bat what was going on downstairs. Charlie looked out. There they were again having their picture taken with another little crowd. He opened the window and shouted, "Alfred, if you and that slut are not out of here in one minute I'm calling the police."

Porphyria looked up. The pink cap fell off her Rudolph Valentino coiffure. "Up thine, Strangelove. We have a license."

"The police!" shouted Charlie.

It was a poor session, the painter left in a huff. But when Charlie looked out the window, there was nobody there.

That night he tried to get hold of Alfred. The last number he had for him had been disconnected. He had a number for Porphyria's mother, a St. Louis caterer. "I'm sorry," the woman told him. "I haven't had anything to do with her for a year. She's the bane of my existence. You wouldn't believe what a sweet girl she was through ninth grade. It was after her period started," and so on, till Charlie extricated himself.

The next day they were back again, this time dressed in formal evening clothes. Porphyria's heart-shaped picket read, "To the patients of Dr. Grasmuck: Want a positive transfer? Leave him." Alfred's said, "I am Grasmuck's damaged goods."

Charlie called his lawyer and told him to get an injunction

and the police. Police cars arrived, but after camera crews from the local stations. Reporters came up to Charlie's office. He read a statement. "It is profoundly sad when a family tragedy becomes public. The two young people are seriously disturbed. I'm not sure they realize how much trouble their pranks are causing. As a doctor and as a father, I grieve for them."

That night, the local news included old footage of Porphyria's stunts and a statement from Alfred regretting that his father was unfit to practice psychiatric medicine. "I owe it to him to alert his patients." The final seconds went to a demurely dressed and coiffed Porphyria saying gently that psychoanalysis was discredited and that Freud had long been exposed as a chronic liar and fantasist. "Our actions are a form of public sanitation."

Charlie had been made ludicrous. Nothing's worse for a psychotherapist.

Which Charlie knew. He found it difficult to work with patients; one by one, he directed them to colleagues.

"You can't imagine the straits I'm in, Annushka. I'm much worse off than a patient. I see the structure beneath the symptoms, which doesn't relieve them. Knowledge doesn't help. I know I should be able to get out of it, but I cling to it. I won't use the exit I point out to everyone else."

"Charlie, you're not strong enough to be your own analyst."

"I'm embracing my weakness. I need it. It's time for me to shut down."

Christmas Eve he took a long walk and caught a chill which turned into pneumonia. Hospitalized, he improved, then went back to an office barren of patients.

Annette said, "Let's forget it, Charlie. We've got money. Let's go to Italy for a year. When we come back, if you feel like it, you can start again."

Charlie said, "I only love it here. I love only you and the children; you're still here but they've turned against me."

"You of all people understand that."

"You'll turn against me too. You don't know it, but you will. I embrace my situation. I no longer like my life."

—— 20 ——

Alfred and Patricia came to the funeral, heavy with the guilt of those who have had a terrible wish granted, silent with the silence of those who can no longer be absolved or corrected by the one who can absolve or correct. They stayed in their old rooms, and after the funeral, went over their father's possessions. Alfred took his watch, gold studs and cufflinks, his underwear shorts and shirts. He told Annette he would work on his father's notebooks, "to see if they're publishable."

Patricia remembered that thirty-five years earlier, Charlie had appeared as a walk-on in a film with Edward G. Robinson. (The director had been one of his first patients.) She got hold of a print, and, with Alfred, ran the film, studying the crowd and party scenes. They pored over them frame by frame. There were two men that might have been Charlie, but one walked with a walk that wasn't his, and the other appeared through cigar smoke. They settled on the smoker and had a still of him made, blown up and framed.

—— 21 ——

How quickly days die in our northern Januaries. Charlie dead before dawn on the tenth, buried before noon the fourteenth, Alfred, Patricia, Annette and I, the executor, listening to his brisk attorney read and parse his uncomplicated will the next day. Three weeks later, Charlie's old film image in tow, the children took off, Patricia to Brazil, Alfred back to St. Louis.

A few nights earlier, they'd given me a cassette of the film and watched Charlie's scene with me. Even through the distortions of the small television screen, despite the smoke, the years and the sophisticated mimicry of the cigar smoker, I saw the Charlie I knew—and cried.

I hadn't mourned Charlie. The tears came from that internal confusion the Master called melancholia, the guilt of an answered wish for destruction. I mourned the part of me that had failed him, at least failed that part of myself that might have made me the mother of some Alfred or Patricia. (Charlie drew me as no man I've known. I only found my emotional ease these last years living with Roberta de Freitas, whose residency at Michael Reese I supervised.) The tears were for the path I hadn't taken, hadn't been invited to take.

—— 22 ——

With Francine's death, the children suffered deprivational reactions. Alfred's was more severe; he showed the signs of anaclitic depression, which I helped alleviate, maternally, not professionally. Yet when he saw that I was the prop and confidant of his father, his deprivation was reinforced. He entered the long, affectless mildness of his late adolescence, then started with the wild girls who diverted him from reintegrating his ego.

After Charlie's death, I could have taken him in hand. I didn't. Clearly I didn't want him around. I won't analyze this. He went back to St. Louis, to Porphyria, his Cromwell studies and the typewriters. Three blanks. The Campus Shop was now Campus Computers. He took a course in computer maintenance, "but"—he wrote—"it involves more than my mechanical knack. It's not for me." Cromwell, too, disinterested him: his king was dead, and he didn't have the energy or will to rule in his place.

Charlie had left him two hundred thousand dollars. He put it into a Vanguard fund, "which gives me enough to live in a small way. I've got no desire to live any other. As for Porphyria, she's taken off."

She showed up a week after Charlie's death. "I need you," she told Alfred. She wanted to become pregnant, then have a public abortion.

"I was to be the lucky almost-father. I declined. It took her a week to find a more enlightened Seed Donor."

Modern chivalry! A year later, just before he moved to Tucson, where he studied cactus and desert insects, Alfred bumped into her mother. Alfred wrote me:

Apparently pregnancy transformed Porphy. She married the Knightly Donor and, according to her mother, was "a model wife and mother." Her last scandal was normalcy.

Not quite. A week ago I read, in a piece in the *Tribune*, that she was organizing a Mother's March to the White House Against the Destruction of the Cradle of Civilization.

I had only one letter from Tucson but could sense that Alfred was losing what little grip he had. Then he was struck down by the Guillaume-Barré virus. Patricia and I were listed as "those to call." Patricia was unreachable. I flew down. He was in terrible shape, unable to move. The virus attacks the nerve sheaths and paralyzes the body functions. Two days after I arrived, he died.

—— **23** ——

I sent a message to Patricia though the Red Crescent.

She'd worked a year in the Amazon state of Para, working as a volunteer for the Rural Workers Movement against the destruction of the rain forest. By the time I heard about this, she was in a Jordanian camp organizing supplies and nursing care for refugees from Kuwait and Iraq.

Amman
Oct. 14, 1990

Annushka, dear,

A line to let you know I'm all right. The world's one hell after another. I'm in the city raising money. Can you get some to us?

The secret is losing what gets hurt, yourself. That's easier here.

Still,
Patricia

—— **24** ——

Yesterday, on CNN, as I watched a parade of fury against the United States in the streets of Amman, thinking, "the ugliness and beauty of mass hatred," I caught a glimpse— I'm almost positive—of Patricia, her clear-eyed face lit with passion. She was both ugly and beautiful, the ugliness that terrifies because it shows unleashed destructiveness, and beautiful with the repose of abandonment. Was I seeing things? (I'm not going to ask CNN for a tape.) It felt right to me, Patricia part of a foreign mob crying out against her fatherland.

.

Part·II

A SHORT NOVEL

VENI, VIDI ... WENDT

—— 1 ——

From Los Angeles to Santa Barbara, a paradisal coast bears the permanent exhaust of the automobile: shack towns, oil pumps, drive-ins, Tastee-Freeze bars, motels, service stations. At Ventura, the coast turns a corner which sends the Santa Ynez mountains east-west and lets the sun hang full on the beaches for its long day. A hundred yards or so off the highway there are a few sandy coves almost free of coastal acne. One of them, a mile north of a red boil of tourism called Santa Claus, is Serena Cove. A wooden plaque over the single-gauge railroad track gives the name. Cross the track to a cyclone fence. Behind that, in a lemon grove, is an amber villa shaped like a square head with glass shoulders. This is the Villa Leone, for which our place was the Changing House. (The villa has been turned into apartments.) Our house was— is—low, white and gabled. It has one grand room windowed on three sides, three bedrooms, a kitchen, and three bathrooms, two of which function. It is hidden by odorous bushes, palms, live oaks and great, skin-colored eucalypti, some of whose sides have been gashed by lightning. A wall of honeysuckle ends the driveway; behind it, the south lawn leads thirty feet to a red-dirt bluff covered with vines threaded with tiny blue flowers. They hang to the beach, a half-mile scimitar of ivory sand. Three other houses, hidden from ours by palms and trellises, share beach rights. You see them from the water, glassy monocles snooting it over a subdued sea.

Actually not the sea, but the Santa Barbara Channel, which

is formed by the great private islands you see only on very clear summer days. The islands are far enough away to preserve a sense of the sea, but, like a lido, they break waves down to sizes which keep you from worrying about small children.

We were there ten summer weeks, in the last five of which I wrote the first version of an opera. I've never had an easier, less-forced time, and although, now, back in Chicago, I see that what I did there on the coast was not much more than take out the ore, and that I now have to build the factory and make the opera, at the time I didn't know it. During these weeks I never turned back to see what I'd done. Day after day I coasted (yes), writing away, feeling the music and story come with an ease which, till then, I'd never known.

Everyone seems to know that opera is on its last legs. In fact, music itself isn't doing too well. A fine song writer, Ned Rorem, says that the Beatles are the great music of our time; I suppose they are more inventive than most. Our best composers spend a lot of time stewing about audience-teasing and other art-world claptrap. Only Stravinsky seems like a wise inventor who happens to use music instead of words or mathematics. And he is enjoyed more as a Dr. Johnson than as an enchanting musician. A man like me who's spent himself writing a musical drama is led to feel his work has no public significance, that, at best, it will be endured by a few friends and an occasional audience bribed by free tickets and a party in honor of the composer. ("Honor" because he endured the long boredom of working out what bores them only an hour or two.) An "enforced loss of human energy," wrote Mr. Khrushchev about armaments. Of course, writing music is not enforced (though one must pass time doing something), and music is a few wrongs up from armaments.

Though down from political action, as the hierarchy of 1968 had it; and I was influenced by such mis-estimates as well as by my inner tides. I lent a very small public name and an equivalent public gift to the better-known victims of institutional brutality. Last spring, I marched in the Loop, collected fourteen draft cards, made a speech in the rain beside a Meštrović Indian, was photographed, televised, went home to look at myself on the local news, and had bad hours waiting for the FBI to turn me into the local Dr. Spock. In short, paid the debt to my consciousness of being in so frivolous a trade.

On the one hand, I dream of my own Bayreuth, the Wendt Festival, with, not mesmerism and fruited myth, but classical wisdom and common sense made engaging and novel by the least duplicitous of contemporary musical lines. On the other hand, I feel the shame of luxury, of a large—rotting— house, of privacy and silence, of a livable salary and easy schedule, of an entrée into the little circles in which I whirl— college music departments, two-day festivals in Mexico City and The Hague, occasional mention in a news magazine's music section.

For this opera, which, with luck, will be given a truncated radio performance in Stockholm and a workshop run-through in Bloomington, Indiana, I'm trying to do, I suppose, what writers do in prefaces (or what my Uncle Herman did fifty years ago as advance agent for Barnum). I'm writing an account of its genesis or composition to serve as a kind of a trailer (which, as usual, precedes what it "trails").

Any thoughtful man who types the solitary "I" on the page as much as I have these past weeks must consider its perils. This is a great time for "I." Half the works billed as fiction are just spayed (or Styrofoamed) memoirs. This week's literary sections are on Malraux's *Anti-Memoirs*, apparently an unravelable mixture of real and fictive "I"s, pseudonyms, *noms de plume* and *noms de guerre*, mixed in with fictional guises and life roles (in which "the man" tells Nehru that he is a "Minister of State" the way that Mallarmé's *cat* becomes *Mallarmé's* cat). I suppose this need to multiply oneself is one of the billion guises of libido. (Professor Lederberg found gender in bacteria; perhaps gravity itself will turn out to be the lust of particles for each other.)

That genius Nietzsche, whom I still read in a Modern Library Giant bought at fifteen after reading Will Durant's *Story of Philosophy* . . . No, I'll begin again; I'm not writing autobiography. Nietzsche asks, "Aren't books written precisely to hide what is in us?" Granting the exceptional concealments of his time, isn't this still the case? I know the authors of some of the frankest books ever written. The books are mostly trailers or self-advertisements, letters to women saying, "Here I am, come get me," or to parents saying, "This is the reason for my condition." Or sometimes, they're just brilliant drugs of self-assurance.

Every book conceals a book. But as the great old fellow (F.N.) says, every thinker is more afraid of being understood than misunderstood. Wants uniqueness more than love and gratitude.

In Nietzsche's day, the pose was to be *simply* grand; in our time, to be *complexly* grand. The good artists I know are more credulous than *smarter* people. (So you hear stories of their naiveté or—its other face—mean shrewdness.)

Writing your own story, you can report, pose and judge all at once. Not as blissful a cave as music, but not bad at all.

So here's my little *Enstehung des Walpole's Love (Opus 43)*, my yet-to-be-finished opera. I pray it's not a substitute for it. (In fact, I'm willing to send a Xerox of fifty pages of score to anyone who sends ten dollars and a self-addressed, stamped return envelope to Holt, Rinehart and Winston, Inc., 383 Madison Avenue, New York, N.Y. 10017.)

[Owing to personnel changes in our office, Mr. Wendt's invitation must be considered null and void. H., R. and W.]

—— 2 ——

I don't begin at the beginning, but with my then seventeen-year-old son, Jeff-U. (For Ulrich; I'm Jeff-C, for Charles. Ulrich is the great-uncle from whom I inherited not the two hundred thousand I expected, but fifty.) Oedipal miseries were, I thought, ruining my summer. They were at their worst when Jeff-U invited his friend Ollendorf to stay with us.

I was not anxious to have Ollendorf around. The presence of an outsider inhibits me, if only for a time and from walking around in my skin. Though notches up from the loudmouthed adolescent ignoranti who fill up our Chicago house, he would be extra presence, an absence of dear absence; he'd be swinging baseball bats against the vases, tackling Jeff-U into Sackerville's stereo; I'd be forking over six hundred for that in addition to the hundred and eighty-five it cost me every week just to hook our trunks up in Sackerville's place. (Which turned out to be Donloubie's place.)

I did not want him.

But there was small recourse: Gina, my almost sixteen-year-old, had had her amical quota with Loretta Cropsey.

I laid it on the hard line. "He can come if you, One, specify dates: ten days and not an hour more; and Two, he's got to fly into Santa Barbara, which means the three-thirty out of San Francisco. And Arrival Day counts as Day Number One."

Since Jeff-U daily stretched his six and a sixth feet of unemployed body upon a bed from one A.M to one P.M., it didn't strike me that Ollendorf's afternoon arrival constituted an important loss of a vertical day. "Besides which, it takes half an hour to get to the airport. And before that you'll have to work your way into a T-shirt. Even shoes. Maybe even a pair of socks. Not matched or clean, of course, but you can see there's more Ollendorf to the day than his arrival at the house." (Not that Jeff-U wore the same piece of clothing three consecutive hours. Except for dress shirts, which I told him to pay for himself. Since which the San Ysidro Laundry had been deprived of his custom.)

It turned out I won't let him pick up Ollendorf anyway because (1) he could drive only our New Yorker, Sackerville limiting the Volkswagen to "licensed adults," and (2) "I'm not going to burn a quart of fuel to fetch your effing pal when I'm up at Goleta anyway." (I rehearse the chamber group Mondays.)

He wished to telephone Ollendorf. "Sixty-five cents won't kill you."

"*Kill* me?"

"I paid for most of the calls."

"Not the tax."

"Here's a buck," fingering the besanded back pocket of the early-afternoon pants for one of the crushed bills which remain from spring poker triumphs and his grandmother's indolent generosity—substitute for the physical birthday presents which would force her into the dangerous byways of Fifth Avenue.

I take the buck. "This covers about ten percent of them." If it's but a week of weeding nasturtiums or washing windows, I am bent on seeing his hairless arse erect before one P.M. Without myself having to chain and toss it into the local office of the California State Employment Service.

Of course he knows what I'm about, knows I bait him, but though down to fourteen bucks (if I haven't overlooked some of the pockets or the change which overflows to every couch and bed in the house), he throws me another bill. Which I don't make him pick up or unroll; because if his theatrical arrogance caused him to toss a five instead of a one, he will be down to nine bucks. (I didn't unroll it until I was in the john: I have theatrical bouts as well. It was, unfortunately, a single.)

—— 3 ——

Every other weekend, the cove fills with the landbound children of my Los Angeles relatives and summer colleagues. (Especially those unable to keep progenitive tools from progenitive work: George Mullidyne has six, the odious Davidov has pumped five into the beauteous Patricia, and even the emeritous Krappell manages to churn junior Krappells out of his third wife.) They turn our half-mile of beach into a sty.

I buy twenty-four cans of pop at a crack; they don't last an afternoon. The be-Pepsied urine threatens the brim of the channel and, for all I know, brings on the underground coronaries which the *News-Press* attributes to "settling of the channel fault." The last of these, 4.5 on the Richter scale, had our chairs leaping around for half a minute, and, up the coast, severed an oil pipe which poured a hundred thousand lethal gallons over the lobster beds of Gaviota. (Note: Winter '69, after the rig across the way leaked millions: I hadn't seen anything.) But I found a local grease called Gorner's which looked but didn't taste like pop. Two giant bottles last a week. (The better mousetrap.)

Three days after I made the first sketches for *Walpole's Love*, my Aunt Jo, her son, Sammy, and his three children, Little Lance, Indian-colored Sabrina, and my favorite, the Golden Triangle, Mina, drove up from L.A.

Sammy's a cetologist at La Jolla. He spends his life in a bathing suit taping the conversation of whales in the green-and-silver tanks of the Marine Biology Laboratory. Whales, it seems, are the wisest of creatures, fearless, sensitive, cooperative. They tend their distressed kind, nudge them to the surface, and skim their pallid flanks for circulation. (Such stuff goes well in Santa Barbara, where the daughter of Thomas Mann used to escort a dog she taught to type to parties where parakeets supposedly chirp *Traviata*.) In such pursuits, Sammy has grown whalish himself. A pink cigar of a man, he rolls out of his Squire Wagon with children, mother, and fly rods. (At the service of the deep during the week, on weekends he murders there.)

Mina is Jeff-U's age. Two strips of psychedelic cloth hang on five and a half feet of intoxicating flesh. Her vitaminized breasts are those of Hungarian spies; her golden triangle—how I imagine its secretive fur—her pure, thick lips, her winking invitations to the ball I think are meant for me. I have seen her beauty spill over since sixty-four. Even then, she was ready, lolitable. (We watched that film together on the late show. How she understood.) But then there was Wilma Kitty (Velia and the children were back in Chicago), I had less reason to act out Nabokov's dreamlife. But while the earth gnashed hot jaws under channel waters and the Impulse to Lobsterhood searched new stuff, I dreamed madly of opening Mina's Northwest Passage. (One day, driving her east, to Grinnell or to Penn State, at dusk, by Winnemucca, Nev., or Provo, U., we pull in to a desert motel, we swim, Mina, you and I, in a silver pool and come back dripping to our cabin, brassy droplets on our golden flesh. Silent, regarding, we strip wet suits—I have lost ten or fifteen more pounds, my pectorals are weight-lifted into buttresses of depilated chest—you walk to me—no, turn from me—flipping suit from ankle, I pull your back to my front, Hungarian breasts within my palms, and you, struggling for me, go belly-down upon the double bed, glorious snow-white rearward twins aquiver for the locomotive rod.)

Aunt Jo is gray, gap-toothed, powdery, hard of hearing, repetitive, with our family appetite for the fortissimo monologue. When she, her sisters, and her surviving brother, my father, the Optimist, assemble, it looks as if an Eastern rice village on stilts has been given life. (All are on canes.) They enter, four octogenarians with octogenarian spouses. (The spouses, except my father's, are all second mates: this family survives. Survives and kills.) They surround the children with their gifts, old arms and puckering lips. "Open, darling, open and see what Aunt Jo (Belle, May) has brought her precious." They vomit triumph, praise, self-adoration. All is right with the world. (Why not? It has endured them.) The cities they inhabit are crimeless, the water pure, the streets immaculate, their children extraordinary, known over New York, Scarsdale, the world, on the verge or aftermath of incredible deals—mentioned in *Textile Week*—their grandchildren are peerless beauties of rare and promising shrewdness. The gashes of their lives (children dead in auto accidents, bankrupt sons, psychotic grandchildren, doomed conditions, stymied lives) are scarred over with such noise. They stagger into the living room, drop into sofas, and, huge voices aimed at the room's imagined center, begin their simultaneous, uninterruptible spiels. Canes gaveling carpets for emphasis and control, voices crashing against each other, they solicit, they demand recognition of their life performances.

Only one mortal thing can suspend their arias: Food. Velia's thin, West Hartford voice inserts, "Would you like a bite?" Convulsion of struggle, sofa arms crushed, canes gripped to bone, the gravity of sagged flesh reversed by visions of repast. And commences the Long March to the table. There, stunned moment of formality, who will sit where? Velia leaves them struggling—monarchical whales—but appetite dissolves precedence, they fall to, moaning about the splendor of the vittles; though their old hearts are sunk at the thin New England provision, the cellophaned corned beef, the thin, presliced rye bread staled in the Protestant markets which magnetize Velia, and, for sweets, dry wafers in lieu of the thick snail curls of raisins, nuts, and caramelized dough, or the scarlet tarts, the berries swillingly augmented by terrific syrups. No, nothing is right, but then how should a thin-nosed aristocrat know what keeps old Jews alive? Mouths liquid, they compliment—and so enrich—the sober fare. They live, they eat; the juices flood. This is what ancestral migrations have aimed at (Children of the Book? Yes, quick. Sons and Daughters of the Schnecken, the Custard Tart.)

Aunt Jo and I sit in Sackerville's beautiful living room, Japanese-free of furniture, windows on three sides, in front, the flowered lawn, empalmed, honeysuckled, grassed to the great bluff over the ocean. The noise is of bird and wave, the Pacific is blue, snowy. Aunt Jo takes my arm, pulls herself up by it so that her lips are at my ear. In a voice that is part puzzlement, part revelation, she says, "The Lord has been good to you, Jeffrey."

The gap-toothed, powdery, great-nosed face tosses back toward the drained cans of pop, the scarlet paradise flowers, the spread and noise of children, and what?—the pretty, apparently undemanding, apparently giving wife. She remembers the commissions from Tanglewood and Fromm, the write-ups in *Time* (three harsh slaps), the full-fledged attack by Winthrop Sargeant ("The complex aridity of Wendt's music, commissioned, composed, performed and—hopefully—buried in the academy"), which she has read as professional compliment. And this is all set in the ocean-cooled, semitropic poster-dream of paradise.

"Things look good out here, Aunt Jo."

We both know that childhood friends are dead in the wars, drunk, bankrupt, or, at best, anonymous. She knows the deceptions of the present, this powdery old aunt whose first husband died returning a crosscourt volley from her sexagenarian racket and whose second was struck by a Yellow Cab as he hurried to her summons at Madison and 72nd Street.

I press the skin bag under her elbow and lead her where lawn and bluff meet in the line of insane-looking palms (spiky umbrellas, vegetable porcupines). On the beach below, dowitchers snap beaks for red beach ants, waves flush iron gleams. (Their metric genius is something I try and try to figure and employ.)

I hand Aunt Jo into a rattan chair, squat beside her ropy legs, and keep my ear alive. I am figuring a sequence.

Yes, for the other night, after a dismal sixteen months in which my only opus was a setting of Definitions from Hoare's *Shorter Italian-English Dictionary* For Wind Instruments, Radio Static and Audience Coughs—I tried to be of the brave new laboratory world, and it crippled me—mooning on the beach, watching the murderous oil rigs lit like rubies in the channel, I hit upon Something Grand, Out of the Blue. And, while Velia snored in the double bed, I sat at Sackerville's cypress work table and sketched the plan, laid down the lines, established a tone row, and worked it all up around a story.

Yes, the opera. In this day and age, surrounded by aleatory gamesmen, vatic pasticheurs of Mozart, phony pholkistes, electronic adolescents, employers of blow-torchers, Caged mice, and concrete crapistes, I fell into this antique pit.

And it's no surrealist cop-out, no twigged-out Clarsic (*Carmini Catulli* or miserable Yeats play with less action than a cigarette ad), no neo-Wagnerian Geschwätz but something new, fresh, off the morning paper. Urban dew. In brief, the story's about a police sergeant and a black hooker he woos with precinct and other stories. In particular with the old eighteenth-century story—he's a night-school reader—of the icy bachelor Horace Walpole, blind old Mme. Du Deffand who loved him hopelessly, and then, decades later, young Mary Berry, whom the old Walpole loved and who milked him of his wit and knowledge as he had milked the old Deffand. Girl and cop conjure between them the characters, who show up on scrims, on a screen, and on the stage (like the Czechs). The musical lines drift with the actors, or, like motifs, fade into other time schemes. No dominant style (the sign of this century), no batting the company into shape. Deffand sounds like Scarlatti and J. C. F. Bach, Walpole like Haydn and early Beethoven, Berry like Beethoven and early Wagner, the sergeant like Arnold Pretty-mount, Igor the Penman, my dear Webern (the musical laser) plus a bit of Elliot C. and Pierre B.; the hooker will swim in every love song, east and west, that can squeeze into the tone row. Yet the lines are never to blur, there are but chordal shadows round the sparse, informative line.

"Sam found marijuana in her drawer last week."

"What?"

Aunt Jo waved at a gold twig in the blue water. Mina on a mattress. "She said everyone takes it."

"Foolish, foolish. Hardly started, they want life to have italics."

"Maybe if you speak to her, Jeffrey. She respects you, you're the artist in the family, she thinks it's wonderful to have a famous cousin." (Aunt Jo received one of the ten *Who's*

Who in Americas my mother bought the year I joined the Kansas morticians and General Electric VPs.)

Gravel scutters—my sequence has dissolved—a car pulls in the driveway. A gray Bentley. Must be a mistake. No. Donloubie.

Donloubie is the owner of Sackerville's place. He has come on a mission, foolish and remote as himself.

"Murder."

Two days before, this golden corner had suffered its first Caucasian murder in ten years. Donloubie's neighbor, Mrs. Joel, the candy maker's wife, was found under the closed lid of a heated swimming pool (ten yards back from the Pacific).

Donloubie is hunched, muscular, immensely rich, is said to own much of Columbus, Georgia, his wife a goodly portion of Jacksonville, Florida. The Santa Barbara story is they met and married to stretch their desmesnes until they touched. Mrs. Donloubie has contrived the Theory of Three. The week before, Slochum, a broker, was found at the foot of stone stairs in a pool of his blood. Now Lydia Joel. "Who'll be the third?" ask the Donloubies. (Slochum was drunk, fell and broke his own neck.) The Donloubies tremble. They alert housemaids and chauffeurs to departure. But can they depart? Their neighbor has been found floating in eighty-five-degree water, gray head bashed with unknown instrument. They cannot flee the coop, despite the fabulous tracts of Florida and Georgia which underwrite their Bentleys and their orchid garden.

Donloubie comes to his tenant's tenant. I am a University Professor, the only one he has ever known. The University conjures up for him the investigation of exotic fauna. Can I suggest a way of getting sophisticated sleuths into the case past the befogged and bungling local officers? "Perhaps your criminologists up there." He means the University of California at Santa Barbara. Doesn't he know I am as remote as can be from university life, that I am a summer-quarter visitor, that I know no one but two colleagues in the music department and a few student instrumentalists and composers-in-the-egg? The Donloubies have lawyers, brilliant manipulators of their tax returns and real estate transactions. Is he afraid to let them know his home touches a house of violence, that he himself has been questioned by police?

Donloubie appears on our—his, Sackerville's—lawn with his Japanese chauffeur who carries a tremendous basket of fruit. Nectarines, peaches, plums, Kadota figs, Persian melons, a pair of golden scissors agleam within a leathery grapple of dates. Aunt Jo rises in tribute to this gorgeous heap. Donloubie, unknown to her a minute earlier, has *sur le champ* become a Personage of Note, a future embellishment of her litany of triumph. She receives him, I am sent for a chair and shout Jeff-U off the Angel baseball game to fetch it. (Argument coagulates in his long face. He is invited to stay, his social charm contrives important business with the National Broadcasting Company.)

Donloubie gives a nervous appraisal of this half-forgotten sliver of his holdings, frowns at an active sprinkler on the south lawn, an unshaven quality in the wall of honeysuckle—I see anew with his landowner's severe eye—but he is on deeper business, he hardly knows what. His gray-blond haycock, his reddish eyes, his sixty years of salted tan, his beauteous chestnut sport coat and fifty-dollar Charvet shirt command the lawn.

Did I know, he begins, that Mrs. Joel had had eight housekeepers since the first of January, that she was a vicious, half-mad woman, that Mr. Joel, slavish in devotion though he was, was on the verge of having her committed, that he had begged him, Donloubie, to keep an eye out on her while he, Joel, gallivanted? Yes, indeed, and the blond cock of hair tossed but did not—a wig?—waver in the air, old Joel had greater interests than in, ha-ha, Tootsie Rolls; for a man of seventy-six, Joel was in—if the Missus will excuse the phrase—terrific sexual form, that if he, Donloubie, were not an old acquaintance—not friend, mind you—and had he not received a call from the man at the very time the miserable woman was having her head beaten in, he, Donloubie, would look very closely at Mr. Joel's whereabouts.

Fascinating, but where do I fit in?

—Well, I thought you ought to know, for one thing. I feel responsible as your (pause) host.

Very nice, but isn't—

Yes, perhaps, but I was from a city where they—as it were—specialized in murder, and therefore, surely, in its investigation. Then, too, I was in contact at the University with all sorts of knowledgeable types. He was not entirely persuaded about local competence in these matters, and since he and Mrs. D. were friends of the deceased, if one could be a friend of a totally disagreeable woman who so antagonized her servants that they dropped off like leaves—though, oddly, the present housekeeper, a rather genteel woman, by the by, had stayed more than three months—at any rate, as neighbors, friends, and, too, as people who both were obligated elsewhere yet felt they could not leave until at least the preliminary matters were cleared up, they wanted to bring in proper investigators. I, surely, or, at least, *perhaps*, could help them find someone, either in Chicago or at the University.

Strange, but it was a glorious basket of fruit, and the man did not summon me to write a dirge for the dead woman—I was once offered such a commission, as if my lyric mathematics could serve an antique ritual—he was clearly anxious to talk, yet nervous about talking to Mrs. Erwin or any of the very few locals he deigned to talk to, or who deigned to talk with him. It wasn't clear how Donloubie—strange name—perhaps a Creole—came to own Columbus, Georgia (if he did). In fact, it occurred to me then and there that his wealth was squeezed out of young girls' thighs and bloody needles in the port streets of Marseilles and Genoa, and that he was damn scared the dumb locals might dig up this history, that even the local rag would publish it, and that, who knows, he would have to give up the Pacific villa he'd chosen to live and die in. I had better try out those dates on the neighbors' cat.

"The Missus and I would like you and yours to come for a drink this evening."

Sorry, pressure of society—we are invited to a party—ditto tomorrow—no party—but he is unstoppable. "Monday, then."

"Splendid."

Aunt Jo shines with solution. "Jeffrey, call the FBI."

Donloubie's tan fingers sink to the basket of fruit, grip a melon, raise and jam it against the dates. "Missus. Donloubie learned to dial a phone some years ago."

The cock of hair waves, the red-pit eyes shiver, the mustard sport coat and hundred-dollar beige slacks rise from the rattan. "See you Monday, Professor. A strategy session."

"I'll be there, Mr. D., don't worry."

"Donloubie don't worry, Professor."

"And thanks for the fruit."

"Enjoy it in health. Good day, Missus."

The chauffeur is spun from the house, where he and Jeff-U have divided the misery of the California Angels.

I too have had it, the breathy clucks of the old aunt, the local bloodshed, the noise rising up the bluff. "Aunt Jo, will you excuse me a bit? I've got to," and left hand is up to tap the hair above the ear. The Composer's Aunt understands.

Past Jeff-U and the Cleaning Velia into the bedroom, where the Muse has stripped her toga, and where, conjuring up the golden body of the impossible cousin, the composer pours generative sap across Sackerville's rough sheets.

The Party

That is, a select company invited to participate in some form of amusement.

Tonight's amusement: musical assassination.

The company: Davidov and Mullidyne, the University Musicologists and their wives; Donald Taylor, my old sidekick from Hindemith's Harmony Class at New Haven. Invited, but not attending: a Montenegrin serialist employed by the Disney Studios; Mme. Hortense Reilly, local alto and graduate of Mme. Lotte Lehmann's Santa Barbara master classes; and Benedict Krappell, sociologist, emeritus, whose musical credentials were playing double bass for Damrosch in the twenties to support—his words—his academic habit.

The inviter/selector: Franklin B. Ritt, an ex-Morgan, Stanley broker and active Patron of the Arts whom I'd met in a Spanish museum five years ago and with whom I have been semi-annually afflicted ever since. (Ritt takes no planes, and stops off in Chicago changing trains.)

The ostensible purpose of the gathering was to introduce me to the musical high life of the area. As I already knew

Mullidyne, Davidov, Krappell, and Donald Taylor, that left the Montenegrin, Miss Reilly, and Mrs. Ritt. Or, as it worked out, Mrs. Ritt, a woman of either great discretion or puissant ignorance. Between "I'm so glad at last" and "So sorry your wife," she said not a word.

Of course, in such company, it didn't show.

"They all know your work," said Ritt in telephonic invitation. Stunned by this rare celebrity, I did not sufficiently examine the reticence of the verb.

Velia does not take much stock in human variety and seldom goes to parties. Besides, her small capacity was exhausted by the Angeleno Wendts. "I'm not going. It'll be one more hellish evening cutting down every absent musician in the world."

This is not my line. An exception to the celebrated vicious-ness of my fellow craftsmen, a good piece from them gets a loud cheer from me. "Perhaps La Mullidyne will have some tidings about psychotic blackies, and you can feel at home."

"That's sweet talk in front of Gus." (Gus is fathoms deep in a game of solitaire.)

"I said we'd be there at nine. The party's in our honor."

"Your honor."

"I regret the dependent state of the second sex, Velia, but you'll have to play along with it till the kindergartners have had their day. You can star tonight: you're two thousand miles closer to hot gossip than they."

"I don't feel like starring. I don't feel like going."

I fear—to the point of idolatry—the unreason of women. "Come on, Vee, it'll put color in your cheeks."

"If I'm so pale, I'd better not show myself. I don't want to humiliate you."

The bee's suicidal aggression is one of the pathetic drives of nature. And poor Vee's.

La pauvre femme n'est pas méchante.
Elle souffre, tu sais, d'une détente.

This in the bathroom getting on a maroon turtleneck (cotton, to spare myself in heat and pocket) and California sport coat, a rose-and-magenta plaid. Large teeth white in the sunlit skin, blue-black eyes, remnants of black hair, I conjure irresistibility out ot the mirror. Though who'll be there to resist? Draggy crones, perhaps one with splendid legs and chest, a wrinkled Frau Musicologue who'll drop her lip my way and, *piano piano,* "Call, I'm in the book."

To Jeff-U, in his sixth straight hour before the enchanted glass: "Get your arse erect and go play Casino with Mom." Rage and disdain darken his long face. "I thought you were going to read *The Possessed.* A whole month, and you're still in Part One. Gina read *Martin Chuzzlewit* in two days, she's halfway through *Children of Sánchez,* and you can't fight your way off Page Sixty-Five."

"I don't feel like reading."

"Then write. I bought you that notebook for graduation."

"Whyn't you get off my back?"

"Oh, that's lovely filial talk. Once more, and I'll whack the indolence off your bony hide."

Jeff-U is mortified by skinniness. Strong and good-looking, he feels he has to knock everybody dead with perfection. Horrific vanity of adolescence. Now and then I look at Erikson or some other Guide to Life's Hard Stages, and muzzle my particular fury in generic analysis. Not tonight. "You get no backtalk from NBC. No criticism, no testing. That's the source of your infatuation with that machine," and I slap the button which blanks the screen. Jeff-U continues staring at it. "*Amour-impropre.* Your mind'll sink so snake-low it'll be unable to rise. You'll perish an idiot. A McLuhanite bum. And looka the mess here." Moated by a carton of orange sherbet, the butts of four frankfurters, a quarter-filled bowl of tuna fish (he never finishes anything), pear cores, two cans of Pepsi (he must have bought them himself). "What a spectacular bloom of human culture."

"Good ni-ight, Dad," D gliding to B flat. Softening my heart, transposing the exchange. A dear boy, wiser than his savage pa, and no power-mad know-it-all, no instant-revolutionary, pimpled Robespierre shrieker, no louse-ridden Speed-lapper, hardly a drinker (innocent fifth of vermouth in his closet, beer to fatten up), not even a bad driver. Only vanity, sloth and narcissism blot him. "All right. Take it easy," and I pull out the button of the magic casement.

Why does the party count? I suppose for the musical jaws within which lay Patricia Davidov.

Another tale of Middle-Class Adultery (Genus: The Academy; Species: Music). Human beings have comparatively few ways to express themselves. We swim in a sexual sea, we measure our affective lives by sexuality. Patricia Davidov was the yeast of *Walpole's Love*. Or, at least, what happened with her was partial expression of what it also partially expressed.

She was there, a long, golden, big-boned woman, and across from her, the dark-faced, sandal-wearing, tieless, white-toothed megaphone and music-hater, Davidov, author of *The Blindness of Donald Tovey, The Deafness of Ludwig Beethoven*. (Democratic hater of titles, Davidov removed Sir Donald's "Sir" and, ignorant lout, Beethoven's plebeian—Dutch—"van.") His dissertation, bound in the black spring binder which constituted its only public presence (i.e., it was never, could never be published, except by a vanity press, which Davidov's vanity would prevent his using), this dissertation graced my desk the entire summer and was returned in a manila envelope, unread, to Davidov's box. Unread, except for certain comic dip-ins, here and there, when this musical wild man lashed the finest noncomposer analyst in English or, yes, emptied the cerebral intestine which substituted for his neural matter upon the sublimities of Opera 109, 111, and 131. Davidov's egoism permitted him to struggle against only the greatest. (The drunkest punk takes on the greatest gun of the west. Except that Davidov had not been shot down, could not be, for he was down to begin with, could hardly have reached lower depths.)

We sat amidst Ritt's Collection. This fantastic assemblage of the abortions, blotches, and illegitimacies of grandeur needs a word. In Ritt's hillside house, an immense stucco-garage affair, this insanely penny-pinching prodigal had collected or piled every cut-rate piece of artistic junk his wide travels had brought him near. There were lithographs by the nephews of Matisse's nurse, oils not of Carraci but of Garraci, dreamscapes not by Redon but Virdon, abstractions done by imprisoned mensheviks, graffiti from Bombay streets, earrings fashioned from the teeth of Goering's schnauzer. The statistical improbability of so flawless a pile of criminal *merde* bespoke the kind of genius which marks California. With San Simeon, the Franklin Ritt Collection is the prize of California *Schweinerei*.

In this setting, pictures smeared on walls, clumps of sculpture squatting by perhaps-ashtrays, within this prison of creative shit, there were its living voices, Davidov and his junior partner in crime, Francis Mullidyne, and their beautiful wives, one on each side of dear old Donald Taylor (tiny, bespectacled, timid celibate who had deserted the musical zoo for his antique shop in the Paseo and satisfied a scholarly itch by writing articles on eigthteenth-century France). (It was his article on Madame Du Deffand which launched my libretto.)

The musicological jaws were biting the throats, ripping the flesh, and drinking the blood of every composer living and dead (with the conspicuously humiliating omission of J. R. C. Wendt). Within the hirsute, vibrant nostrils of Davidov, I read a terrible question: What somatic deficit kept Bach from the proper mode of human expression, murder? What sickness glued Einstein to his numbers, defrauded Shakespeare of dirk and pistol? Where had I gone wrong, squirting out musical sperm instead of poison?

Even Donald Taylor, minute, and cyclops-eyed behind fishbowl lenses, was forced from timidity to question the Davidovian Scheme of Musical *Schrecklichkeit*. "I don't follow that bit about Schubert, Bert."

Charmer Davidov responded that if it were a pair of tight trousers, Donald would follow it close enough.

A company gasp, except for the impassive Venus whose Davidov-inoculation was renewed each night.

Into the gasp plunged the fury of Wendt. "You're a creep, Davidov. Why Ritt here trots you out as social decoration, I don't know, unless to let his guests enjoy a sight of the sewer. As for me, I've had it," and having calculated that a man with a mouth like Davidov's is probably at least the coward I am and that my extra fifty pounds and six inches will pacify if not tranquilize him, I got up, snarling.

Ritt mentions something about seeing his "latest buy," Donald Taylor says he guesses he'll come with me, Davidov manages, "Wait a mo.' Wait a mo' there, buddy. We gotta talk this thing out," two of the ladies are shivering too much to respond to my farewell nods, the other, the long golden obbligato to the malodorous Davidov, puckers and opens her lips in recognition of the farewell blast, perhaps divining that it was she as much as her husband who excited it.

The Bleeding Jellyfish, or Masters and Servants

with—for bows to antiquity and other concessionary spice—one epigraph from the saint of English humanism, Dr. S. Johnson: *"There is nothing, Sir, too little for so little a creature as man"* (which has, with its hidden injunction to the objects of Gallupian inquisition to regard the recalcitrance of small things before blowing stacks of utopian fury, more force in the Age of Gallup than in Dr. J.'s hierarchial time) and, for musicians, another from A. von Webern: *"Life, that is to say, the defense of a form."*

or The Persistence of Uoiichh

— 1 —

Eight A.M., slow getting started, not from Ritt's select company and bargain booze, but from sheer sludge of time, skeins of fat in blood, layers of surrender stacked in the passage from sleep to waking.

Up, on with shorts scissored from denims shrunk in the Carpinteria Laundro-Mat, haul Gus off the morning cartoons and descend the three tiers of sixty-nine pine steps (only this morning do I notice the pretty mathematics) to the empty beach.

Gus: "You better not run on em pockmark things."

—Em pockmarks is bloodworms.

I avoid them, raise heavy, archless feet and clump up the beach trailed by Gus. When he senses a race and goes into high, my overreacher's need drives my gross pins, and I beat him by a mile. With frequent stops to assure him that I'm watching his progress, really to mute the hard pumping in my not—quite—unflabbed chest, the diaphragmatic tremor after deep breaths. This morning, I look round from one of my markers, a nude, fallen eucalyptus, and Gus is furiously waving me back, his stickpins flailing the terrific morning air. I lope back, Air-Rider Wendt. Gus, gorgeous, blue-eyed, big-mouthed head split between hysteria and joy, points me to his feet, where lies, sits, squats, a frightful purplish glob of what I would elsewhere take for the fecal deposit of a hippopotamus; or perhaps the aborted hippette itself (gluey within the placenta). Vomitous, wrinkled glob. Uoiichh.

—Look, Daddy, a jellyfish.

Shall such things live?

Closer, one sees incipient differentiae, rubbery pincers, a kind of mouth. Gus nudges it with a eucalyptus prong. The thing gathers itself, wrinkles up for a kind of progress. (Is this what our wrinkles spell?) The pincers shift, the ocean rolls closer, a bubbled fringe breaks round the glob. "It lives," I said. "It's alive."

—I'm going to bring it up to Mom.

—She'll collapse.

—You carry it.

—You're out of your little mind, lovey.

—I'll get the bucket.

—Leave it alone. Let it go back to the ocean.

Which almost happens as the next wave, lapped by its twin, floods the creature and brings it homeward a foot or two.

"I'm gonna get the bucket." Since I have a sweet sight in mind, the presentation of this uoiichh to the sleeping Jeff-U, I say nothing. The little pins mill up the first tier of steps.

I regard this miserable presentation of the sea. Wordsworth had not wasted a cubit of his verse on such as this. Yet it by no means deserved the terrible fate Fellini gave its giant, plastic cousin at the end of that rebuke to (and wallow in) grotesquerie, *La Dolce Vita*. Among jellyfish, it holds its glob high.

The water embraces it. I pick up Gus's prong and urge it seaward. At which, there issues a squirt of thin, pathetic ink. Gus is back, fist round the loop of a metal bucket. "What happened?" A wave comes up, flushes feet and fish. "Help me, Daddy."

Gus puts the bucket edge on the jellyfish's. An inch of glob is on the metal. And then again, squirt, tiny hemorrhage from hidden wrinkles. "Gus, this jellyfish is bleeding. He's in pain."

Gus laughs at this splendid joke, takes eucalyptus prong in right, bucket in left hand, and tries to fork up glob. Another discharge barely misses his foot.

I take the branch, throw it into the water, and detach his fingers from the bucket. "Leave it be."

Oddly enough, no tantrum. But we run no more, ascend with the story of our discovery to awakened Davy, who doffs pajamas for shorts, runs to the beach, and ascends to tell us he can't find it. What relief. The Wounded Vet has made his way home. (*Histoire d'un Uoiichh.*)

——— 2 ———

On the wall of the Davy/Jeff-U bathroom (unusable toilet) there's a painting, "one of a series by Emil G. Bethke interpreting the world of ophthalmology." This Kandinsky cluster of globes—eye, earth, lens, sun—"illustrates the persistence of roundness, a simple derivative of the roundness of the eye, the solar bodies and the very instruments with which we examine them." I discharge medusa-shaped phlegm into the sink and meet Herr Bethke's globes. ("Medusa," for I have looked up "jellyfish" in Sackerville's big Webster and seen the picture of the rag-of-bone-hank-of-hair creature named by some witty naturalist.) My yellow-brown glob trailing its thin throat reins supports the thesis of Emil Bethke's art.

Roundness. Persistence. Tonal row. Row nothing. It is roundness, circular. A trap.

In Chicago, the Department's musical electrode, Derek Slueter, corners me weekly with the latest advance in musical slavery, "Dumbandeafer's Solipsism for Electro-Encephalograph" (a pianist playing while hooked to the apparatus whose record of his reactions to being hooked dictates what he plays).

I say to Slueter: "I compose for liberation, not tyranny."

Secretive, snaggle-toothed, Jesus-bearded boy, he smears Game Theory, movies, computers, and synthesizers on our departmental head (and budget). The peace of Santa Barbara is, in no small measure, a Slueter-less peace.

Yet today, at the cypress work table, I sink not into the delicate shoals of my dear Deffand's exchanges with the icy bachelor, but into the calluses, cancerous boles, and labia-shaped knots. One week ago, they drove my fantasies, then me to the Ali Baba Café on Salsepuedes Street, where I slipped in behind the blue-lit teamsters, soldiers, adolescents, iron-eyed, gray-headed ex-sailors and watched the bumps and jangles of Miranda, the Gaza Stripper, almost stiffened enough to ask the mini-skirted dank blond waitress what time she finished. In the living room here there is a table made of a stump of eucalyptus. Its almost flesh-colored (Caucasian) gap faces the couch. I have not been able to joke about it. The persistence of need is a prison.

This morning, everything underlines enclosure: the staves I rule on the white paper, the sharps turning keys which fail to open doors, the annual striations of the cypress, the marine wrinkles raised to purplish bars of cloud. The persistence of uoiichh.

—— 3 ——

We sit, the four of us, Donloubie and his Missus, Velia and I, in a stupendous room before fifty feet of treated glass within which preen five miles of crescent beach and untold acres of moon-and-oil-rig-lit ocean.

The room is modeled after the Double Cube at Wilton, but "fifty percent larger," says Donloubie, stranding my small mathematics. A crystal mass, twenty feet above us, draws mild glitter from a hundred gold and silver objects—trays, decanters, dishes, whatnots. Soft light seeps from ivory walls indented with bas-reliefs of mermaids, plastery mock-ups of stonework in the Church of the Miracoli.

We're couched on fifteen curved feet of gold and rose drinking some vodka concoction reddened by a raspberrylike offspring from Donloubie's hothouse. A black-tied, hunched-up butler (not the chauffeur) approaches with heaped tray.

"Ooh," says Missus D., "China Chicks." Butler leans with his great offering, I study the crusted containers of herb and dribblings, reach for a couple, and then—they are so small— as the servant withdraws, reach again, causing him to miscalculate, so that the tray tips and one of the tiny globs falls over the edge to the golden tundra of carpet.

—Swine.

Donloubie, eyes like red ice.

I, momentarily taking this qualifier to myself (who better?), flush, swallow, cough. Butler, hide leathered by frequent whips, mutters apology (to me, Donloubie, or perhaps the injured Chick), scoops, large tray perfectly suspended in one hand—had they recruited him from the defunct Twentieth Century Limited?—and begins a second passage of the Chicks. Persistence of roundness. Velia utters profound thank yous against Butler's perhaps-humiliation. His back, in retreat, humps an extra centimeter, hours nearer its grave.

Masters and servants were having and giving bad times in Santa Barbara. The police had arrested Mrs. Joel's housekeeper, Mrs. Wrightsman. Donloubie: "Not that I blame the woman. Joel said his missus threw her dinners on the floor."

Is the floor Santa Barbara's sacred space?

Perhaps to Mona Wrightsman, who, bent there to retrieve her spurned veal chop, there gathered the final fury of a hundred such rejections, from there rose to the vicious spurner, and, there standing, rage and pan still hot, beat and beat again the thin, hated skull.

Home, I read in Roger Caillois's *Man, Play and Games* of the romantic toys of boys, the practical toys of girls. Had the child Mona been given miniature skillets? And Butler, had he been given by mistake a broom instead of a three-master? (So China Chicks instead of China Clippers.) And Mrs. Joel, who refused meal after meal, not to find what slaked her appetite, but—Donloubie's version—to fill the day's tyrannic quota. What had her Christmas gifts been? Dolls? Which cried when squeezed? Ninety-five-pound Caesar in rose bathrobe and puffy slippers (Mrs. Wrightsman's doll) to be swatted, sponged, stripped, lifted by those muscular arms, carried to lidded pool, dumped, and lidded up again.

Velia, in rebellious connubial servitude, once again determines nevermore to take master-talk from Julius Charlemagne Robespierre Wendt, turns her back to him and reaches bed-edge. Wendt, Servant, if not Sum, of Appetite and Ambition, conjures up from opposite edge the golden spread of the Musical anti-Christ Davidov's wife, and breathing, grunting, manacled, and sinking, covets, covets.

Names and Games, Tales and Flails

—— 1 ——

News drifts in muted to our still cove. Plains, mountains, and deserts do something to televised accounts of Cleveland riots, political treks, the Politburo in Prague, or even, just north of us, the trial of Newton, the Black Panther. The palms, the waves, the dowitcher trills, E flat, G, make it all remote.

Chicago devotee of *The New York Times*, here Velia skims the eight-page *News-Press* and reads California history. She likes to snow me with unexpected expertise, and hides her sources under pillows, behind Sackerville's pathetic library, or her boxes of Modess. A literary Geiger counter, I find them all. I leave no print unread, cookbooks, cereal boxes, Jeff-U's *Pigskin Prevue*, Davy's *Mad*. From the toilet seat I spot behind the blue Economy-Size box, Professor Bean's *California, An Interpretation*, and read how this hundred million acres of mountain, desert, parboiled valley, and paradisal cove received its name from Calafia, Queen of California (an "island between India and Paradise"), a black beauty who trained griffins to feed on men. Recruited to fight Amadis of Gaul and his son Esplandian at Constantinople, her winged assistants chewed up both sides. Broken, she turned Christian, married Esplandian's son, and took him back to California. All splendiferously rendered by Garciá Ordóñez de Montalva, and read by the deputies of Cortez who sailed up the difficult coast the year after downing Montezuma.

Friday afternoon, for the first time in my daily racket encounters with Jeff-U, my arm could not deliver the cannonballs which plunge him into errors, despair and double faults. My smart drop shots, volleys, slices, cuts, and crosscourt lobs were countered by confident drives. Jeff-U bounced up and down in wait for my patsy service and swung like his dream of Pancho Gonzales. Six-two, six-one. I walked off with a dry-mouth whistle, asweat from black eyes to limp crotch, drove wildly home on the freeway, neck too sore to check the approaches, honked at by swerving Jaguars, missing the Serena turnoff and forced to double back from Summerland along the railroad track.

Saturday, after three hours of flubbing Walpole's aria at Mme. Du Deffand's death, music which I must repeat when Mary Berry hears of Walpole's death, I was ready for revenge. I hung around Jeff-U's prostrate form, his immense, bony, but well-made back. (Ah, I thought, I have given him something, Velia's back being a less-distinguished feature of her body, curved by some displacement of vertebrae into a flattened S.) The back was being tickled for a penny a minute by Gus and Davy, alternately.

"Wanna play?" asked Jeff-U. Cut-rate Medici of Titillation.

The boys said, "Yes."

I said, "Why not?" and we were off in Sackerville's VW to the beautiful court set in the California oak grove of the Montecito park. There in Act II of the agon, I lost the first set 6–1, went silently into the second, won the first two games, lost the third out of sheer weakness, not having the strength to serve consistently hard, arm aching with previsioned defeat, lost the next four, and then, going to position on the base line, heard Jeff-U say his finger was blistering, and "Let's quit," meaning, "We've made the point, why continue?" I left the court silent, trailed by the three boys—the little ones having played during warm-up time—and went in silence home. There, before my shower, I sat down at the little upright I'd rented for our room, and worked out with terrific speed a perfect aria. I haven't played it over, haven't dared, but I feel its rightness, its place in the score, its power, felt its words (a line of French, then one of English) as the sybaritic bachelor imagines writing a letter to the dead woman who, from the screen, interprets his words in such a way that they drive small, elegant stakes into her heart.

The explosion—to use the word which in the 1960s stands for every exacerbated encounter, chemical or human, mental or physical—the explosion at Jeff-U came out of the void the next day, an hour before he is to call for Ollendorf (who changed flights at the last minute and arrived a day early). "Better put clean sheets on your bed for him," said I.

"O.K." He gets up, surprising me a bit by the speed of his accession. "I'll put one sheet on."

—Better put two.

—He's my friend. I know what he wants.

I get up and follow him to the linen closet. "Take two, please. Your mother and I are his hosts, it's up to us to see things are done right."

—Bullshit.

I take this in stance for a bit. He has gone inside with the two sheets. I follow, notice his bathtub is filled with sand. "I've asked you to keep the sand out of that bathtub."

—That's Davy. He comes in the back way, washes his feet in there every day, five times a day, and the sand just stays there.

"Will you clean it out please, before you go?" My words are polite, but, Walpole-like, there is the undercurrent of menace in them.

—Let Davy do it.

"I realize you've had a tough day, a tough six weeks," I say. "I know you're exhausted from having your back tickled, but I want you to clean it, so your mother doesn't have to further twist her back doing it herself."

"Eff-u," says Jeff-U. (Despite almost universal literary freedom, I am a child of repression in print and usually refrain from writing out what is a not infrequent presence in my speech. ((Let the Edwardian guff of this sentence express my feeling.)))

I approach him, eyes aglitter with rage. "You say that to me once more, and I'll knock the living crap out of you."

His eyes show scare, but he forces his voice through it. "You better not hit me. Ever again."

At which, the rage of days touched off, I shove him across

the room onto the bed. He yells, his legs, very long legs, sneakered, start kicking wildly, pumping him up. I crowd him, daring more violent response. "You effing bastard," is the response.

I punch his arm hard.

He leaps up, I punch and miss, he gets out the door, and now amazed (for I've never hit him like this), as well as fearful and furious, he calls to the closed door of our room, "Cmere, Mom, cmere, Dad's trying to *hurt* me."

And I, hearing the wonder in this, O brave new world that has this in it, feel my fire flooded, doused, and think, My god, this is Jeff-U, little beauty-boy whom I showed off to Mlle. Boulanger in Paris (a picture keeps this memory refreshed), to whom I gave milk bottles in Cologne reciting the *Inferno*, singing the *Well-Tempered Clavichord*, dear companion and confidant, and he is just learning that I am—*was!*—trying to hurt him.

I stride out, whisper in the muted menace-voice of Jimmy Cagney (fellow alumnus of Stuyvesant High School, along with Lewis Mumford and Daniel Bell), "Don't upset me like that again, Jeffrey. Never again."

"I'm not upset," he says.

My rage starts up, my tone rests monotonous. "You haven't the emotional richness of a pebble," and go into the bathroom, heart throbbing terribly, mind so swept with self-disgust, disgust at Jeff-U, disgust at my violent failure as a father, I'm unable to speak to him with any ease at all for four or five days, even with Ollendorf there. (Ollendorf turns out to be a jolly, decent boy, who comes in on a happy roar and jokes the entire two weeks he remains.)

—— 2 ——

Velia has accepted an invitation to a "peace-making" dinner at the Mullidynes.

"Why did you accept?" I yell. "You know I can't see people when I'm working."

Not quite true, sometimes I have to see them. "Is that effer Davidov coming?"

"I assume that's what the peace-making is about," said Velia, who has had a triumphant version of my squelch, without, of course, its sexual basso rilievo.

The Mullidynes live in the hills on the lip of the desert. Donald Taylor drives us up in Ryan, his convertible (bought from a man named Ryan who never put the top down but liked the style of convertibles). The drive is up the Riviera, Santa Barbara spread out like a cupful of Genoa, then into the strange broken, mocha-colored hills nudging and nuzzling each other, the most artful, Cézanne-looking hills I've ever seen (and I was once in Aix-en-Provence for the playing of the *Drang Nach Bach* songs, my opus 9).

All the way, the body of Patricia Davidov rises from those hills to calm the agitation raised by the menacing apparition of her husband.

But when we arrive at Mullidyne's house—a fine eyebrow on a noble hill—the Davidovs are not there. Nor do they come. Had he refused? Or had Mullidyne managed to unhinge his lower jaw? (The evening supplied the answer.)

Mullidyne is quite decent out of Davidov's presence. And his wife turns out to be quite remarkable, very long and soft and smart, a cabinetmaker, fisherman, linguist, mother of an immense, well-mannered and—tonight—inconspicuous brood, an honest person who does not press for intimacy yet is quickly your intimate. (Life—she seems to say—is too short for anything else.) Finally, a marvelous cook. We have a terrific kidney dish. I see the Escoffier open in the kitchen, it must be Number 1339, *Turban de Rognons à la Piemontaise*, "Fill a ring with *rizotto à la Piemontaise* (2258), press into the mold and keep hot." And, after, marvelous melon balls and strawberries from the valley. Says Sandra, in a voice you would expect a rose to have, "I wanted to have valley grapes in hard sauce, but Chavez has called for a boycott of table grapes. I don't dare buy them." Velia, who has just lugged home a mountain of green grapes, receives a punishing stare from me, and says "I'm not a Californian."

"Don't buy them again," say I, though kindly. Velia has a new dress, a Finnish print (she has read the Finns have learned to stain materials a new way), full of blue and yellow balls and great stripes, a kind of sack but better formed, light, but you know (she says) you've got something on, a knockout, it almost restores her looks. (She had them, her legs are very fine, her body thin, but neat; but that's over.)

It is a night for stories. Of a pattern, as I see it four hours later, riding down the hill in the dark, each story so much more final in its way than a tennis match. (Though who knows. The people involved may have emerged from the fierce predicaments in which our memory abandoned them.)

The one that tells for me is about the Davidovs, but its trailer, another account of domestic fury, also stays. It's Sandra's psychology professor at Duke, a man who, infected with J. B. Rhinitis, took to a Jungian strain of it, the so-called "substratum of certain memories which were 'not one's own.'" the apparent ability of some semi-mesmerized people to "recall" experiences of psychic ancestors, "Bridie Murphys," or "Viennese court ladies." His wife, a student of cell conductivity in frogs, expressed the contempt a lifetime's Scotch-Presbyterianism had schooled her never to express by telling him that she too had strange inklings of an antecedent life. "Oh yes?" he said, from his worldly, husband side. "Were you a cigar butt in Sir Walter Raleigh's mouth?" But weeks later, short of a willing subject, he decided he had perhaps overlooked a local treasure, and asked if she were still smoldering in Raleigh's jaws.

"No," she said, "but I was bending over the microscope last week when I had the strangest feeling that I was gathering fernshoots by a river with a name I knew deeply but which now sounds strange to even pronounce." She had never used, and he had never heard, the word "fernshoots" before.

He removed his Roi-tan from the ashtray, inhaled for steadiness, and asked what name that was. "Huai," she said.

"I'm curious, why do you think?"

"The River Huai," she said. "A broad river curling around a kind of cape of firlike trees."

"We can begin tonight," he said, and had her lie back on a couch, and switched on his tape recorder. There she registered her month's secretive research into fourth-century Chinese history. She was, she said, a Sinic farm girl living near river fortifications worried by Sienpi troops; her father Li Huang-ti, grumbled in Chinese—she'd spent twenty hours in the language lab, playing the records—about taking his turn as sentry on the wall. (Sandra's account was more detailed.)

The Jungian husband, blank, like most of us, to any Chinese history between Confucius and Sun Yat-sen, had the notes transcribed and taken to the American professor of "Chinese Civilization: A Survey," not at first revealing the extraordinary source, but when told that, yes, there was such a river, there was a repulsion of nomadic invasion attempts in the fourth century, said, "It's my wife," and asked if the strange sounds that issued from her were authentic Chinese. "I've never bothered speaking it," said the scholar. "Though I pick out what might be a few words. But here," and he smudged out a few characters, "see if she knows these characters. I'll transcribe the English sounds for you." That night, the Chinese peasant girl disclaimed ability to read, that was only for administrators of the rites.

So it went for weeks, until a book-length monograph was transcribed from the tapes, the West Virginia farm girl translating more of her feeling into fourth-century China than she had ever revealed on her own. Her husband was enchanted with this metamorphosis of dogged student of cell conductivity into naively sensuous Chinese village girl (raped by Uncle Su-i Chen, taken up as concubine by a weaver from Shang-Chi, dying of a sexually ignited pneumonia)—all mimicked on the green Grand Rapids sofa while he, the rapt psychologist, fell away from all his domineering cynicism and behavioral training. After he submitted the manuscript with full complement of annotation to, not the *Journal of Parapsychology*, but Basic Books, his wife told him over his four-minute eggs that she'd played this little joke on him, she thought it was the way to lead him back to proper experimental work, some of the books she'd used were in the upper shelf of the linen closet, would he perhaps return them to the library, they were overdue, and his first class was nearer to it than her lab, she would bring him home a nice sirloin for supper.

When she came home that night, he had not left the chair, she drove him to the hospital, and when, six weeks later, he came out, the term was over and she had gone.

Watching Sandra stroke her husband's browless little head (tactile conclusion to this gruesome tale), I thought, "Aha, this soft jewel of a woman, this fruit goddess with her great bowl of rose and golden balls, has suffered terrible blows somewhere. Mullidyne is her rock. He must have his facet of tenderness as she must have hers of toad. Soft jewel with toad in head. Such beauteous carats congeal only from secreted poison. Brutal father. Psychopathic mother."

"Tell about Davidov and Pat," she told Mullidyne in her lovely voice, and in white virgin's dress, passed the crystal bowl of strawberries and melon balls. Behind her, a great window showed night squeezing a line of sun-fire against the blunt point of the hill. "Davidov," said Mullidyne, and laughed. "Davidov." And with what one then could see was indeed a bit of forehead, contrived a wrinkle or two of frown.

Davidov, he said, sprang from the bowels of the Brooklyn ghetto. Ugly, squat, an atheist broken from an orthodox cigar-roller's home, "saved for scholarship" by the public library, where, each week, he read B. H. Haggin in *The Nation* and resolved to study music, not for love of music—"He's next to tone deaf"—but for love of the destruction he sensed—wrongly—in Haggin's devastating columns. Native shrewd-ness sent him to the top of Boys' High and into City College. In Forty-two, despite feeble vision and flat feet, he was drafted, pulled like a rodent from New York, and sent, dazzled by fear, to a Kansas army camp, where he stayed, goldbrick-ing and clerking. Knowing he'd need proficiency in an instru-ment to pursue musical studies, he got a local drummer to teach him the tympani. In Forty-five, he was transferred to San Francisco, and aimed like a broken arrow for the Japanese invasion, but, with Hiroshima and the end of the war, was discharged in Oakland. He walked over to Berkeley, enrolled with his G.I. Bill, and became the first World War II veteran to get a doctorate in music, his dissertation, *The Failure of Opus 109: An Analysis of Tovey's Critical Blindness and Beethov-en's Musical Deafness.* (The manuscript on my office desk had been revised for a publication that was never to be.)

In Berkeley, he taught two freshman musical appreciation classes. Enrolled in one, and soon auditing the other, was a beautiful co-ed from the Napa Valley named Patricia Mulhol-land, the poor, smart daughter of a workman in the Mondavi bottling plant at St. Helena, a cousin of the Los Angeles aqueduct-builder. That this long, great-titted, golden beauty with a famous California name should be hanging on every word dropped from his muzzle (my memory has altered

Mullidyne's more straightforward vocabulary) so intoxicated Davidov that his lectures became wilder and wilder, more and more notorious. The destruction of every musical reputation past and present fused with the discovery of sexual perversity or ineptitude in nine-tenths of the great composers of musical history. He called the fusion the Myth of the Castrated Orpheus. It had the post-war co-eds slavering at his very name. But Pat was there first, and with the most, and, age seventeen, she let her untouched cup run over the parched, violent instructor. With the ferocity of a miser, he whisked her down to City Hall, wrote Davidov after her name, and within a month had impregnated her with the first of their five children, two sons who but faintly darkened the generous gold of Mulholland genes, three daughters who stooped under the squat Davidovian darkness. And down the coast they moved to Santa Barbara's new campus, where he took over as chairman—though then but assistant professor—of the Music Department.

Here revolts began. First, his colleagues protested his tyranny, obstinacy, and musical ignorance to the chancellor of the University, who removed him from the chairmanship and threatened to withhold tenure unless he mended his tattered ways, and then Patricia, who told him that she loathed him more than any human being could be loathed, felt she was married to the devil himself, and was now ready to have affairs on any street corner with any man who'd deign to look by her ever-swelling belly to the great promise of her never-fulfilled-by-Davidov interior.

Under these twin assaults, Davidov, like rotten wood, broke apart. While Pat picked up astonished flutists in his own department, took them to motels, paid the bills, and shed her extraordinary graces on their graceless heads (this from the unbeautiful, browless Mullidyne), Davidov stayed in the hot mesa apartment, warming the bottles, changing the diapers, driving the kids to school, and hiring sitters when he had to stagger to the University to give his but slightly less fiery lectures on the febrile contortions of Handel and Pergolesi. At night, he would call down the list of graduate students, till he traced Pat's lover-of-the-day, and beg him to release her for the night. Then, said Mullidyne, he found me at Alabama, liked my little article in *Musical Quarterly* on the "harmonic blunders in *Le Nozze de Figaro*," brought me here, and then, from the moment I arrived, poured into my ear his tribulations with Pat, with the Department, with the life he led, he, the great Davidov, who should be shaping the strong intellects of men who would rewrite musical history, transform the flaccidity of contemporary composers and performers, and water this Sahara of the Arts with the kind of criticism which had lifted literature from caveman grunts to the heights of Miller, Dahlberg, and Selby. "I," said Mullidyne, "who had my friend, Sandra, waiting here at the hearth for me, though we were on Anacapa Street then, couldn't tear myself away until Pat would grind up in their Pontiac—exhausted but triumphant—and brush past poor Davidov with, 'Did you remember to put the vitamins in Gloria's bottle?' "

What vengeance. Yet if she hated him, she hated herself worse. (This seemed reasonable to even Pat-lusting me.) "Sash here had to go to her sister's funeral and take care of her kids for two weeks; and Pat was on my doorstep every time I came back from class. 'I've told Bert I'm here, he's not to bother you,' and she'd lie on the couch, shoes off—she has beautiful feet, kind of thick ankles but terrific legs, I nearly went out of my frigging mind. She begged me to run away with her, I should leave Sash—Sash knows this—Sash, she said, was too soft for a man of my mettle, whereas she'd become hard on Davidov's brutality, she was basically soft as Sash but would stand up to me, improve me. And I'd just shake my head and say I wish she were happy but couldn't she make it for her children, if not for Bert. And she said, 'They have his heart. They can think of nothing but what's in front of them. Or worse, what's in front of each other. They live to eat, they lie around, they have no curiosity.' But I couldn't believe it, I thought the children amazingly good in view of what was happening in the home, helpful to their father, sympathizing with him, yet, as far as I could see, not harsh to their mother. And then she'd go, and half an hour later, Bert would call and ask what did she say, what did she do, and I would say, 'Please keep her away from me, she just complains of her unhappiness, she's such a child it's tragic.' And he'd say, 'Just let her talk to you for a bit, it's better than her picking up these bastards in the street, maybe she'll talk herself out of it. At home, she never says anything, she never talked, ever, except dumb-ass women's questions, why this and why that, why's the ground down, why's the sky up, and I'd have to knock the shit out of her, here she'd been my own student, I'd given her a couple of A's, I still think she earned them, but she was probably just giving me back my own words and I was so blinded by my putz I didn't see what I was getting into, Jesus Christ, I wasn't made for this, Frankie,' and on and on, till I'd say, 'Bertie, I've got to go to sleep, Sash is calling me and forgive me.' He'd scream, 'You effing pig-sticker, you're nothing but a mouse-brain pig-sticker, I saved you from George Wallace and pellagra and you can't give me the time of day, you're an effing sonovabitch,' and so on, until the next day, or maybe two days later, he wouldn't call, but he'd know what time I went to pick up my mail, and he'd bump into me, and say, 'Francis, I was wrong, you and I are the same type, we're both married to dumb pigs, we both know music, we oughtn't to quarrel.' And it would start all over again."

Sandra, on the couch by her husband, smiled as if she'd not heard this story, as if her husband had repulsed the proffered detente with, "Don't say my wife's a pig. Or even yours."

"But she's still with him," said Velia. "I saw them holding hands downtown in the Paseo." (And my heart bumped in fury, at Velia, at Davidov, at Patricia.)

"What happened," said Mullidyne, "was some kind of contract he made with her. He let her have a round-the-world trip, and in the interval, he built her this house on the shore, it must have cost him sixty thousand even seven years ago, and he hardly had a nickel. He taught night classes, lectured all over, though nobody's ever heard of him, he wrote book reviews at twenty dollars a shot, not even taking time to open the books, just pouring them out, on any subject, he did a stint on the roads in the summer—he's still got muscles under that flab—everything, and she came back after four months and she's stayed down there and I haven't been asked once, and though I see her at parties, it's one nod and good-bye, and that's the way it's been for seven years. Oddly enough, I still care for him. And for her. He's a brute, yes, but he's got standards. He cares deeply. He thinks, maybe wildly, but how many think at all?"

Snaking down the Marcos Pass in Ryan, Donald Taylor, as if reborn in the foam of these passionate stories, said, "My God, how can Mullidyne take him? How can he go on all these years with all that he knows about him?"

"He has to have his Misery Vitamins every day. Maybe to have something to amuse that great wife of his," I said, taking a look from mine.

My bed-reading in dear Deffand's letters offered a better answer. Wrote the old poison pen about Buffon, the naturalist, *"Il ne s'occupe que des bêtes; il faut l'être un peu soi-même."*

Gradations of Effing

—— 1 ——

That night, stimulated by this storied bowl of untasted goodies, I slept with my dear wife for the first time in a month. A certain, special pleasure, old acquaintance newly met, though with P.D.'s imagined opulence fresh on my mental bones, I was scarcely replete after the short-order feast. (Of course the polar breeze of imagined betrayal gave its own zing of sadness and soft revenge; what a rummage sale sex is.)

In the Tacitean tradition, my Walpole was a great comparer; surefooted, though procrustean. This morning, while the lawn sprinkler makes instant rainbows in its whirl, and there is otherwise a stillness in pine, palm, and fir, it strikes me I want a musical comparison between such elegance of gradation and the rough-hewn, grandly uncertain gradation of my own mind. Music has splendid means of articulating such contrasts. I think my opera may be about the difference between oceanic passion and terrene order; policeman and prostitute, each a social control for other people's passion, summon up Walpole and Mme. Du Deffand to control their own. Something like that.

But it's not enough. Judgment and action live on fine-honed distinctions; verbal ones. ("Galba had the capacity to rule, if only he hadn't."—Tacitus; "Pitt liked the dignity of despotism, Mansfield, the reality."—Walpole.) Velia and the thought of Patricia offer different things. What to choose? (Maybe the policemen should fall in love with Madame Du Deffand. Like the detective in *Laura*.)

I'd waked up choked with such thought; or, not choked, soaked. In that estuary-inbetween-state, I heard a thickening of line, a gulf of bass, E C sharp D D flat. Pressure: and into mind Voltaire called out by Rohan's bullies, beaten in the street, Rohan, chaired, saying, "Spare the head. It can still amuse us," the crowd watching Voltaire, bleeding, mad with fury and astonishment, the crowd saying of Rohan, "Oh, that was decent. *Le bon seigneur*." "Enough," says Rohan. Voltaire, up, bony, long, bemudded, back to the drawing room, where he had been the light of the company, answering their gaping faces with his story, seeing them freeze, sympathetic emotion not available for the likes of him; a solo bassoon, staggering in fifths, a clutch of cello, a slash of violin, and then, orchestral rumbling, a small structure building. From this day, Voltaire's dazzle will burn, the Revolution is ten years nearer.

Pressure. In the bed, a sense of leg, Velia's. I roll over, lift an interposed valley of blanket, the leg shifts away. Cold, dangerous, selfish, womb-raddled, public-minded, hating.

Yesterday, in the San Ysidro Pharmacy, buying wine, I waited by the magazines till the afternoon *News-Press* arrived with the latest on the Joel case. By the fifteen-dollar cribbage boards and Japanese television sets for the beach, a barefoot girl, with fantastic legs and rear. Bare-armed, face pale, blond, a little blunted, but with that sense in the nostrils and mouth that she wanted someone. Her breasts. No great matter, but there, in an easy flowered blouse. White pants, a bit cozy for her beauteous rump. Wrenching legs. I looked up from *Scientific American* and caught her sense of being looked at. She came back, examined the paperbacks. Had she ever gone through a book? She came to the magazines. In a minute, I turned and brushed her arm. How old? Statutory-rape age. I couldn't tell. Hopefully eighteen, more hopefully twenty, but not unlikely, fifteen, sixteen. Too young, even in this new world where anything goes, where anything that can be called love is applauded—cows, leaves, watermelons, Krafft-Ebing sweetened for mass production—like "Château Laflute" made out of horse blood, cow urine, and the discarded skins of Marseilles grapes. The Revolution's won, we are all privileged, it is not kitsch, mass culture is for real, though it is plain style for all. I stoop for *Life*, my bare arm, tanned beneath short shirt, feathers the fantastic leg. All I need is "Can I give you a lift?" or "Shall we?" or "Let's go outside" or "I'll be in the VW." I have Sackerville's plates, I'll use a version of his name. There is a whole string of new motels, half-empty. Or, hell, in the fields, bugs crawling in us. *Life* has investigations of Masaryk's defenestration, and of thalidomide children learning to cope, a crack at American doctors who didn't know about the Heidelberg clinic where the child learns how to zip, walk, eat and, as they put it, "toilet himself." Why doesn't every doctor call into the World Health O., which has all the stuff on a computer? Like that Hemingway story of the doctor who carries the guide to medicine indexed for symptoms and treatment. *Life* quotes one of the benevolently lethal Rostow brothers: Never a time when so great a percentage spent on armament, yet Donald Taylor told me we're almost back at the Renaissance, when the Napiers and Da Vincis refused to publish their lethal inventions. Only vacant-minded puritans and bright tinkerers will work on weapons. But there's the rub. I stoop again, the leg is there. I take my seven-buck Château Lafitte and depart. I will not be refused, I will not be arrested. (Though I know the symptons and the treatment, I will stick with my disease.)

—— 2 ——

I look up Davidov in the Faculty List, dial, but hang up before the tone, then sit by the phone and look at the eucalyptus, a huge salmon, its terrible insides exposed by the old fire bolt. I ring again.

A child's voice: "Davidov residence."

—May I please speak with Mrs. Davidov?

A flash of music, a terrific theme. I leap to score paper, phone stretched in left hand, pencil notes, De, dom, dom, dom, de, da-da, dada, da-da, dee de dom. Heavenly, and then more, a flood, transpose, shift, work in the tonic, a depth of bass, a figure.

—Yes? Yes? Who is it?

—Pat?

—Yes. Who's this?

Sigh: Defenestration of Inspiration. "It's Jeff Wendt."

"Oh. Didn't think I'd hear from you." Meaning?

—I want to talk to you. Not to Bert. Just you. Think we can manage that?

Pause. "Mmm." I was in.

—Your body's on my mind. I want to see it. I want to see you. I can hardly wait.

—Mmm.

—Can you meet me at the Safeway in fifteen minutes?

—Half an hour.

—I'll be there in fifteen minutes, in a yellow VW. I'll park as far from the store as I can, in the southeast part of the lot.

—I can't figure directions.

—I'll see you. What'll you be driving?

—A beat-up powder-blue Ford station wagon.

—I can't wait to see you. So long.

—Good-bye.

I haven't shaved. I haven't shat. Bowels crucial. At home, I shave, shit, and read at once. Velia has taken a picture of the three-ring activity. If I write a sequel to this memoir, in the new age of freedom, it will be the dust jacket. Here, the plug is too far from the toilet. I first squat. (The equalizer: Shelley, the Kennedys, Bonaparte, Walpole, Anaximander; Thales fell into a pile of it.) I am too nervous to let go. Then shave with my Philips, bought two years ago in Amsterdam after they played the *Quartet in No Movement* and after the only visit of my life to an official whore.

—You off?

—Yeah.

—I need to get a few things at the store.

Christ. The Safeway. "I'll pick 'em up. Give me a list."

Grumble, but she writes one.

Jeff-U has my car keys, he has lost his ninth set. ("I suppose you never lose anything." "You jerk, I pay for what I lose and pay for the replacement. And still I haven't lost a key since nineteen-sixty-one." Arbitrary figure. "Or anything else. Not only is your mind a sieve, but your pockets are full of holes. And the main thing is, you just don't give a damn. Well, that is going to change, buster brown, you are going to be paying your own sweet freight very soon.") The keys are in his back pocket, along with a besanded dollar bill, gum wrappers, change, and, Lord love us, a hairpin with a blond hair therein. Nobody but Davy has blond hair in the Wendt family. My God. When has he had the time?

I have lost all feeling in my gavel. I may not be able to do my stuff. Fantastic.

But I'm there, baking on the asphalt lot, fifteen reflective minutes before the station wagon wheels up the ramp an indiscreet thirty miles an hour, whirls down the last row, then the middle, where I am, and finds a place two empty cars away. My God, she's a big woman.

—Hlo.

I lean in the half-open window. It is the east, and Patricia. The alba is the blast of a Jaguar. ("Ah," says Donald, driving into Montecito, "a Jaguar. I'm home." He saw a black Cadillac the other day. "What are things coming to?" There are more Rolls-Royces for these ninety-three hundred people than in any four blocks of Park or Fifth.) "Glad you came."

She has on one of these psychedelic prints which women with small figures can use as camouflage but which a great beauty like this doesn't need. All she needs is a strip of burlap, one single color with maybe one odd streak of another, the rest done by that great corpus delicti (though not, as yet, by me). "Where you wanna talk?"

—See that motel down the corner. That's where.

—Climb in.

I go around. The door is stuck. Davidov hasn't thrown a new car in with the house and round-the-world. She leans over, and it is then, lightly through the glass, that I catch the outline which cements the runny swamp of my belly, stiffens the gavel, the resolve, here in the noon parking lot of the neo-Aztec center (bougainvillea empurpling the latticework, a gnarled oak brought in from the hills to make a jungle nook).

The *patronne*, back from making beds and distributing packets of soap, comes in from her betwixt brunch-and-lunch coffee. "Wife and I have been driving since dawn. We need a quick snooze. Up from . . ."

—Fifteen dollars. You can have Number Three, not on the highway.

I sign in "Mr. and Mrs. J. Mullidyne."

We enter the blind-drawn, shadowy room with the double bed. Patricia kicks off her shoes, she is down to five-ten, turns around, her face flushed, her pointed nose huffed with breath, thin mouth open. She holds out her arms. I lean toward the burst of orange and purple sun between her breasts and kiss the rough material, wrap my arms around and drive her awkwardly backward to the bed. Our breath would have terrified Mme. Du Deffand. (Did Walpole ever breathe like this?)

A deep kiss, her mouth rich with Filter Blend. Is there no Lavoris in the Davidov compound?

We rise. I take off my blue sport shirt, breathe hard, flex muscles.

She rises, Venus, barefoot, bends for her hemline—she has somewhere unzipped—removes the dress so that, like a great banana unpeeled upside down, her immense, beauteous legs show to the pants, then her waist, ribs, the bra, marvelous, the neck. I manage out of my Bermudas (despite new obstacle). I wear no underpants. She steps out of pants, I kiss her copious rear, draw up my arms, hers are unclasping her bra, I cup the haughty twins, flip off the cloth, she is mine, I hers, *Himmelweiss*. We fall back, we entangle, she mouths my home base, I hold back, agony, she is no novice, fortunate Davidov, this Napa Valley bottling queen. I make my way out, down the valley, hands on the hills, lower over the great hump, into the sweet divide, oh my, why is this not my daily life? What have I done not to deserve this?

What a sight from beneath, great palisades of peach, she bounces, she jounces, I manage with beach-hardened legs to upend her, I am on top, in the holy saddle. (Paul has just issued the decree from Rome. God, I assume this beauty is in touch with Dr. Rock's pill. Upon this rock. Poor Paul, will you go to your last resting place innocent of this huffing sweetness? In abundance, I think of the underprivileged.) And then, as always, and not when called for, the great maiden humming, noising, "Unck, oonck, yeyeye," and there we are. "Og God, maw, maw, maw." I try, I exert, I limp without fuel, she crushes me. Fiat. It is done.

I sink beneath, I work the tongue, oh crushing, those eucalyptic thighs. "Ahhhh," she says. My eardrums.

Done.

We lie. In a minute, I look over. The great body is working, it is gauzed with sweat. I feel a twinge of surge. It grows apace. I wait. It grows. I lean over, I mount. "Hello, Dolly," she says. We wrestle, we throw each other about. I enter, we somersault, we twist, we bite, we hug, we sniff, taste, we hurt, we work it up, we go, we keep going, we are there again.

Basta.

We hug each other. I sleep.

Awake. "We'll take a shower."

I can hardly walk. I am ashamed to be seen, so limply small am I.

We're in the shower. We soap each other's hair, back, chests, the sun breaks on the line of sea, she touches my aching swell, it is tender, retreats, she is back at my rear, I lean into her, we are face to face, we kiss under the jerking spurts of water. Wet, we track our way over the polished wood onto the sheets, we work our way, I slowly, she but fed by what has wearied me, though inside, she squeaks, is tight. I come up to the mark, there is a muscular spasm, there is something else. "I love you," says foolish old undergraduate I.

"I love this."

We agree to meet tomorrow at the Safeway. Two o'clock. I will have a longer time to work.

—— 3 ——

It turns out (what I have but suspected and hardly cared about till now) that I am not the only one in the family making the record. Velia's notebooks, which I thought contained merely digests of her occasional course work at the School of Social Service Administration (her premenopausal contribution to urban wreckage), contain personal observations as well. I should have married Roz, the constricted Connecticuter, whose bowels would not move for days (what a partner for Igor, the Constipated Penman), or the culturally silenced

Cholonese girl in the biology lab in Paris—was it Vo Ban?—
who was so mad for navel-licking and the presence of oranges in the love-bed.

This record-keeping, though it is much more than that, is a
late and perverse development. It must derive from our reading, in succession (me, as always—almost always—first), the
novel of Tanizaki about the couple who leave their diaries
open to stimulate each other's jaded impulse.

But what purpose has Velia's epic catalog of my smells,
warts and deformities (hairy toes, unbalanced ass, flabby
chest, hawkish nose—black hair rampant within)? And is it
intended for me? Or the children? (The notebooks lie all over
the house).

And, astonishingly, there are analyses of the unhappier
traits of our (I assume) children: Gus's rages, Davy's stub-
bornness, Jeff-U's narcissism, Gina's sharp tongue. Are these
her notion of the proper Annals of the Gens Wendt?

She is moving the vacuum around, the striated hose leash-
ing the noise-box, which, she deeply knows, prevents my
work. Barefoot, I sneak behind her and stamp the green
circuit breaker. She heaves, breathes fright, turns.

She has on yellow pants bought from Magnin's, a surge of
Californianization, but her legs and rear are so thin, she
cannot fill these glaring funnels. They droop pathetically
below her coccyx, jounce, unpressed by sufficiency. Her face
is red with repressed fury.

"I can't work with that." Courteously. "I'm sorry."

Her mouth sucks itself in, the cheeks dimple, not in female
courtship, but in advertisement of displeasure at male pea-
cockery.

"Translating your charming diary notes into music is a job
that needs concentration. I can't simply transcribe them. I
need a template. Music can't take such acids. Like the body,
it needs solid stuff, proteins." And I pat the limp rear of the
trousers. Her beaux yeux, a pure hazel, no one has such
single-colored eyes as Velia, how long is it since they en-
tranced me?

"You've been reading m-y private notebooks?" That ascen-
sion for Miss Berry, end on B flat.

—You left them on the right—the northwest—corner of my

very own work table. It was the clearest passage to Inda ever not-supposed-to-be traversed.

—I can't follow that. I don't read your notebooks.

—I don't keep diaries. My notebooks are sketchbooks. If you wash your hands, you can read them.

—I don't open your letters.

—I wouldn't say that.

—I haven't opened them in years, unless I know they're also meant for me.

When a marriage fails, the couple which has opened each other's mail, ceases to do so. And vice versa.

She sits down on the golden couch and covers her small face with her fine hands. Her grandmother's ring, weaving bands of emeralds, diamonds, and sapphires, glitters from the third finger, right hand. She hasn't worn her engagement ring for years. (Its diamond came from the navel of the little gold lady on my Uncle Herman's favorite ring. I won the ring in a Casino game when I was six. "That's what you call Big Casino," said Uncle Herman, and could not be made, even by Aunt Lillie, to take it back.) Velia says, "What did you read?"

—About the hair in my rump, the cruelty in my voice, the smell of my body.

—I was furious and controlled myself by writing everything down. Everything that annoyed me that day, I mean.

—It was very well written.

—Thank you.

—I myself don't think it's advisable to do this. It's not like taking a cold shower, or singing away your miseries. It's more like gastrulation, or, let me put it this way. It seems that internal organs are made from material on the egg surface. I mean, if you start showing, even superficially, your discontents and dislikes, like that face you made when I turned off the vacuum, or these little body Travel Notes of yours, the stuff won't go away. It'll seep and steep inside and become part of you. So a bit of care, or even living together as we do will become impossible. You know when we behave decently to each other, even on the manners level, we soon get to care more for each other.

Velia is crying. Noiselessly. Probably was during my physiological analogy. She asks whether it would be all right to go in the room. (The room where we sleep and I work.)

—Let me get my paper and pens out first.

She goes in, the yellow pants so pitifully ugly I can't watch them. They are now curled up, her face is in the pillow. I take up the sheet I'm working on, then put it back. "I can't work this way. I'm sorry I read your notebooks."

She is heaving and humping in the pillow. No response. The situation is transformed, the apparent meek—who were never meek, just quiet in persistence—inherit the earth.

I grab *World Scriptures* and *Ideas of Modern Biology* (source of my analogy), and, in the kitchen, open a plastic cup of boysenberry yoghurt, whip, whip the scarlet juice in the low-fat whiteness, and read about the fly-catching feed-back of a praying mantis. And for minutes keep from myself Velia's state, holding off from that puritan, judaic, masochistic analysis which will show me as tyrant, betrayer and brute, and will see Velia as Ariel calibanized by me.

Mencius's disciple asked why some are great and some little men, and Mencius said the great men follow that part in them which is great, the little men that which is little. Hypocrisy, arrogance, wrath, conceit, harshness and *Dummheit* enslave; fearlessness, steady wisdom, almsgiving (I gave the Negro shoeshiner in the shopping center a buck while I waited for Pat), self-restraint (I've never hit Velia), austerity (I've lived for months like a monk), truth (*oui et non*), mildness (*non et oui*), vigor (I run on the beach), forgiveness (mostly), absence of envy and pride (not absence, but overcoming)— these are the divine properties which liberate.

"The success of a given population structure is the probability of survival and reproduction, the fittest genotype that which maximizes the probability." (So pills, abstinence, then sheer attrition of sentiment prevent more Wendts; more Wendts diminish the scope of existent Wendts; so loveless-ness is that trait which maximizes the survival of the Wendt population.) Walpole, Mme. Du Deffand, and Miss Berry survive by not marrying. (The generic energy went into what makes them survive.)

Behold, thou art fair, my love; thou hast dove's eyes within thy locks, thy hair is like a flock of goats that appear from

Mount Gilead, thy lips are like a thread of scarlet, and thy speech is comely, thy temples are like a piece of pomegranate within thy locks, thy two breasts are like two young roses that are twins, which feed among the lilies. Until the day break, and the shadows flee, I will get me to the hill of frankincense . . . camphire with spikenard, spikenard and saffron, calamus and cinnamon, myrrh and aloes, a fountain of gardens. Awake, O north wind; and come thou, south; blow upon my garden, that the spices thereof may flow out. Let my beloved come . . .

Yoghurt and boysenberry, magnolia, bird of paradise and plastic, honeysuckle and Velia, peaches, roses, VWs, New Yorkers, come my life, pasteurized homogenized DELICIOUS served just as it comes from the carton. Excellent with cheese. Net wt. 8 oz. Distr. by Safeway Stores, Inc., Head Office, Oakland, Cal. 94604.

History Is Made Morning, Noon, and Night
or
When Nixon Runs, the Grunion Don't

—— 1 ——

Ocean noises, a piper's flatted G. No one in the house, even Velia making safari to the sands. At the cypress table, my four pens, red pencil, point like a shrew's eye, cubes of india rubber, the stylus with which I draw my own staves, the Weyerhausered trees on which I commit whatever will be my residue (I am not what's swimming in the waves below). I usually don't compose at the piano. A defect? I simply hear the music, I trust what I hear, I have never felt discrepancy between the graphite smudges on the stave and the "sound" in my head. Orchestrating or instrumenting, I am somehow up on almost every blown, bowed, plucked or hammered sound. When I, rarely, "hear" something whose instrumental elements escape me, I just sit it out, going over sections and choirs like a schoolboy till it comes.

Honeysuckle hanging in the nasal follicles, doubling in the brain. Neural rust. Elicits a "shadow horn" (cf. Ives's "shadow violin" in Decoration Day) I have my orchestral narrative shadowing

Baritone sounds from horn, bassoon, cello, transforming, as if under water, a serial current born in the overture foam and never absent, even in the silence which fills a gap in the row. Pacific. Continuity. Humanity. Genes.

Bonaparte's musing aria, "Robespierre, *fauve* modeste," as secco as a Mozart recitative, a carefully charged *Sprechstimme*, followed by a broken shadow of the row:

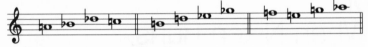

"Giii-nnah." (I can insert that call.)

Three, four hours, I am still fresh.

Hand cramped. No erasures. Confident. I don't look back. This score will go.

—— 2 ——

I drive up 101 (El Camino Real) to get mail and library books at the University. A pretty, wise-faced Chinese librarian, barefoot and mini-dressed, tells me they've moved the Mss and shows me where. I take out Webern's Opus 5 (with the sonata movement in 55 bars), Eager S.'s String Concerto with its "motionless measures" (his term) and flutters of wind, some electronic gossip of Stockhausen (*Carée* with its pale glissandi at 67), and the latest *Die Reihe* (to up my adrenalin).

The mail is for Gina (envelopes bleeding impassioned

afterthoughts: "Disregard stuff on TP—he just called from H's!!!"), Jeff-U (parietal instructions from Oberlin), an invitation to a McCarthy "Blow-Your-Mind" during the Convention (Chicago socialites in alert modulation; though not quite alert enough), a letter to my mother returned for misaddress (Santa Barbara instead of New York—no further comment today, gentlemen), and The New York Review of (Each Other's) Books, XI, 2, minus one of Eager's unearthly/worldly Swan Songs of an Octogenarian. (My—of course secret—competitor.)

I flip through the Review, whose effect is to make me wish to top everything I read there except for the stravinskies, which are sheer joy. I read H. Morgenthau's harsh entombment of Robert Kennedy (the marble thrown at the corpse's head), admire its Tacitean errors (capax imperii nisi imperasset), but, but, last Shakespeare's Birthday (April 23) in Indiana, I went on RK's campaign plane and made speeches (for what was not to be) to the Butler and Bloomington Music departments. ("We tried to get Irving Berlin," said Bobby.)

On the front cover, a Levine of Hubert Humph-er, knitting with barbed wire, crocodile tear hanging off left eye, fat face squinched half into John Garner, half into Mirabeau.

I feel left out. The music world is fierce but not half so fierce, not a tenth so populous with brains, pens and venom as the literary-political world, and of course, not within light-years of influencing events or feelings. We have only our subversive time schemes to insert in half-deafened men (fewer each year).

I don't know whether to leave the Review in the men's room (where I've cleared my roughage—alerted by Morgenthau's citation of Cromwell's, "I beseech you, in the bowels of Christ, to think it possible you may be mistaken") or to take it home to raise Velia's conversation level and keep her from her catalogs. Or—and this is what I do—take it downstairs for the lovely Chinese girl. (That accursed Exclusion Act which kept this great race of brains and beauties to so dangerous a minimum that the meeting of East and West will, at best, take place above the Dewline.) As she stamps the scores, I ask whether she'd like it.

Her face, scotched a bit at the cheeks (how smallpox must

have devastated her fruit-picking ancestors), is now alight with sweetness; eyes, mouth, cheeks, even the ears tremble with response. But no words. A shrug: I dunno.

—It's pretty good this week. Gass on Lawrence, Morgenthau on Kennedy.

—I'm an Ag. Sci. major.

"That's life," I say. "Thank you," taking up my books, my *Review,* my marbles. I have an abnormally short torso and long legs; the turnstile, which she releases for me, strikes at the testicles, my torso hangs momently over. Ag. Sigh.

—— 3 ——

12:30. An hour and a half before my engagement.

In the Volkswagen, zipping past Sandspit Point, ten snooty palms surveying the bikinied beach, I suddenly want to see some pictures. I haven't been to the museum since '64, when Wilma Kitty and I surveyed it and each other in confused simultaneity.

I turn off the freeway onto State and park around the corner from it. In the white courtyard, Greek vases, marble torsos ("after Praxiteles," "after Phidias"), limestone bodhisattvas, beaded, their small sweet breasts soliciting touch (but there are French tourists looking on).

There is a wall of aluminum-and-black-enamel panels, the trick being to arrange the aluminum squares so that the thread differs from section to section, making in-and-out peaks of reflected light, then diving in with a black-enamel cavern; handsome enough, more work than arranging groceries and, happily, unaleatory ("Arrange the blocks as you wish"). There's a splendid Zurbarán Franciscan (I remembered it), Tintoretto-lit, brooding, greenishly geometric. At the desk I buy Macedonian gold-coin earrings for Gina's sixteenth birthday next week.

The VW is being leaned on by a barefoot Chicano who smiles at me easily, without apology. "Never apologize, never explain," the Balliol aristocrats were taught. Six hippies on the grass are passing—is it called—a joint from pinched fingers to pinched fingers. One is a beautiful girl with a weeping willow head of hair who gives my long look a second look, pauses, looks too quickly away, but not before I recognize her as a Mullidyne.

—— 4 ——

"How," asks Patricia Davidov, "can you tell that the house has been burgled by a Pole?"

I am making a Greek cross for her verticality. We are between rounds on the second and, it turns out, penultimate day of our affair. "Well?"

"The garbage can's empty and the dog is pregnant." Her head rises from my stomach, and she gets a not-yet-, not-ever-to-be-eliminated roll of my side flesh in her teeth, then licks. "Salty."

"Who," I respond, "was Alexander Graham Pucinski?"

"Mmm," she says, arching a long neck northward, till I lean southward far enough to place my tongue within her mouth. Small revival. I slide around on the pivot of my stomach. We are parallel, head to head. "Well?"

—Get in first.

—The first telephone pole.

"Mmm," says Patricia, great knees up, great feet on my rear flanks. "What," she manages, "is a circle, huh, of, uh, Polish intellectuals. Oh. Called?"

"Oh, Patricia."

Three-o'clock Augustan sun through blinds. On the wall, sun-barred, a beautiful Japanese print of two ladies, hands on their Frisbee-shaped hats, skirts blown up to show sandals like those by this bed, thongs between first and great toes.

—A dope ring. Now.

So be it.

But, oh, I am feeling it. Whoever hath, to him shall be given, and he shall have more abundance, but the capillaries of my rear bulge sorely, my mouth is clogged with canker sores, there is a drowsy numbness in my chest. By mentality Cyrenaic, I am in body Stoic.

I flop. Patricia encircles me, front to my back, a divine burden, but a burden, a weight. "Had it?"

—Had it.

She plants hands on the sheets and in push-up position attempts a sweet abrasion.

I turn slowly, struggling. Embrace and kiss, deeply sweet. But my legs are weary, my gavel without authority. If I could represent the future in the present, storing away for the hundreds of unsolaced hours the abundance of Patricia, I would even vote for Richard Millstone Nix-no. But nix, but no, Heinz has not yet canned her goods.

—— 5 ——

Full moon. The tide chart says high tide is 9:45. From Miami, Nixon has spooned up the worst of cornball syrups, his plugging history, and received the cheers of the hard-hearted and the surface-sentimentalists. The rich dropout, Scranton (of P-ay), leans to Mrs. P. Ryan Nixon and forms the words "terrific," for he can't match such poorboy sagas. Nixon huddles with the newsmen, faking an intimacy his face can't manage.

From down Padaro Lane, Davy's friend, Willy, walks to tell us that the grunion will come streaming in to lay their eggs at 9:54. We go down the steps to the beach. The moon is there, plowing the water silver, we kick off moccasins and wait, Davy, Jeff-U, Willy, Ollendorf and I. The waves roll toward us, lap each other, come to pitches, crash, lap each other, fan toward the shore, our feet, the steps, leaving behind bubbles of fringe. But no grunion. No grunion eggs. Perhaps the rigs of some of the men gathered in South Miami have let lethal oil slip into the channel. Or perhaps, when Nixon runs, the grunion don't.

Exemplary Lives and Barbecues

—— 1 ——

Exemplary lives. Stripped of detail by model-seekers, the saints, heroes, and witnesses (Kierkegaard's men of significance) are reconstructed by the new democracy of neurosis: Everyone afflicted, the race is even. So new Bokes of Governors, Mirrors for Magistrates, Model Courtiers.

Webern. Banal except for his music and his death. The

engineer-official father, the parochialism (though he con-
ducted often in London), the poverty, the domination by and
idolization of Schönberg, the friendship without (expressed)
rivalry with Berg, the teaching and chorale-directing jobs
(Jewish Blind, Workers' Chorus), the hated work in the oper-
etta theater at Stettin, a couple of prizes from Vienna, the
mountain-climbing, the uxoriousness, the absorption in children, then, broken by the Nazis (no funds for Jewish Blind, no
Workers' Chorus), proofreader for his publisher, the war, air-
raid warden, only son killed near Zagreb, he and wife pack
rücksacks, age sixty, take to the roads to see their daughters,
cooped up in house with son-in-law's parents, the sons-in-law
return from the front, Webern scarcely ever leaves house,
timid, laconic, yet, September 15, son-in-law Mattl working
the black market and currency exchange, has found him a
cigar, the Americans set a trap, Webern lights up first cigar in
years, goes outside to keep smoke away from grandchildren
and is shot by stumbling North Carolina army cook (drunk,
trigger-nervous), twice in abdomen, once in lung, stumbles
into house, "It's over. I'm lost." Webern's wife denied pension,
soldier claims Webern attacked him with iron bar, he shot in
self-defense.

Exemplary?

Schönberg, dominating, fierce, teacher, writer (*Harmonie-
lehre,* the *Letters*), painter, tennis player, world citizen, late
father, excused by Austrians from military service (as was
Lehar) after Loos, the architect, spurred by Webern and Berg,
appealed; rejected, age seventy, by Guggenheim Foundation
for grant to finish *Moses and Aaron* ("I have had some pupils
of note . . . My compositions are . . .") though pension from
UCLA was only seventy dollars a month; fading in L.A., which,
said Mann, in the war was only livelier than Paris had ever
been (Vera Stravinsky concurring).

Stravinsky's life, looking in from outside, the finest; the
intimacy with the best (known) of men, women, whiskeys,
food, music, books, places (Vevey—Ravel down the street—
Venice, Grasse, Hollywood), visiting the rest of the world, fine
wives, children, but then, the mania for bowel talk, the materia
medica, the morning headaches, the hypochrondria (above
the navel, the old seat of melancholy), the jousts with fakes,

critics, imitators, thieves; the preference for thinking to understanding (the first continuity, the last conclusion), composing
to composition (ditto). Yet in the Rio Zoo, before the anthro-
poids, he wonders "what it would be like to go about on all
fours with one's behind in the air, and with a plaque on one's
cage identifying one with a Latin binomial and a paragraph of
false information." Is not the good fellow thus bravely exposed
in those elegant books of R. Craft?

After my run on the beach in the dankest of all our Santa
Barbara days, it strikes me I have been taken in by the charm,
the silvery bustle, the off-the-cuff wit. (Glassy the currency of
Bobsky and Eager.)

For us, heritors, auditors, watchers, better the laconic failure
types (Giacometti, Webern), the mordant and silent (Schönberg and old Pound), the fabling, courteous, twisted invalids
(Proust, hiring men to torture rats in his presence), the mani-
acally narcissistic, vain, jealous, nephew-tortured (Beethoven,
Michelangelo), the clipped, snubbed, shunted, but world-
relaxed (Mozart, Shakespeare), and finally, the old tea leaves,
broken spars, drifted seaweed, odd roots and unforeseen
shoots that make up, for better and worse, till death parts
one, oneself.

—— 2 ——

Donald Taylor gives a farewell barbecue for himself (he's off
to see his mother in Louisville). He lives in the gatehouse of
the princely Gossett estate, more or less watching the place
while the princes Gossett stay in their château in Normandy.
The party takes place in the Orangerie, the company larger
and more menacing than I'd guessed it would be: Donloubies
(triumphant at the confession of Mrs. Wrightsman, their release from having to depart), Mullidynes, Krappells, a Count
and Countess Czaski, he, the piano player in the Hotel Biltmore, infinitely more musical than the musicological jaws.
Amazingly enough, Donald has invited the lower half as well.
Davidov is in evening sandals (over white socks) and a shirt
he wore only twice this week, Patricia is pale but triumphant.
Her clumsy beauty contrives a modest slink; to me she is
distant, ridiculous. "How GOOD to see YOU again." (It's like
publishing banns.)

Davidov clumps up darkly, a smiling menace, "Hear you and Pat had coffee together."

"I don't drink coffee." That golden pump has sprung a leak. In order to call for home repairs? (Every story is a minor detail of another story as the librettist of *Walpole's Love* well knows.)

The moon is like an advertisement for the Orangerie. It sits low, reddish, almost full, it lacks only a Gossett gardener to belong exclusively to us. We mill around bushes carrying glasses of gin and quinine, picking limes and lemons, Donald, nervous, tinily cyclopean, stuttering, rallying everywhere with ice buckets, soda, a silver bowl of caviar and lemon. I turn around a jacaranda tree, smell its vanilla and honeysuckle bark, think of Walpole at Strawberry Hill, his editor, Wilmarth Lewis, Jackie Kennedy's uncle, in Farmington. Life's princes. *Crack.* Agony in my ear.

"Lover."

Pat, body shadowed behind the odorous trunk, has kissed into my ear.

"Cheeeristpat," I yell—under control—in whisper.

"Shhh." Lips on mine. She has on a white dress, sleeveless—though the night is cool to chill—cut in the classic female V so her body dominates everything. In the moonlight, she is the lit-up movie screen.

Sure enough, eye never off her, the smirking, tortured torturer, Davidov. "Playing games, kiddies?" Mousing over in sandals.

—Human flesh in moonlight, Bert. You've seen *Figaro.*

"Sloppero," said Davidov. "Why not get out of the cold, Pattie? They're serving up steaks in the house."

—Scat outta here, Bertie, you make me sick, like some private eye or somethin', always trailin' me around, Christ.

Behind silver glasses, a dog's low look. Its fury is driven by his wife's excited beauty, at himself, then at me. "Don't lick his crumby hide. He can't write his way out of a paper bag. Derivative, sloppy, and look at him, the ex-chorus boy."

This is a coward who will fight. I am a coward who almost won't. But am big, even strong, and say with Gary Cooper quiet, Bogart menace, "Be a good idea to cut that out, Bert. A kiss on the ear isn't a week on Capri. And I'm a little sensitive about my work. I know you're a great critic of the art, but I know a little bit myself. I'd just as soon we saved debate for another time." Or some such put-off drivel, the speech, as usual, feeding on itself, hardly related to the heavy breathing, the sense of each of us—I'm sure—that our hearts were thumping our ribs, dangerous to all over thirty-five, especially to three running-to-fat types like us.

Pat, cheated down below, transfers her energy and cracks Bert's cheek, the sound is a snare drum, *thwack,* over the garden.

—Hey.

—Wha' was that?

This through the lemon and lime trees. Pat retreats. Bert moaning low, doggily, on his knees, feels for his glasses. I edge away from Pat's exit toward the servants' garden, feeling my way to a plaster cast of Bacchus and Cupid, onto the Old California porch, past pots hanging from its ceiling, into the warm house, where Krappell, mouth pink with blood juice, delivers to Velia, Mullidynes, Donloubies, and the remote, petite Czaskis his old prediction that the Czech filmmakers were the harbingers of the Dubček revolution. "The movie-in-the-round, every man in the driver's seat. The psychological anticipation of the end of serfdom."

Old Count Czaski, small, red-faced, a chuckler and man of spirit, says, "Much as I love Charlot, I would have wished they had never brought the cinema to Prague if it had such terrible effects." The Count escaped in 1939, taking out nothing but a pair of dueling pistols whose sale in London enabled him to keep his family for a year. Now he is suing the Polish government for his stables and furniture. The Countess studies law books, writes letter to U Thant, Gomulka, Ambassador Gronowski, Dean Rusk, the Quai d'Orsay. Without a typewriter, on Woolworth stationery which her spidery script dignifies to parchment. She receives no answers. Only Czaski's Biltmore clientele pays attention to him. Mrs. Sears, a cousin of Woodrow Wilson, drinks brandy Alexanders with him every night after "Smoke Gets in Your Eyes" and the E-flat Polonaise. He had complained about the old Baldwin stand-up he was forced to play, and last Christmas, she'd given him a six-thousand-dollar Steinway which he leases to the Biltmore.

Donald's steaks are marvelous. Davidov is vegetarian. One

of the world's brutes, he has the habits of a saint. Dark, brooding, he bears his misery into the room, a billboard. Pat creeps after. Thank God for noisy Krappells. Count Czaski tries to immerse Patricia in Polish memories. She says, "Know who Alexander Graham Pucinski is? The first telephone Pole." The most boorish patron of the Biltmore has never told the Count a Polish joke.

End of Summer

— 1 —

Signs. August 4, summer's height, the sun halfheartedly (cloudily) sweeping the coastal fog out of the cove and lawns. I look out the great-glass rectangle of ocean front and see a single magnolia leaf fall lawnward. Last night, I heard what I thought was a man's voice saying, "No, thank you," thought in fury, "Velia's got someone in here," turned over, saw it was Velia herself, talking in one of the strange sleep voices that have for years made the nights theatrical for me. (Gina, too, is a great sleep talker; many a night I have laughed to hear, room to room, these fragments of sleep talk, almost dialogue.)

— 2 —

Yesterday, Mina, the Golden Triangle, made her first solo drive on the freeway, stayed with us, and went out to swim at midnight with Jeff-U. Skinny two months ago, Jeff-U has added tan to muscle, his idleness has paid off. He is quite an admirer of his body, hugs himself, partly to articulate the muscles, partly to enjoy himself. And tonight he enjoys another body. They go down bare-arse, I watched from my magnolia-veiled window and almost get charged up enough myself to wake Velia up for discharge; but don't, and twenty minutes later, when they return and slip around to the back lawn, I shift to the kitchen window and watch them embrace. There is much beautiful mingling, but despite knee-raising and other somewhat-educated hints from the Belle Triangle, Jeff-U remains—as far as the not very good sight of them permits my knowledge—innocent of the triangle's contents.

All is sign, felt prevision of the end of summer, this easy absence from Chicago life where I seldom bother to buy newspapers, have not read *The New York Times* in two months, listen to the distant noise of politics as bird gabblings on morning air. What's the difference, I think. Even that old con man Nixon—whose Cheshire smile passed right through me at Newark Airport a few months ago—has been ground into reasonable enough shape by American life to make him palatable; even the slick little dollie, Reagan, will speak as many right as wrong answers. Though could I think long enough, I'd moan here, just two months from and eighty miles north of the struck-down Bobby. (Of our house of Atreus with its new patents of nobility: books, beauty, sailboats, poems, the public weal. Oh happy oedpial bloom: Ritt has remembered Joseph Kennedy negotiating for RKO, had seen him with local beauties while the gracious daughter of Honey Fitz told her beads and raised the children. Though Lord knows how it worked out for us all. Us all?)

On the campaign plane, late April, yet zero weather, tornado weather in Indiana, Bobby came in after John Glenn (the pure-eyed astronaut elated by his world tour for Royal Crown Cola). Blue suit, blue hooded eyes, mouth latent with smile over squirrel teeth, graceful, dear little fellow, working the crowds like a medieval jongleur, feeling every response as new energy for the old themes. That last day of life, out on Santa Monica beach, an hour south of this one, diving into waves to scoop a son from the undertow, banging his head, weary football of the lights and American noise, which, that night, would be irremediably punctured. Two months ago today.

Life flies by so quickly, "a field mouse in the grass," sped by that hourly communication of event about which Wordsworth complained in 1800, separating us from every precious thing in our lives. We are so full of the world, this great age of wounding and repairing, moving for movement's sake. Hoping feeling will stick.

An almost impossible time for an artist.

At a Contemporary Music Jamboree in Flagstaff, Arizona, I went to the annual exhibit of Indian arts at the museum. There among the Hopi sand paintings and Navajo rugs, pots, jars and turquoise pins, sat the old men and women who made them. I elbowed through a sportive crowd to a silent, pipe-smoking Indian gentleman who sat on a kitchen chair beside his wooden name plate, smiled, said how much I admired his work, and then threw in, "It's not easy being an artist in America."

Perhaps his English was poor, the noise too great. The words did not mean the same for him. (Hadn't I said them more or less to have an anecdote for the exhibit?) His look did not differentiate my white-jacketed self from what it hoped to be distinguished from.

— 3 —

Mid-August, our beach shakes with autumnal tides which strip the sand and expose more and more of the smooth rocks. In winter, the neighbors tell us, the shore is all rocks. Even now we spread towels and beach seats behind a narrowing sand fortress, and still dig out rocks which press on rear and ribs. Television tells us that Kosygin and Brezhnev have been summoned from vacation to a full Presidium meeting, and, that night, the results of the interruption are announced: troops are marching into Czechoslovakia. Johnson, enormous face grooved by depths nothing in his life or reading prepared him for, returns from a fierce speech to the Veterans of Foreign Wars in Detroit to confront advisers summoned from their own long weekend in Virginia and Chevy Chase. (Johnson advisers, unlike Kennedy's, do not, apparently, stray as far as the Vineyard, though my ex-colleague, Katzenbach, has ventured there, to be assailed in the local gazette by literary sideswipes from the off-season editor-writers from New York.)

For the last ten days, we have new neighbors, the Loves, up from Louisiana, father and eight or ten children by three wives (all absent, he's separating from Number Three). The children saturate the length of beach between the felled eucalyptus and the bluff from which it fell. They come in with surfboards, Polynesian bikinis, mattresses, rainbow towels. The loveliest of them speaks Cajun French with me, "*Que voy que zhe zire, cherie?*" and to this cane sugar nineteen-year-old with her flawless Sea and Ski-oiled body, the old music

perfesser says, "*Que tu m'adorasse, m'belle.*" She and another of the stepsisters (the tangle of marriages is as complicated as the kelp which meduses the end of the bared tree)
are shopping and cooking for the mob of Loves, Williston-
Loves, and Freers. "It's lahk the quahtuhmaster caw." Her
father, it turns out, owned the beach before Donloubie, was
raised in the Villa Leone, and the real-estate advice I've
passed him ("The bank buys the property, in five years you
sell, pure gold."), he politely lets fly over his head. He
stretches, auxiliary bellies mounting to the volcanic navel, and
asks if I've read *African Genesis.* I haven't, but concede the
events of the day make me think more of sharks defending
territory than modern nations. He hasn't heard the news of the
Russian move on Prague, nor of the innocently forked address
of our President talking of great powers crushing the will of
free peoples; he's given up the boob tube's hourly communi-
cations.

The sugar cane turns her oiled belly and says, "Daddy, you
doan do nothin' but sleepn read."

"Readin' I enjoy, sleep I need," and he tells me, from his
Kremlinic isolation, of the good relations down his way between negroes and whites. One would think the last years
had seen him at a permanent eight thousand feet above the
delta.

I tell him our smart black cleaning woman is supporting
Wallace because he tells it straight and nasty.

—It's best to know whah you stand.

I agree. On the other flank the disturbing beauty peeks a
smile out from under her lambent arm. She has loved Bobby
Kennedy, she can't figgah out that man Nixon, she thinks after
leaving Sophie Newcomb she'll fahnd some perfesser to
marry and lead a good life goin' different places every summer, she loves travelin', learned maw in Colombia up in the
mountains with Indians the term she was on probation, than
she's evah done.

Jeff-U and Gina are part of the Loves' night parties; they
swim in the midnight surf. Tonight—I say this loudly—I will
swim myself, will risk turning pumpkin, rat, or tubercular; my
hope is to draw my sugar-caned left flank down from her
party to a strange once-in-a-lifetime moment with the transient

perfesser. Why not? Twenty-one years separate us, but in this smorgasbord age of kinky love, what is this but digested bread and water? (In Jeff-U's new *Playboy*, Kinsey's assistant, Pomeroy, tells of a "mild-mannered man" who'd had relations with seventeen members of his immediate family, including father and grandmother, and had gone on from this good training to most varied experience among the world's flora and fauna. "What's your preference?" asked Pomeroy. "Women," was the rapid, surprising answer. "But," reflecting, "the burro is very, very nice.")

That night, the house quiet, I flip on Sackerville's playful outside spotlights and make my way down the sixty-nine stairs. It is dark below the reach of the shore light, I feel along the banister and, on the newel, brush Love's bourbon glass onto a surfboard. It cracks, my big toe steps, is cut, bleeds. I howl, furious, but take off my trunks and run off the pain along the shore. The tide is starting to flow back, but the beach is still wide enough, the lights and waves oil it to lubricity, I run five laps and plunge in. The water is rollicking, warm, intimate. I lie on my back, rock, stare at the starred gauze. The shore outline is a recumbent dragon, no, a turkey. I try not to await, but I await another body on the steps, removing the Polynesian strips from the generous doves and happy wedge. I wait, I roll, I loll, swim, and, by God, I hear hum-bump, hum-bump, and make out a figure on the steps, a girl, the legs buckling in, the hips swaying. I swim up, "Hi," yell I. "Hi thah."

"Who's that?" calls Gina. "Dad? You swimming too?"

Something in the region of my heart dives through something like my intestines, slaps my bare gonads, sinks in my bowels. "No, dear, I'm just cleaning off my rump. Throw me my trunks there from that stump." You clump.

Upstairs, I sit in the—except for the colored-television light—dark and hear that President Svoboda, broadcasting from a hidden radio station, has asked the Russians to release Premier Dubček and leave the country. There has been scattered fighting, the people in Prague, filmed by their television cameras, gather in the squares, sit in front of tanks, the iron muzzles wave over their heads.

While Velia snores, I read in a Sackerville anthology Dr. Browne's vaunting cliché that the world he regards is himself,

"the Microcosme of mine owne frame . . . my life, which to
relate were not a History, but a peece of poetry . . . that
masse of flesh that circumscribes me, limits not my mind."

Dumbhead boast.

Gina, back up, watches the late show, one cell of the
electronic plasmodium. Some cosmos.

Outside, magnolia leaves and canary-headed flowers on
the vine against the window lit by the reading lamp. Beyond,
night and ocean, *what lasts*, extinguished by reflections of
the room, the electric clock-radio, the sleeping Velia, my work
papers, india rubbers, pens and ink cones, the anthology
(plasmodium for Dr. Browne), score paper, stylus, my own
bulging head, bed, ashtray, cigars, wallet, checkbook, maps,
and, source of the reflected deception, the lamp itself.

—— 4 ——

I am to meet Pat at the Safeway parking lot again. The
"scene" with Bert has intervened since our rendezvous-mak-
ing, yet, last night, no signal passed between us, no note of
cancellation. We parted without handshake or acknowledg-
ment. But, a man of my word, I will show up on the asphalt,
ready, mind and body.

I do. I wait. Ten minutes, twenty. Five minutes more. No Pat.
I turn the ignition key. The state is restored, family, morality,
ultimate sense. But now, my need is large, pressing. I pull up
two parking places from the exit, go change a dollar into
dimes, and telephone from a glass booth by the market.

"Hell-O." Bert.

I must hang up, but a lifetime of nonwaste and, yes,
straightforwardness inhibits. I cannot even disguise my voice.
I but soften it. "Hello."

—Oh, it's you. I suppose you're making a shack-up time
with Patty.

—Whatinchrisname you talking about?

—Fuck you. Stumblebums his way through elementary
harmony and thinks he can fill every hole in California.

—You miserable dung-heap Davidov. Waddy think your
wife's legs are gaping for if you weren't such a hopeless
dragass and shitmouth. "Don't hurt me," "don't hurt me," and
the next day you're coming on like Mussolini. Christ, I can see

why these rubes around here won't give up guns, lice like you rushing around waiting to be crushed.

—You want to try a little crushing there, Wendt? You just wanna try something?

I am blowing sky high. This glass is fogged with my heat. My glasses (I use them for driving but haven't taken them off) are fogged by it. The physiology of rage.

There's another element. At the newsstand, I bought this morning's *New York Times,* thirty cents, flown in the same day. First time this summer, a treat to remember what the great world's about. And what happens? Agony. There's a big We're for McCarthy Ad, painters, writers, musicians, entertainers, the "health professions" (to spare the feelings of dentists and veterinarians), and lo and behold, I, a McCarthy supporter now, haven't been sent it, have been sent an Artists for Humphrey (but that's because they can't get many), but apparently they have enough Musicians for McCarthy not to need me. Half the lousy composers of New York are there, there's even a Wendt I never heard of, probably some stage designer, but me, am I fallen this low, that on a list of a thousand artists, I'm not there? So I sat cramped in the miserable VW, my body steaming for Pat, my head raging at exclusion.

And so stayed in that glass booth by the Safeway market ready to tear Davidov's guts out, wrong though I am. And challenge him. "Here I am, you sac of envy. Creep. Come and get me." Though don't tell him where; nor does he ask. He comes back with throaty gurgles, and I say, "Spit it out, Davidov. Cough it out, you slime."

Three feet away, I see, waving at me, out of some Hal Wallis movie of the thirties, Gus, Davy, Gina, Velia, and Jeff-U. Fog, sweat, my face parboiled. The fish is hooked, cooked, and yet alive. Davidov breaks through his gurgle and splits the phone with a yell. An unearthly yell, they must hear it outside the booth, I have to hold the receiver a foot from my ear. I grind my mouth into the speaker and say, "Davidov, if I see you, I'll turn you over to the De-Lousing Squad. I'm taking to the Public Prints if you ever dare drop your pissy pen on a sheet of paper. I'll expose you to the Chancellor, you watch your step or I'll shoot the guts out of your fat head. Tell your wife to zip your prick to her arse, I have had it with her, I wouldn't touch a cunt you touched with a revolver. Fuck you eternally," and put the receiver gently back, emerge from the glass tank, sweating triumphantly.

"WELL, what was that all about?" asks smart-eyed, rather pretty Velia.

—I forgot to turn in a report on the chamber group it's the deadline I was cussing the secretary for not reminding me I told her fifteen times I needed cigars from the market here I couldn't go up to the Havana Nook. This town heat is killing me!

"It's not hot here," said Velia. "You're just overagitated by little things."

By Bei Wendt

—— 1 ——

September 6.

House empty. I'm orchestrating Scene 7. The sergeant is telling the girl about Walpole and Mary Berry. It is his first sure sense of his own love. Dry recital, but I want caverns of love music under it. There are woodwind choirs, all breathy, then a solo cello breaking into, stopping, breaking into, stopping, and finishing out the declaration. When the girl speaks, I have Miss Berry's music in back of her, but in plucked violins, flute, vibraharp, wood percussions. The sergeant is shadowed by Walpole, by Napoleon (who read the letters to Madame Du Deffand en route to Moscow), yet is held in by commentary music and by the tone-row spine shifted from choir to choir, instrument to instrument.

An hour, two hours, more. I keep lighting and relighting the Muriel blunt, chewing Sour Cherry gum, tossing my neck, working with Jeff-U's wrist-strengthener. My scores are neat. It is a crucial condition of getting played in our time. A slob elsewhere, I am a beautiful scorer, copyist. I love these notes, I make quarter-rests like a cinquecento Flamand, I rule my crescendos into beauteous horns, I rank with the better calligraphers, if not composers, of mid-century.

The telephone. Ignored. It persists. The house must be empty. I've worked long enough.

I answer it. A boy for Gina. I shut up shop, brush the amoebic curls of india rubber into my wastebasket (*Embarcation for Cythera* in rounded tin), put my pens in the red earthenware jug from Arezzo (bought at the museum there after a joint concert with Dallapiccolo), add my score sheets to the flat-top snowy mountain. The phone shoots off again. And again for Gina, Loretta Cropsey. I tell her Gina's at, I think, the Point, hang up, and hear from the first floor Gina calling, "Hi."

She comes upstairs, I go to her room with her, deliver messages, cannot say who the boy was—"Dad, I've asked you to get the names of callers"—lie on her bed while she cuts up skirt material and pins it, puts on Aretha Franklin, "Love Is a See-Saw," a very good singer, the music wretched, stiff stuff, put Gina's shell ashtray on my bare chest (I have a convenient cavity), smoke out my Blunt, and listen to her morning picaresque. Gina gives the lie to Beast City, she wanders everywhere, speaks to everyone, gets invited for coffee, tells them easy lies, "I'm from Omaha, my parents are French, my father's a mechanic, wounded in the war, I'm a first-year student at UC," and so on. The day's bag is, "I went to the Point, it was beautiful, I swam, read *Portrait of a Lady*" (my birthday gift to her, along with the earrings), "a well-dressed Negro, quite good-looking, about twenty-five, asked me what I was doing out of school, he was a truant officer. I told him school hadn't started for me. He wasn't a truant officer, he recruits people for jobs. He said he only liked to swim with flippers, and someone had taken his flippers off his boat, would I have breakfast with him tomorrow and go swimming," I am shaking my head, but with Gina in front of me, this pure dear fruit of girl, what is there to say? We are surrounded with rapists, head-crackers, she wanders on like a nymph in a pastoral. She went into the shelter with the Recreation Director, a bored physiology student, "quite good-looking," he was working on heart banks, enter a policeman who "asked me if I was a hippie," said he hated them, had been at the Convention last week, he hated Paul Newman, but when Shirley MacLaine had walked in he'd said, "Come on in, honey." "You sure you're not a hippie?" She'd played chess with the physiologist, had been beaten in ten moves, "he was very bright," then ran into Ollendorf at the Unique and was driven home. "A great day."

—— 2 ——

Saturday, September 7.

I wake at seven-thirty, eyes amidst the darkening green of the Tree of Heaven, a trimmable branch of which loops over the second-floor porch and, in a stiff breeze, scrapes the window screen. There is no breeze, the day has the pure deep gleams of an early fall day here. Shall I put on sneakers and run in the backyard? Or down toward Dorchester, dodging the glass bits, the dog shit, the paper bags and Seven-Up bottles left by Friday's school lunchers? No.

But I go barefoot downstairs, open the door to the empty, tree-caverned street. I do ten quick bends in front of the rubber-banded cylinder that is my day's key, the Chicago *Sun-Times.*

Inside, I fill the coffee pot with water and Stewart's Regular Grind, plug in, slide off the rubber band, make a pitcher of orange juice, and glance at the Cubs (the team's Methuselah, two-years-younger-than-I Ernie Banks, has hit his twenty-ninth homer, his biggest total in eight years, good sign for us oldsters). The first page gives Mayor Daley's rapid-fire defense of his elegant behavior at the Democratic Convention, with illustrations of black-widow spiders, razor-bladed tennis balls, and the dented police helmets victimized by these occult and more-than-occult weapons. (Chicago-loving Dick, so monolithic of conviction he will not grasp that television did not register him as the sow's ear without some help.) Onto the whirl of yesterday, I could be reading the Fugger News Letters, the variations would be in detail only. (*Viva* Detail.)

Two cups of coffee. I weaken during Two and spread pumpernickel with saltless butter and urinous peach preserves.

Upstairs, Gus and Davy watch Saturday's horror cartoons, Gina is at Loretta Cropsey's for the night, I wash, shave, and climb another story to the study, why don't I call it "workshop"? There sits the pile of worded notes (noted words?). Slag?

Will some twenty-second-century genius, brooding over "the pastoral, thoughtful, tolerant twentieth century," think of Walpole's farewell aria to Miss Berry and hum its pathetic, chromatic, synthetic loveliness as he plugs in the universal music computer and tunes in on the tonal events of Galaxy Scribble?

I proceed with orchestration, do three pages, rather joyfully, working with end-of-spectrum instruments, double bassoon and piccolo, these bearing melodic burdens while strings and brass police the side streets.

Down the hall, Jeff-U's door is shut. Last night I would not let him take the car because the night before he'd gone to Arlington Park, lost money (his affair), and kept the car until two thirty A.M. (mine). I was waking at each sweep of car light down the street and met him in fury at the door. We had harsh words, rare these last weeks.

He is stretched out endlessly in bed, feet and neck out of his blue quilt, just the way my father, grandather, and I sleep; unblanketable Wendts.

I lift the hand weights ten or twelve times, regarding the musculature—already softened in the two weeks since our return, or so it seems to me. Jeff-U's pants, shirts, underpants, socks, weights, magazines and papers litter the room. At his graduation last June, I tried to persuade him that high school essays on the Economy of Chile were not immortal witnesses to his intellectual power, but here they be; his slag. Posters of Einstein and—in color—the Bernini Vatican Piazza dominate two walls, the rest have a Dürer rabbit, an ink sketch of Arezzo by Maniera (which he gave Jeff after I played at the concert in sixty-three, Jeff-U's first appearance at a Wendt concert), and a panel of a Tree of Jesse from either Chartres or Lincoln (stained glass is his forte, not mine).

"Please don' lif' weights here now." Mumble from the bed.
—Sorry.

I sit on his bed and pat his head, a harsh tangle of brown hair. I rub that a bit, his skull is narrow under the hair. He loves to be rubbed and tickled (another Wendtism), and I rub his shoulders. Unblemished, soft-skinned, very strong, tan. The little boy who's spent seventeen-plus years in Wendt houses and in one week leaves for college. Yes, a classic scene, but I surrender to it, I play my part. (We fit into such a small repertory.) Back against the wall, I rub his shoulders. *Der Rosenkavalier* flies up from WFMT below. I stare out, through and above the trees, and remember life with Jeff-U, the frightening announcement by letter from Velia—would we have lasted that first year if it hadn't come?—the room in— was it Cherbourg?—she on her way home, I to stay to finish up with Boulanger, the long birth, twenty-six hours in the American Hospital, the noise of carnival drunks below the window, my first sight of the brilliant bright eyes, the heart- wrenching child, how many thousand hours, playing, reciting Dante, whistling Bach, while I held the bottle for him, teaching him to throw, to bat, to serve, driving with him around Italy and England, with Gina, with Davy and Gus, with Velia, the boy becoming himself, thinning, hardening, his will becoming his own, his lies, his sweetness, swimming in the Neckar, not wanting to go away, staying always with us, no camps, no schools away, reading *I Promessi Sposi,* saving ball cards, climbing in the Dolomites, life, middle-class-American-Wendt life, one of the earth's three billion, one of its hundred million lucky ones, one of my four children, my one and only, unique at least in this, Jeffrey Ulrich Wendt. So long, my dear boy, fare thee well, dear heart. The *Rosenkavalier* dies away, my hand rests on his shoulder, I pat his blanketed rear twice and leave.

—Thanks, *mon père.*

PART·III

SHARES:
A NOVEL
IN TEN
PIECES

A SHARE OF NOWHERESVILLE

—— 1 ——

Illinois is tornado-shaped. Its southern funnel spins out of Kentucky, Arkansas and Missouri, swells at the Carbondale parallel, and is widest at the line between Bloomington, Carthage, and the old Mormon town, Nauvoo. Willsville, fifty miles southeast of Springfield, is in the tornado's eye.

It is a county seat, a town of four thousand with five restaurants, seven bars and a movie theater which opened on weekends until it closed in 1975. There's a 120-year-old college and an eighty-year-old courthouse (which cost three quarters of a million dollars and raised a still remembered scandal). In 1852, Abraham Lincoln tried a case here. In 1908, a seam of coal was discovered in a cornfield; Standard Oil of Indiana bought it and, to house the miners it brought in, ordered eighty prefabricated houses from the Sears Roebuck catalogue, which, in the early 1980's, brought the town its only moment of national recognition. (The *Smithsonian* published a piece suggesting such prefabrication might be a solution to the American housing crisis.)

Now Willsville is the only place within a couple of hundred miles where the world's best old films can be seen, where there is a complete file of the *New York Review of Books*, a twenty-year file of the *Hudson* and *Partisan Reviews*, *Art News*, *Paris Match* and *Der Spiegel*. All this can be found in the Share Complex—six rooms of George Share's nine-room house. Here there are books recommended by *The New York*

Times, the *Times Literary Supplement*, and those George finds in European and American bookshops. There is a discussion-recital room dominated by a Baldwin grand piano donated by Hobie Spriesterlach (who'd lent George the original sixteen thousand dollars for his shoe store). The walls of the house—the Share Museum—are covered with reproductions of paintings from the world's museums, and with paintings done by young men and women of the county who'd been inspired by them.

George's own quarters are convenient and private enough to give confidence to the young women who over the years moved from the deep chairs of the Complex to George's kitchen, bath and living room-bedroom.

Self-taught and, though no spring chicken, still learning plenty, George had been passing out to Willsvillians what he knew—and occasionally what he didn't—for almost thirty years. It had taken a decade or so for Willsville to accept him. Now he is a community pillar, an odd one, as if a marble Corinthian column had been inserted among the courthouse's granite Dorics.

What other Willsvillians had been interviewed by the *Chicago Tribune* (*Tempo* section) and been featured in a half-hour of prime time on WTTW, Chicago's public television station?

The Shoe Store Plato. That was the title of the *Tribune* feature, the usual theme of George's celebrity (until his brother Bobby became Deputy Secretary of State).

Founder, half-owner and manager of the largest shoe store between Springfield and St. Louis, Share had a solid place in town for giving credit to the illiquid parents of the club- and flat-footed, the hammer-toed and weak-ankled. In the *Tempo* article he was quoted as saying, "I wooed Willsville through its feet before I wooed its collective head. Does the word pedagogy cover both? I don't know Greek."

Before satellite dishes replaced Piper Cubs on the lawns of rich county farmers, before computer terminals and video cassettes converted the Dark Age Nowheresville of the Illinois Plain into another sliver of International, if not Intergalactic, Here and Now, George's Cultural Complex—the *Tribune*'s term—was the mental center of Carlin County.

—— 2 ——

What was Willsville for George Share? He was always asked this, the often-asked question of the American small towner. "It's where I live," he told the *Tribune* reporter. "Where I've built what I've built. I wouldn't be a bigshot in Chicago or St. Louis. I wouldn't be needed there. I like it the way any reasonably happy man likes his town or his neighborhood. I like knowing every face, every cat. The way the green looks in the rain. I like eating at Wayne's Grill, even if no one's in the booth with me. Alone, I'm not alone here. (Of course, that's also the danger of a small town.) You can read the world here as well as anywhere. We've got people who know lots of things. Important things. People who know about animals, machines, grain, fenceposts. There's a doctor, there are two lawyers, two realtors, a pharmacist, an accountant. No Nobel Prize winners or Henry Kissinger. (Is he that much different from Hobie Spriesterlach?) We've got books, we get MacNeil-Lehrer, the Masterpiece Theatre. There's no such place as Nowheresville anymore.

"Of course, I live a shuttling life, Willsville-Venice, Willsville-Paris, Willsville-London. I'm at home there too. But I come back to Willsville with more than trinkets and satiety. I'm on top of Willsville, but when I was growing up in Mercer, Iowa, I wasn't on top; I was at Mercer's mercy. Growing up, you don't know anything, until the world leaks in and you see you've been swaddled in pettiness. The books I read told me there was a world out there. I couldn't see much of it in Mercer. My parents were too fine a sieve, nothing came through them. My brother got away first. By a straighter route, but he got away. I guess I owe him the idea of getting away."

—— 3 ——

Since school days in Mercer, George had tried to work out the difficulties that stood between him and the world he read about in the Mercer Library.

Mercer then, like Willsville now, was one of ten thousand American towns called even by its inhabitants something like Nowheresville. Since this town was the center of their lives, the reference was less shameful than proud.

Mercer had never been a center for George. At twelve, he decided he wanted to be at home everywhere in the world but Mercer. He wanted to see the world he read about, wanted to know the way it worked, wanted to be a part of it. Busy as he was making a living—he started at fifteen when he left home and school—George kept reading books, thinking about life, and working out his own.

Europe was a crucial part of that life. Years after Hemingway and Fitzgerald had cooked their moveable feasts, George wanted to dine on them. At first, he wanted to live in Europe, but after a decade of work, he realized he'd never be able to afford that. He was going to have to eat it piecemeal. Even this meant thousands of toiling hours. Still, each year for the past twenty, usually in July, George took off from Willsville for Europe. With him he often took one of the girls he'd met in the Share Film Club, the Share Library, the Share Museum or one of the other institutions he'd formed in order to meet them.

—— 4 ——

The only person from Mercer outside his family with whom he kept up was Leroy Scheuer, whose father had the feed store on what else but Scheuer Street (two local facts that would have swelled any Mercerian's head but Leroy's). He'd had evangelical modesty beaten into him very early. It made him a rebel and so George Share's pal, confidant and collaborator. He'd come close to taking off with him. "But what's the point?" had been Leroy's point. "I don't have your brain, George. I'm just smart enough to admire yours. That goes for guts too. Anyway, you'll need an aide-de-camp here. Somebody to send you care packages."

But George decamped without a lifeline and with no companions or hostages, actual or emotional. He'd cut himself off from regret, censored any impulse toward nostalgia or family piety, and used loneliness to steel his heart, not soften it. He had a berth picked out, seven miles down the Interstate, in the Huron shoe store, the first of twenty such stores he'd work in till he started his own in Willsville. In Huron, he made twenty-eight dollars a week; half of it went for room and board, much of the rest was saved.

His parents were people who accepted what happened.

They were the descendants of farmers who suffered as much as coped with natural disasters. Wallace Share was diffident, laconic, a casual pursurer of the small comforts that got him through the day. His lumpish body expressed the thousands of cattle carcasses he'd hoisted from packing house to refrigerated truck. A strong man who looked and felt weak, physical activity had sapped his capacity for rage and resentment. The relief from bearing carcasses was the core of what *joie de vivre* he had. He embellished that relief with beer, country music, radio comedy and reveries in a porch hammock. There wasn't much time for discontent, not while he paid the bills, fed children, saw his parents, aunts, uncles, cousins and in-laws.

Fifty-odd Shares and Freihofers lived within an hour's drive of Mercer. The Share boys grew up in a network of family events, observation, knowledge, mutual aid and mutual suspicion. Most of the family made out well enough, though two farms were lost in the nineteen-thirties, there was a suicide, a convicted thief and at least four semi-loonies, but the family made it through hard times, helping each other and keeping records so that in better times there were repayments and restitutions. Life did not feel marginal: that was the condition of life. After you were twelve or thirteen, there wasn't much leisure. But George and Bobby Share were raised on the lip of as much prosperity as the family had known, and had time to follow the dreams induced by the radio and the library books, the occasional teacher and friend who dreamed of breakthroughs.

Their mother helped, though obliquely. Erma Share's most intense feelings went into an introverted devotion she pressed on no one, including her sons. It was her retreat. Up at five-thirty, she milked their six cows, tended the truck garden, got Wallace and the boys up and out of the house, washed, cleaned, mended, negotiated with the milk co-op, paid or forestalled the bills. Sundays she sank into hymns and sermons. Evenings, she studied the local news, turned on the national. She voted, and saw that Wallace voted. As for her sons, she watched them grow out of her knowledge into mysteries.

Bobby was the smartest boy in his class. When he got back

from two years in the Air Corps and told them he was going
to the university in Iowa City on the G. I. Bill, Wallace, stunned,
asked him if he was sure it was going to do him more good
than harm.

"In what way, Pop?"

"They'll put you down."

"Why?"

"You are who you are. They're who they are."

"Is it bad being who I am?"

"Not bad. Different. From them."

"What's the difference?"

"They're kids who've had things. We're small potatoes."

"In the Air Corps we were all the same."

"That was war. This is regular life now."

Erma said, "It's meant for him to go." He went, and never
stopped. After Iowa City, he went to the University of Chicago
Law School; after that, he clerked for a federal judge. The
next thing they knew he was in New York, working for a Wall
Street law firm, and within five years, he was in the government. By then, his eminence was as natural, and as distant,
as a constellation. Somehow or other, the boy in short pants
eating cornflakes in the kitchen had been touched with star-
dust. Pride was not part of their emotional palette, but their
feelings about their son went beyond surprise and curiosity.
There was a stunned amazement that began, as most of their
feelings did, with relief from disaster. "At least he won't have
to worry about paying the dentist." (Bobby's dental problems
had caused one of the financial crises of their married life.)

George was a different matter. Whereas Bobby went up,
George dropped away. In the middle of his junior year, he told
them he'd had it with school.

"But," said Erma, "you're good in school, Georgie."

"It's not hard for me. And I'm average, not good. Not like
Bobby. It's a waste of time."

"A diploma's not a waste of time. Bobby wouldn't be in Iowa
City without a diploma."

"I don't want to go to Iowa City. Or any school."

"A diploma's not a waste. You may want to do what Bob's
done. No diploma, no college."

"I want something else."

What he wanted would "take too long to explain," even to himself. She saw him reading, the books meant nothing to her, but she saw it was a display turned into pleasure. Fine with her, that's what the library was there for. That it could change a life didn't figure in. George read and read, and what he read of was far from Mercer. What he read had been written by people who'd come from places like Mercer, at least weren't all that far away, St. Paul, Oak Park, other small towns and larger ones in the midwest and south. What they wrote of though was Paris, Madrid, London, New York, the Riviera, Rome.

When Leroy's uncle, Homer Scheuer, asked if he wanted to work on Saturdays in the Huron shoe store, George saw which way he wanted to go.

OBIE AND JOCKO

—— 1 ——

Odd, thought Obie. Her bureaucrat father thrived on crisis; her husband hid from it; her son was too young to put a word to it. What they had in common, maleness, was an instruction book on the avoidance of it. Yet maleness was behind their troubles. All that strut, just to keep the idea of themselves. Even eight-year-old Wyn.

She was not good at drawing lines between other people's troubles and her own. Her brother told her that her strength was the use she made of her weakness. Too easy. Reg cared more for paradox than truth, but she was weak and unsure about many things, her ability, her looks, the impression she made, her very nature, her self.

Growing up, the burden of dependence on good parents became intolerable. All that affection, masterful generosity and good humor closed off her energy. After an apprenticeship of devotion and propaganda—telling everyone how wonderful her parents were—she became a student of the system in which they flourished. Their classy words and gestures were unearned legacies. She mimicked and mocked them, not to their faces. That would be crude, and it might rouse the anger she saw her father direct at Reg as well as at congressmen and newspapermen. Her father was known for having a temper. She herself had been its object. Why then did she want to cause him pain?

What she really wanted was to end systems of unfairness. Right now, her energy was moving in one direction, eight blocks north, to the Kimberley Plaza Apartments, where Ivy Kandel had been mistreated.

Ivy was the twenty-year-old sister of Rosa, Obie's cleaning woman. She was modest, gracious, ignorant and ambitious. Two months ago she'd gotten the best job of her life, as a rental agent at Kimberley Plaza. She earned five dollars an hour, came in five days a week at eleven and left at seven. She showed apartments to prospective tenants. Dennis, the manager, required rental agents to memorize a spiel suitable for each class of apartment, the one-bedroom, the studio apartment, the two-bedroom with view of the Loop, the three-bedroom with a view of the Lake, and the three-bedrooms on the top floor which offered Loop, Lake and the West Side. "I memorized it, Miz Cramer. Everything he asked me. I did whatever he told me, I didn't make any fuss. I signed the agreement to pay back $100 for the uniform if I left before a year. I didn't complain about this tin badge he wanted us to pin on our heart. It tore through my blouse. I did everything, and never gave him sass."

Obie'd seen enough people and read enough books to know that one never really knew anybody—well, maybe she still knew Wyn—but she could testify that Ivy didn't lie. She was materialistic, limited, sometimes inept, but she was not a person who could do what Dennis had accused her of doing.

The master key, which hung by Ivy's desk and which she and other rental agents used to show the apartments, had disappeared. When Ivy came in Monday, the key wasn't there; it had been there Friday when she left. She was sure of that, for she had shown an apartment on the twenty-first floor and she was positive she'd put it back on the hook at seven o'clock, just before she left. She'd remembered that Hannah and Bill, the mother and son who came in every evening to do the office, came in, said "Have a nice weekend, Ivy," and left. Obie asked, "Could they have taken it?" "No ma'am. They been working for the company four years." Yet anybody could have taken the key. The office was open. (That was the point: to invite prospective tenants in, make them feel what a friendly place Kimberley Plaza was.) People were always coming in and out. Yet, as far as Obie knew, Ivy was the only one "investigated." Obie knew why. She was investigated because she was young, because she was new, because she was black, because she was weak, because she was a she. She was investigated because Dennis, crude, energetic, mean and male had to blame someone.

Dennis yelled at Ivy, told her that she had cost them ten thousand dollars. They had to change every lock in the building. When she denied she'd done anything, denied and redenied, he called the police and told them to arrest her. The police refused. "The man said they had no reason. Dennis was ma-ad. I could tell when he drove me home."

"He drove you home?"

"Sure, it's on his way." (It was in moments like this that Obie felt left out.) The next day Dennis made Ivy go downtown for a polygraph test.

"You didn't need to."

"I was too scared not to." She'd gone down to West Adams and been strapped into the machine. "I was so nervous, Mrs. Cramer. I flunked everything. I flunked my name, I flunked my age, I didn't get one thing right."

"I would have broken down too, Ivy." At Smith getting a C on a paper brought on such headaches she'd had to go home. Even in the street, she couldn't bear what went on: some creep's sexual compliment unleashed such fury in her she could barely hold back. The Great Tyranny was everywhere.

"You're emotionally involved in this, Mrs. Cramer. That doesn't mean you should be involved. It's an internal affair."

That was the line Mr. Stalwardt took with her on the telephone. It was the line men took with women, even men as free of lines as Jocko.

"Everybody is emotionally involved in everything that counts for them, Mr. Stalwardt. That's the basis of my complaint. Dennis—and for all I know, you—are so emotionally involved that you bullied, harassed and brutalized a young woman who's trying to make the best of herself. Just the sort of person you should be helping, as you did when you hired her, though at a salary nobody could live on. Of course I'm emotionally involved. Any human being with an ounce of care for justice and decency would be emotionally involved. How dare you belittle me with your threadbare patronizing?"

None of this came out. She'd been raised to be courteous, a patcher-upper, a charmer. What she said instead was, "I'm speaking as a peacemaker, Mr. Stalwardt. I know Kimberley Plaza is trying to establish itself in the neighborhood in which I've lived most of my life. I know this neighborhood as well, I think, as you do, perhaps somewhat better. It's one that's sympathetic to people who have been unjustly treated."

"Mrs. Cramer, I don't see your point, but I sense some innuendo. A threat."

"I don't think 'innuendo' is the right word, Mr. Stalwardt. I was describing this community. People here are sensitive about the way things are done."

"Mrs. Cramer, this is why I'm talking to you now, though you're not a member of Ivy's family. In fact, I fail to see any connection you have to this matter at all—"

"I'm her friend, and her sister has worked for me for years. I've known her since she was a little girl."

"The girl is not the sister, nor has the sister talked with me. As I see it, this is an internal affair having to do with an employer and an employee. You have a one-sided, emotional view of the matter. There are facts which you do not know."

"That's why I called, Mr. Stalwardt. I would like to know the facts on the other side. I'm not interested in seeing Ivy get off if she was at fault, but as far as I know, her only fault was not reporting the missing key as soon as she thought it was missing, and the reason for that was she thought it would turn up. You—or at least your subordinate—tried to have her arrested, you—or Dennis—grilled her and then when she was"—she had to keep herself from saying *au bout de ses forces*—"completely distraught, you—he—forced her to take a lie-detector test. She couldn't even give her name—"

"Mrs. Cramer, when you manage an apartment building, you may run it as you wish. If master keys disappear, you may do nothing about it, but I tell you you won't have any tenants. We are fair to our employees. We gave Ivy every chance, but our relationship is dissolved. It is over, and I will not tell you or anybody else any more about a purely internal matter. I appreciate your taking an interest in a friend, but that cannot affect the management of this business."

"She is owed money for her last week's work—"

"She will get every cent she is entitled to. I make a clear separation between that and what happened."

At least she'd forced that out of him. Her father had settled for less and been called a great diplomat.

—— 2 ——

As for Wyn's crisis, that was the easiest to understand and the easiest to fix, but the one most painful to her. Wyn appeared to be so self-sufficient and insouciant a boy that even Jocko didn't realize how fragile he was. He looked so impish, even she could forget how deeply he felt things. He'd stopped crying early, when he was three or four, even stopped complaining sometime in preschool. What he did do when he was hurt was get very still. It took subtle interrogation to open him up.

Twenty-five years ago, she'd overheard her mother and father talking about her. She'd just suffered what appeared to her the worst thing she could remember. Her friends at the Lab School had been asked to join the Delphine Club. For a year, they'd all been making fun of it, talking about the snobs who had nothing to recommend them so they joined a club which nobody worth anything would think of joining. Now her friends had been asked and they'd joined. She hadn't been asked and was therefore in no position to persuade them to decline. Her world collapsed. She felt like nothing. She couldn't tell her parents, and there was no one else. She pretended nothing happened, but her friends couldn't pretend and avoided her, embarrassed at what they'd done and embarrassed for her.

Mother said nothing. Days after Obie's moping and sobbing, she'd come in and held her. Obie had been ashamed of her shame, ashamed she could do nothing about it. Mother understood, which helped, but she was at the age when maternal consolation wasn't enough. Then she overheard Mother telling Dad, "We used to be able to fix everything in her life. Now there are things which can't *be* fixed." Dad came into her room as she was pretending to read *Madame Bovary*—a book she'd not been able to read since—stroked her hair, kissed her cheek and said what he'd never said before or since, "Dad loves his Obie very much."

What happened to Wyn was not snobbery but accident. The second grade had written paragraphs about baby brothers, old grandfathers, flowers, wind, rain, school buses, teachers and friends. Wyn's composition was called "Going to Sleep" and it went

---

GOING TO SLEEP IS DIFFERENT FROM SLEEPING. WHEN YOU GO TO SLEEP YOU THINK ABOUT ONE THING BUT WHEN YOU SLEEP YOU THINK ABOUT SOMTHING ELSE. THAT IS CALLED DREAMING AND YOU CANT HELP IT. DREAMING IS KIND OF A PRESENT. YOU DONT KNOW WHAT IT WILL BE. SOMTIMES ITS BAD AND SCARY LIKE YOU OPENED A PRESENT AND IT BIT YOU. IF I HAD TO CHUSE BETWEEN GOING TO SLEEP AND SLEEPING I WOULD CHUSE SLEEPING ANYWAY BECAUSE I LOVE PRESENTS.

Miss Lomnitzer had typed the twenty-five compositions on her word processor and printed copies for each pupil to take home; but she'd misplaced Wyn's. It was not even listed in the Table of Contents. It was as if he had never done it. He brought the class folder home and left it on his desk. Though Obie made a point of not looking at his things, it was there she found it. (This after two days of unusual stillness.) She apologized for finding it on his desk, telling a lie, which she hated to do. "Wyn, I was washing your window and saw the folder of class stories." (She washed the window to cover her story.) "Did something happen to yours?"

"I don't know."

"It was a very good story, I'm sure Miss Lomnitzer liked it."

"I guess she didn't. She didn't put it in." And he went outside, though it was clear to them both that more needed saying, which is how she called Miss Lomnitzer and found out that she'd just found Wyn's story behind her desk and was on the verge of calling Obie to explain and apologize.

"She's going to post it on the bulletin board in a special place tomorrow, darling, and she's going to copy it and send it home with all the children. It was just one of those things that happens."

There was tremendous relief in Wyn's face, his head lifted and his eyes were brighter, but something had happened that changed things for him, as she had been changed by what had happened to her twenty-five years before. The incident was a magnet that picked up smaller incidents and arranged them in its lines of force, small snubs and omissions, little lapses of attention, no longer haphazard events to be taken in stride by forceful and successful people. Neither she nor Wyn had suffered as ninety percent of the world's children suffer, there was nothing remotely traumatic about what had happened to either of them, they were whole, in fact, wiser and stronger for what had happened, but everyone lived in the peculiar dimensions of his own life and as their comfortable lives went, the snub and the omission helped form their being.

—— 3 ——

Jocko Cramer believed his work wasn't serious. Early in his legal career, he'd been attracted by the prestige of writing first-rate wills. He'd written three or four that distinguished him not only in the firm but in legal circles. Yet these extraordinary charts of tax avoidance nearly did him in. The delicacy of phrase necessary to keep unwanted hands off worldly goods required a concentration that would have served a cosmologist. "What a waste." For years now he was incapable of drawing up an important will. A partner, there was nothing to do about his incapacity but give him the firm's garbage. He met undesirable clients, represented the firm at unimportant meetings, and was judged a man who'd frittered away his life.

There was something else. Years ago he'd caused the death of the person dearest to him. It was both the clearest and most obscure event of his life.

It happened after his brother Henry's second wedding. Henry's first wife, Rowena, was the oldest sister of Jocko's girl, Frances Gregory. Henry had told him about Rowena's death. "We'd had a terrible argument in the middle of the night. I went out to cool off, walked around Rock Creek Park, got back around two and went to bed. In the morning, I noticed there wasn't any heat coming from Rowena's body. I'd been preparing an apology, leaning over to kiss her." A heart attack. A hundred days later he married Sabine Flanagan.

It was during that wedding in a Chevy Chase garden that

Jocko, standing a few feet from Henry, decided he would not marry Frances Gregory. It was those heavy words modernized by Sabine—the *thees* becoming *yous*, the *thys yours*, the *plight my troth* becoming *pledge my fidelity*— full of tremendous obligation and metaphysical conceptions about identity and interchangeability, devotion and purity. He couldn't live up to them. Bees gorged in blossoms, birds skimmed trees, lizards did their business in the woods, and here, in a rented cutaway before a judge, he stood, the best man, handing Henry a ring of fidelity for the second time and thinking, "Nature doesn't use, morality doesn't need, this contract." To his left, Frances was restaging the ceremony with him and herself. "Never," he thought. Couldn't she understand the immorality of oaths that had to be broken?

So Jocko told himself, and then told Frances. A week later, Frances, feeling that what she built her life around no longer existed, ended it.

Obie, a friend of the sisters, consoled Jocko, becoming his lover. She was no Frances. After a month, she said, "It's time."

"Anytime," said Jocko.

"The whole works? Orange blossoms, kids?"

"The whole works."

—— 4 ——

Futito. That had quite a history. Out of Indo-European *peig, evil, hostile.* By way of *faege, fated to die,* as in *fey.* Going clannish in Old English with *fehida,* yielding *feud,* or Old Dutch *fokkan* meaning something like *die before your time.* In northern ears this expulsion and palatal crack became *fuck.*

Shoeless feet on a hassock, Jocko thumbed through *The Latin Sexual Vocabulary.* Three shelves of one bookcase in this room of bookcases were filled with dictionaries, etymologies, Chomsky on syntactic structures, Sainte-Beuve on Port Royale, a French monograph on *Nicanor ho stigmatias, The Punctuator,* a life of St. Cyril (of the Cyrillic alphabet), a collection of runes, a collection of curses.

He had no confidants, no real friends. Pedantry was his companion. Obie and Wyn were people to talk to, though his talk became more and more oblique. So he said to her, "You're wise to convert your discontent into crusades." "Crusade" had been a pejorative word for years, but she did not guess that he meant, "You ruin the peace of everyone around you." "You're like dawn, you and your father. You think every day you renew the world."

"I couldn't live without that."

"It's wonderful. *Gefrühligkeit*, earliness. Dostoyevski said that's what reformers had."

"Somebody's got to do something."

"Exactly."

"The trouble is Daddy does it wrong. He thinks the presidents he works for are sacred. He's like an English child seeing the King."

Obie typed her letter while Jocko read the entry on *merde* in *Harrap's English-French Slang Dictionary. Merder*, to screw up, *merdique*, very difficult, *merdouillere*, to flounder. *Semer la merde*, to cause confusion. *Avoir un oeil qui dit merde a l'autre*, to be cross-eyed. Face red, hands sometimes trembling so that she had to stop typing, Obie wrote

---

Dad—I'm so furious, so upset, at what you and those you work for are doing in Central America I cannot bring myself to use even the formal endearment. My "dad" you are, biology made you that, it cannot be undone, but at this moment, "Dear" you are not. Your daughter—this person raised and educated by you and those you sent her to—this daughter cannot rest easy in opulence while her father inflicts brutality and hypocrisy upon the people of Central America.

For years I've kept still about your public life. How different from those friends of mine who rage about their fathers' private lives, sometimes in silence, sometimes not. No, your private life, and I think I know it, is exemplary. It is a terrible puzzlement to me that you have been so good a father, husband and grandfather.

A good man! Yet how can you be a good man when you collaborate with the bullies of the world?

Every morning I wake up with acid in my heart, knowing that all over this world not hundreds or even thousands but millions of human beings see my father

as the instrument of oppression. I think "Oh, if Dad had only studied history instead of economics. His boss too." But you know enough history. You know about Somoza, the Marines, the American filibuster William Walker who just walked into Nicaragua and delcared himself President—no, you probably don't know about that. You don't know the hundred and fifty years of humiliation, of bullying, we North American gringos have visited on these southern people, using one excuse or another: Monroe Doctrine, economic well-being, need for a canal, preventing a communist foothold.

Unlike most of the people in the world, who throw darts at your picture and your boss's, I know you for a man of sympathy and intelligence. I've talked with you and with Mr. Stubbs and Mr. Hatch, and you've been kind enough to see I talked a bit with the President. I know none of you is a caricature. Yet, on certain subjects—the presidency, the evil of your opponents, world conspiracy—your intellectual level sinks drastically, wit, tolerance and flexibility go out of your faces, and you become the men—and occasionally, very occasionally, women—who fit the caricatures drawn by equally narrow-minded, mechanical thinkers on the other sides of these issues . . .

On she went, citing the cases, the outrages, the patience of the people, Sandino, Ortega. She quoted a poem from a volume of Nicaraguan verse. And ended:

Dad, I can't live a duplicitous life. My beliefs are too important to me. It is not that you're not important as well, but if the education you gave me means anything, then I can no longer live as I have been living, smiling and laughing with my father while I know that mothers and sons and daughters all over the world are suffering because of you. So awful do I feel that I cannot sign off as I have in letters all my life, "With love."

Obie

A SHARE OF GEORGETOWN

—— 1 ——

"Obie's worried about me," said her father, Robert Share. He held up two sheets of white paper typed rim to rim, north-south, east-west, some words broken to incoherence on the margin. The letter, unlike most of hers, had come to his office and been opened by a somewhat embarrassed Miss Fisher. Against his better judgement, he read it there. Now he read aloud to Eileen: "I think, If only you had studied history instead of economics."

For fifteen years, since Obie's last year at Foxcroft, such letters had come his way. Usually Eileen went through them first, then briefed him and helped formulate his one paragraph answers: "You write of 'the responsibility of the world on your shoulders.' By now, my shoulders are down to my ankles."

"What is it this time? Lebanon? Gentrification? Solidarity? Seals?" Eileen's voice had several tiers, sympathy, amused exasperation, and sheer wonder at the flow of filial instruction. Bobby was his daughter's forum, classroom, congregation, couch and battlefield.

"Nicaragua."

"She'll never see that she and Reg are your real crises."

"They're joys too; at least Obie can still be. When she lets me laugh with her. Not that I've figured out when I can do that. Some time I'll take a month off to work it out."

In Robert Share's life one thing in short supply was time. In the Air Force, there was the time of missions; then there was writing time, his bachelor's essay at Iowa City, and at Law School, course and case outlines, in New York, writing briefs, complaints, analyses, position papers. All that was intense— he often worked through consecutive days—but when it came to time, Washington was special. Yet he thrived—that was almost the official verb for what you did when you suc- ceeded—on his work. Everything he learned and was went into it. He imagined artists felt that way, lost in what they did. His work too was a vocation: to keep the world reasonable and orderly.

Bobby was a solid northerner with clever blue eyes and a long face. He was in as good shape now as he'd been in years, but the first Washington year of this administration had been hard on him. He'd felt dumped on and looked it. His color was poor, he felt his sixty years and then some. That first year, he couldn't bear the endless accountability, the grandstanding congressmen provocatively interrogating him to get their thirty seconds on the evening news. The journalists too set traps; he was their game. When he'd been here in the Seventies, he hadn't had much attention. OMB seldom made news (though he'd had more discretionary power than he had now). The president then made most of the news; his prima donnas made the rest of it. This stint was different; it had taken a year to get used to its duplicities. (Triplicities: what you did; what you told the press and Congress you did; and how you worked it out for the president, Defense, NSC, Central Intelligence, and the Department itself). He'd more or less learned how to do it. At least, he must have done a few things right: the world was still there.

Stolidity was the word people used about him. Others were *solid, calm, unemotional.* "If I suffered about everything, as Obie does, I wouldn't have lasted a month here. I wouldn't have lasted six months on Wall Street or a week in the Air Force. Which doesn't make her less admirable. But why so sensitive a girl should be so insensitive to someone she says she loves I can't figure out."

"Having a Deputy Secretary of State listening to you is irresistible. Wish you could make her your deputy."

When he and Eileen had met in London during the war, she

was attached to Naval Liaison, a subtle, decent girl with gray eyes and a hungry body. Her good sense, fortitude and erotic ease had turned him into an adult.

"At least Obie writes as much to the point as most people down here." Share lay down. The bed took up half the bedroom. This old Georgetown house had not been built to accommodate such beds. When it was built, the average man was six inches shorter, the average lifespan a quarter century less. Perhaps sleep didn't count as much then; as for intercourse, it couldn't have been the gymnastic and gustatory affair he gathered it was in these postwar decades of vitamins and hormone reinforcement.

"Should I read the letter?"

Four decades of intimacy, and Eileen never looked uninvited at a letter, a memorandum, a diary entry. "Our girl keeps trying to do my job. The things she digs up. Poems from the 1930's about this fellow Sandino. There's even a poem by Ortega about thorns and stones cutting the feet of sowers. We're the thorns. Maybe we should start writing poems. Ahh." The only hand he wanted to feel at his throat was massaging it, fingers pressing out the fatigue, sliding over his shoulders to the nervy groove at the base of his head. "Oh, Eileen." Obie's letter faded: Monroe, Bolivar, Panama, Texas, Cuba, the Tampico, Taft, Coolidge, Diaz, Sacaso—who was that?— the Bay of Pigs.

—— 2 ——

There was something beautiful about the way the world was reduced for him. Eight o'clock on his desk were five sheets of paper, beautifully typed and spaced, the reduction of cables from the hundred and sixty-odd countries in which the US had representation. The cables were read and sifted in the Situation Room by some of the brightest people in the country. The Senior Officer decided which needed departmental action. (There were occasional mistakes: they'd overlooked the Peace-in-Galilee offensive for two days.)

Up here on the seventh floor it was beautiful. Getting out of the Deputy Secretary's elevator, walking past the chairs and ribbed tables of Hepplewhite and Duncan Fife, the Chippendale highboys and satinwood commodes, the Boston rockers with their spiral arms, the Shaker spinning wheel, the double-tiered stand-up desk where Jefferson had written the Declaration, he felt that he was in a rational, symmetrical, beautiful world. The paintings of Bierstadt, Church, Cropsey, Marin and Childe Hassam, the tea sets of Lowestoft and Wedgewood, were as important as any Deputy Secretary. They were, in a way, what the country was about. Wasn't something like this in the minds of the visitors who came here to do business with him? The length and warmth of his office, the soft gold and blue, the clocks, the barometers, the easy chairs, the intelligent, relaxed, fluent looks of the men and women who put the right papers on his desk and worked out his appointments and got him here and there to the right auditorium, the right meeting, the right plane, the right country with the right speech, the right briefing, this said good things for human intelligence. Sure—he was half-speaking to Obie—there was the danger that this would become an end in itself. God knows it was hard to give up: the ease, the excitement, the luxury that pillowed the tension. Professionals had made it a profession, and, for some, it was an end in itself, more beautiful than the best music, more important than the peaceful world that was its end.

Public men.

Fifteen years ago, after the first landing on the moon and the drowning of the girl at Chappaquiddick in Senator Kennedy's car, he was having an unusually late breakfast with the children. Obie said that a girlfriend of hers had said that Dean Rusk was a terrible Secretary of State, and he'd said, "I wouldn't say that." In Washington you could never tell when a child's remark would end up in the *Post*. He'd gone on about the difficulties of men in public life. "It's not easy always being looked at, always having your picture taken. You saw Senator Kennedy on the television yesterday." They'd watched the then junior senator from Massachusetts returning to the Capitol for the first time since the drowning. Every square foot of the Capitol steps was occupied, every occupant had a camera, and every camera was aimed at the senator. A large man, he looked like the tiniest fish in the biggest bowl. "How would you like to have to go through that?" he asked Obie, and she'd said, "The moon doesn't mind." "What do you mean?" he'd asked.

"Having its picture taken."

To some degree these public men were like the moon. There was something alien and cold about them. He himself was not a public man. Presidents and senators were, and now and then, an appointed official. (He'd watched Kissinger become one.) They ate attention. It was part of the extraordinary energy that brought them where they were. It was a quality that somehow translated to the skin: they almost all photographed wonderfully, at least while they were running for—and while they were in—office.

The presidents he'd known all interested him. The most complicated one was not of a piece with himself. When he should've been happy, he wasn't, and vice versa. In time he mixed everybody else up, and the country came down on him. Share had gotten out early, just after Shultz. In his years of public life he'd never felt so tired. "Robert's exhausted," the president said, and let him go.

This president was the simplest, the strangest, and the luckiest. He'd never seen such a lucky fellow. A voice, a presence, a joke barrel, he had the shine of celebrity, a variety of grand smiles. He looked like a pushover, was almost Italian in his hatred of making a bad impression, yet had the wit to make himself the butt of stories. Lazy, a poseur, full of obvious contradiction, the man went against the grain of everything he preached and no one spotted it. The only one he cared about was his wife. Tight as a drum, lazy as a lion, capable of winking at everything he spouted. It was unfair to dismiss him as an actor. (Shakespeare had been an actor.) He showed his movies at the White House. Share had seen the most famous one: the father of his girlfriend is a sadistic surgeon who amputates the boy's legs. He showed that one over and over. The sadistic father, the crippled son. Wasn't his father a drunk and an outsider—a Catholic in Waspland who felt isolated and took up for minorities and was saved from disintegration by doing local political work for Franklin Roosevelt? The boy sent fifty dollars a month home when he was putting himself through school. Not bad. Aeneas carrying Anchises out of Troy. Then whom does he marry but a surgeon's stepdaughter, herself a deserted child who'd been disowned by—as she later disowned—her father?

The man was not stupid. There was some theatrical gallantry there too, and God knows, persistence and physical confidence. He'd been spotted by California money men who'd turned his tax delinquency into million-dollar land holdings. They thought they'd ride him into the White House, and, in a way, they did; but you don't really ride these fellows. Once they've been in the world spotlight for a month, they become uncontrollable.

The national curse: news hunger. There had to be something interesting every day. Only personality could carry that cross. Since what was interesting there was its ups and downs, conflict and scandal, the government was Swiss-cheesed to death.

He had been lucky. So far, no tail had been pinned on him. "Maybe that's where Obie comes in. She knows how to pin my tail."

GEORGE FINDS BUG

—— 1 ——

All but one of the Companions, Alicia Venerdy, had left Willsville. She remained a friend, a patron of the Complex, a deflector of the fury which every few years blew up against him and his enterprise. Years ago, one Companion—an unstable girl about whom he'd been less sure than usual—spilled a few beans and threatened to spill more. George bought her silence with a year in England, but from then on the scandal seed was in the ground, and he moved with care. He didn't boast about the Complex. "It's the overflow of shoe store profits. What else should I do with my money? I'm a kind of cultural bake-off. I work with books and films like Mrs. Spriesterlach and Loretta Ottermund with flour and yeast. Willsville should be able to enjoy all kinds of cakes."

George contributed to local institutions and causes. The contributions were made with notes to the effect that his own prosperity depended on the town's, and though he himself had no time for a church or Kiwanis outing, they were as essential to local prosperity as what he did. The generosity blunted criticism. Of course he took precautions: he gave "the Share Fellows" tickets to Chicago; they went there by themselves; he followed. The Fellows were sworn to silence.

—— 2 ——

So this odd life went, the forty-five weeks in Willsville, the seven summer weeks in Europe. Still, there was no way George could get rid of the hundred thousand hours of his business life, the weight of all those soles and heels, the arches, vamps, vealskin uppers, ortho-vents, the breathing leather, air-cushions and tempered steel shanks, the boxes, the crates, the tanned and cardboard smell of storage, the ugly ballet of selling (whipping off the tops, thrusting a box three to four feet below the curious, greedy, suspicious, anxious faces), the order pads, the brochures, *Footwear News*, the National Shoe Fair, the soft trench of the shoehorn, the Venetian bridge-hump of the try-on bench. Forty years of this, of stockings, socks, the weight of feet, the stores in which he'd worked for years, the lumpish, abrupted, hammer-toed, bone-twisted, sheared, angry and pathetic pedals with the complicated formulas and tremendous price tags which had subsidized the Complex and the months away from it.

"For years," he told Don Ottermund, "whenever I saw people, the first thing I saw was their shoes. My head was full of prices, trade names, Balmoral, Cordovan, scuffed tips, heels. I'd think, 'She'll have to come in for a new pair.' The world as shoe store. Before everybody started wearing more or less the same shoes, I used to be able to tell what a person was by his shoes, how much money he made, where he came from. I could judge his confidence by the wear on his heel."

⎯⎯ 3 ⎯⎯

A year or two after he left Mercer, George knew he was always going to go it alone, no kids, no wife; no hours, months, decades of "going home" to other people's anger, needs, demands, habits, smells. It wasn't only the totalitarian convenience which attracted him; it was the solitude of bachelor philosophers. Not, though, their chastity. On the contrary, there was the endlessness of temptation, the millions and millions of amorous possibilities in the world. Every year there were more of them. How could anyone nail himself into the coffin *à deux* of marriage? Of course, years of paying the dues of courtship—heavier in the first decades, but never negligible—wore down old resolve; every once in a while, George itched to settle down, "to get it over with," but he'd never fallen hard enough for anyone to settle down with her. "I must lack the settling glue. Or is it fear?" Superstition about the significance of beginnings set him thinking about his parents: what was it about the awkward complaisance of their interdependence that revolted him? Or was he punishing himself for escaping the standard destiny of Shares and Freihofers? Since he'd gone beyond his father, was he to be punished—or rewarded—by not being a father? But Bobbie was a father.

Whatever, marriage and children became a constituent of his thinking. Meeting someone for the first time, the first question—asked or unasked—was "Is he married?" the second "Does he have children?" As if the world were divided by those facts into hemispheres. As he got less able to imagine himself a husband-father, the more he thought his own hemisphere was northern, frigid and fruitless. Yet he had chosen it, had shaped himself on its terms and knew that his happiness depended on sticking to them.

A March morning. Slow getting up—low blood pressure deepened the morning depression—reluctant to go across town to the store where the aligned shoe boxes were like jail cells, George nearly called Alf, his assistant, to say he was sick. Alf and Maureen, the buyer of women's shoes, could take care of things. He did not want to face the tin pucks of polish, the board of laces, the shoehorns, the reproductions on the yellow walls: Monet's Saint-Lazare Station, Caillebotte's Pont Neuf, the Venetian backstreets of Sargent—caped young women running through them while men with curved pipes looked them over. (At least, there were real pictures for the buyers of boots, clogs, running shoes and Oxfords.)

But he got up and was there as Penny, the stock girl, opened the doors. At eleven, Alicia Venerdy, Companion Number Two from 1960, came in with her daughter. George didn't see the aging faces of old Companions as mirror versions of his own. Over the years, they passed over the hill: he remained what he was when he'd taken them to Europe. Alicia's face was still fine, large, vague, light-blue eyes, brown curls, little ski-slope nose, a slender neck. The Alicia he'd known twenty years ago was gone; a version of that gone, twenty-year-old self was by her side.

"Morning, Alicia, June. How grand you look today. What can we do for you?"

"Hi, George. June needs some of your pretty goods. You're looking spiffy."

"Sure I am, richer and cuter every day." And then, before he quite knew why, he called, "Maureen, can you help June?" He did not want to hold the girl's feet in his hands while she sat beside her mother. He couldn't remember having such a scruple. "She wants something very nice."

"À la mode," said Alicia.

"That's what we have," said Maureen.

"Something minimal," said June. "Full of nice little peek-a-boos."

"Maureen will have it. Or get it."

June's nose was broader than Alicia's, and as far as a glance could tell him, her thighs were heavier. She had an interesting mouth, full and pursed, as if setting up for irony. Her hair was straighter and lighter than her mother's, the eyes were brighter, denser, a before-storm blue. She didn't look as easy to read.

"Hey, Alicia," said Maureen, solid, rapid, youthfully gray. "Junebug, how *you* darlin'?"

He hadn't heard, at least remembered, this nickname. Cute as a bug in a rug.

He said, "Maybe you could find her something Parisian."

"Wha?"

"Those curvy pumps from Barnes."

"You'll like them, sweetie," said Maureen.

George said, "I'm sure I haven't seen you at the Complex, June. Do you like films?"

"She's got a PhD in the late show," said Alicia.

"You'll have to bring her over."

"Can I come by myself?"

"Of course you can."

It was bright now. The sun broke little emeralds on the windows. The Seine, the Grand Canal, the Thames, the Tiber flowed through the store. Wonderful, what girls could do. Just when you were ready to throw in the towel.

"I'll leave you to Maureen." Who was there with an armful of boxes. "Saturday we've got an early Fellini. *The White Sheik*."

—— 4 ——

He'd probably seen June Venerdy five hundred times, had seen her grow up, had tried sneakers and shoes on her feet since she was two, but children weren't as distinct as other people, their charm was lost on him. Being Alicia's daughter had made her a bit special, but he'd never taken her in as a personality; as for growing up, that happened in a blink. Or had he censored her because of Alicia?

Alicia, after all, had been the Companion who'd done more than any other to save his subversive life. In the early days, when there was always a risk he'd be run out of town, she stood for the high-minded innocence of the Fellowship program. It was a bond of conspiratorial intimacy. When she married Hinson Venerdy, manager of the John Deere outlet, the conspiratorial shoe was on the other foot. In the years since, they remained grateful to each other.

Alicia never became a Complex den mother; she would have felt like a madam. She did get used to the idea of her successors, to George's life. There was something deeply tranquil and tolerant in her. She was a woman of exceptional sympathy. Her relationship with her daughter was an extension of this. She remembered what she'd been and felt, and she didn't use her daughter to stage her own needs; nor was she a *laissez-faire* mother. June grew easily within large boundaries. Yet when she began going to the Complex and came home with books, a critical vocabulary, excited eyes and a growing appetite for the world, Alicia felt more perturbance than she'd felt since she herself understood the arrangement with George twenty years earlier. "Do you think we could give her a summer in Europe?" she asked her husband.

"Maybe she can be a Share Fellow," he said. "George seems to like her. Gave her a job at the store, didn't he?"

Alicia took a walk, and tried to work the rumbling agitation out of herself. "Why not?" she forced herself to think. Why should she care so? What was so—so—she couldn't find the word. She walked and walked. After all, in the big scheme of life, why should it matter? That her innards were pounding wasn't legitimate. Did it matter that her darling girl let—let—let him muck about in her? A few hours in her life?

It mattered. She couldn't shake it loose. Things grew in certain ways, leaves, tassel, cob. Nature defined the way things worked, made certain things beautiful, others ugly.

All right, she'd violated the decorum of her day. But this violated more than decorum. It was Sodom and Gomorrah. The noise, the velocity, the beat of things, the ease, speed and carelessness of sex. Who could stop it? But what was a mother, if not a set of signals for stop and go? Could she stop it? George himself would. He was a decent fellow. He'd never dream of—doubling back on her this way. But itch had its own reasons. Even now, parts of her were trembling out of control. But George was in control, and his sense of things had the same boundaries hers did. He wouldn't cross them, would he?

—— 5 ——

It wasn't smooth sailing for George. The only thing going smoothly was his bank balance, and that sent him a sinister message: "I'm the security your old age is going to need." He had doubts about everything, Bug firstly, then the ever-heavier weight of his life. Why go anywhere? He'd been where he'd wanted to go, why go again? The stupidity of travel, the delays, the cramping, the stupidity of crowds.

But the ache of need was still there, if not as madly as it once was, it was there. And Bug was devastating.

Alicia's Bug. The second generation. What about grand-daughters? Would he still be itching? "I hope so." If anyone would tolerate him then. It wasn't easy now. It went more slowly, heavily and fearfully than ever. There was a new vocabulary of signals; new caution; new gestures of refusal. Luckily, since the late Sixties, most girls mastered them early and had been around the sexual mill.

One day he asked Bug if she'd like to go to Europe with him. The "with him" was clear.

"Yes."

The first touch was a surprise, a joke; the second, playful; the third, tense, powerful, initiatory.

—— 6 ——

Alicia said nothing.

THE WALL

The day after getting Obie's letter, Robert played hooky. That's the way he thought of it. He had no business lunch, and instead of eating an apple and a chicken sandwich at his desk, he took the elevator downstairs and walked, unaccompanied, out of the building. The week before, he'd made a speech about international terrorism and had testified on the Hill to get money to beef up embassy security, but, by himself, and, as far as he could be, unobserved, he walked a hundred yards or so across to the scruffy park.

It was one of those nothing Washington days, not hot, not heavy, not light, not cool. It was as if the weather hadn't been filled in for the day. In his all-season gray suit, with his all-weather face, he walked through the park to the strange ditch where that strange black L of polished basalt stood like the foundation of some never-to-be-built building or like some geometric check left as a sign by an unearthly transient.

There were, as always, lots of people looking at the Wall, putting their fingers in the smooth grooves of the names, looking at their own reflections backed by those of trees and people paying their touristic and memorial respect. Unlike almost any monument he could remember, this abstract shape centered or expressed, even transfigured the feelings of millions of people. It was the first time Share had come down to see it, but he remembered seeing it on television news the day of its dedication, and—a sentimental man—the tears shed there had brought tears from him.

Almost twenty years ago he'd been one of the interdepartmental group called to analyze the effectiveness of bombing the Ho Chi Minh Trail. The North was capable of bringing in 14,000 tons of materiel and was bringing in 5,800; the Viet Cong needed only a hundred tons. It was clear that no amount of bombing could be effective. He, Townsend Hoopes and Jack McNaughton had convinced McNamara. It was the straw that broke his will; he resigned, and the president brought in Clifford, whose studies showed the futility of the war itself.

Did those long days earn him a molecule of that black basalt? No.

What had happened to the brilliant Chinese-American girl who designed the memorial and faced down the criticism of its *coldness*, its *abstractness*? He should find out. She was a student at Yale, wasn't she? Remarkable how these things happened: an Asian-American girl had somehow known what would express and transcend the confusion of the terrible Asian war. Chance?

Abstraction, he supposed, was more a Western than an Oriental concept, yet he'd seen enough of Asia to know there was a special investment in letters, characters, words. Outside Shinto temples were trees loaded with tiny prayer scrolls on which worshippers wrote the names of relatives and ancestors. The calligraphy of China and Japan was more than the transmission of messages. It was a declaration of the beauty of words, of what separated men and animals. So here were the names of dead soldiers, almost sixty thousand of them, cut beautifully on the polished basalt and these abstract letters stood for the 60,000 disintegrated bodies. In earlier monuments, the shorthand was a bronze body or two. Those who'd opposed this memorial had raised another down the way, three bronze Rodin-like figures, unmemorable. (At least, he couldn't remember them.) No, this young girl, probably working as purely and unsentimentally as a mathematician, had somehow sensed that this combination of name and graded slab would be what was needed. As its spectators supplied human content with their reflections, so they supplied the feelings, which each day made this indentation in the park across from the massive government buildings a sacred space.

A few months ago, he'd been in La Paz for an OAS meeting. In the middle of the main drag—he couldn't recall the name of the street—was the Bolivian monument, a huge bronze or stone soldier fallen on his rifle. If Share hadn't been what he was—a man trained to keep irreverence to himself—he would've burst out laughing. Poor Bolivia, hung up there in the Andes, its streets filled with the tiny Indian women in black derbies bent under enormous parcels, its mountains filled with the leaves which anaesthetized mountain people against terrible cold and millions of addicts against life, Bolivia had this sprawled icon of defeat as a national monument. No Delacroix—it was he, wasn't it, who'd painted that bare-breasted Liberté?—or the fellow who made the Statue of Liberty or whoever designed the Nelson monument, the Bolivian sculptor had been the tragicomic soul of this man-and-mountain-battered country and set it in sprawling bronze in the middle of the main drag.

Here this black L, not quite holding its visitors in its one long and one broken arm, was also in its way a monument to defeat. Yet the architect transcended it by making it an abstraction, black amidst the white power of the buildings, State, Treasury, Commerce, a tragic checkpoint.

A woman wheeled a blue-and-pink stroller down the wall. Thick brown hair, shoulder-length, a heavy-cheeked face. She lifted a two- or three-year-old baby from the stroller and raised it to the wall, saying something. The baby's tiny palm slapped the stone, the mother reinserted it in the stroller. The child couldn't be the child of anyone whose name was on the wall, she wasn't showing him his father. Perhaps it was a grand-child. Was it the example of the Kennedy nieces and nephews—fewer each year—coming to kneel at the flame and the graves of their father and uncle at Arlington which provoked this obeisant dignity?

Memorial Day, Armistice Day.

Bags of fingers, torsos in trees, metal shards in human meat, brain soup, the sudden goneness of a being. From the sky, he'd inflicted that. Scot-free. Though of thirty-two men in his squadron, only eight made it back. Here on the park bench on this neutral, nothing day, taking this break from this other life, he would not let himself think about that one. Extraordinarily lucky to be on this bench, not dust in a box, name on some other wall the only mark he'd have left in this world.

VENICE

George

An odd town, Venice has always drawn oddities to itself. Feel displaced, unwanted, unappreciated, come to Venice. Too contemptuous, indolent or poor to wash, shave or dress in one of the ninety more or less acceptable modes of the day, come to Venice. Want your nullity glamorized, your vacuity filled, your stupidity mistaken for wit, your silence for sagacity, come to *la Serenissima.* Bums, thieves, con men, frauds, every kind of poseur and viper, they're all in this beautiful, watery zoo.

Something like this is one of George Share's summer tunes. For twenty years, Venice has been one of his pick-me-ups. Not this summer. Not the fault of this summer's Companion. Bug Venerdy is reasonable, good-humored, grateful, patient, calmly enthusiastic, unaggressively amusing. Young enough to be—and often taken for—his daughter, she accepts laughs, looks and Italian insinuations with easy grace. She is also lovely to regard, touch, pass all kinds of time with. George had brought her mother here twenty-two years earlier.

No, there are other reasons, internal, external. The worst of the last is the heat. The sirocco blows out of the Sahara, picks up Mediterranean water and dumps it steamily on the city. People move through the streets like long-distance swimmers, scooping air for forward progress, gasping, sagging. George sits in the long bathtub—it takes half an hour to fill it—drinking the thin Veneto white wine from a mug filled with tiny ice cubes. He reads the *Gazzetino.* It reports all Eurasia is gripped by heat. In Palermo, a man beats his wife to death with a Bible. In Milan, the Moon Monster has cut a crescent into the belly of his third summer victim. Humans are patriotically slaughtering each other in Somalia, Angola, Eritria, Morocco, Chad, along the Euphrates—when the heat reaches 120 degrees, they suspend the fighting—in the South Atlantic, Indo-China. Belfast and Beirut are doing their usual bit for population control.

In Venice, it's thought which is murderous. Wooden shutters are kept shuttered. As much time as possible is spent indoors, in the few air-conditioned bars and restaurants. The one air-conditioned theater is hotter than the street. People walk on the shady side of the *calli,* duck into the always-cool churches. "You see why religion's lasted," George tells Bug. As for eating outdoors, much of the eating is done by a new breed of gnat. "Shrewd buggers," says George. "They give you the soup course, then you're theirs."

Heat, gnats and George's complaints can't kill Venice. Bug loves it.

Bug and the Queen

Bug's new friend, the Queen—what would they make of that in Willsville?—said to her, "Why are you in this hell?"

With her other new, middle-aged friend, Betsy, the sculptress, Bug had come to see the Queen in the Municipal Hospital next to *San Giovanni e Paulo, San Zanipolo,* as they called it in Venice.

"I love Venice, Your Majesty," says Bug.

Says Betsy, "She's with George Share, Serena. You remember George Share."

"I remember nothing."

"I know it's very hot," said Bug. "But it doesn't bother me. Everything is beautiful."

The Queen's black eyes look at her as if unsure where she

stops and the chair beside her begins. "You're probably a pretty girl. It won't last."

George will not visit the Queen. Like so much in Venice, she is "out of date, superfluous, irrelevant. An affront. A front. Like that facade in front of that death machine of a hospital. You might as well go straight to the cemetery. The Queen's too stupid to kill. She stands for generations of organized theft."

"She's human," says Bug. "Not a symbol. You can't be a symbol if you don't have your country anymore."

Betsy is the Queen's dearest, her only friend. The Queen telephones her many times a day. "Betsy can I come see you?"

"I won't be here, Serena. I have to go to Cipriani's." (Or the Lido. Or Milan.) Betsy tells Bug that last week the Queen telephoned her at midnight to say that she'd committed suicide. "I asked her if she were feeling better. She said she wanted me to come over. 'Can you wait till morning, Serena?' 'Depends when it comes.' She's so far gone she sometimes makes sense."

"She must be grateful to you, Betsy."

"She's not grateful to anyone. She was brought up to think her simple existence gratifies people."

Sunk in the gray sheets of her hospital bed, the Queen drinks iced tea in a thermos sent twice a day across Venice from Harry's Bar. She says, "The last time I was in this hospital I got gangrene. I had to go to London to be cured." From a gold pillbox she pours saccharine tablets into the thermos. "The doctor says I can drink six glasses a day." Her voice is oracular; it's hard to tell if something is a joke or an official announcement. "I live on tea and boiled potatoes." These are also brought from Harry's Bar. "How do you like this room? It's the only air-conditioned room in the hospital."

"It's awful," says Betsy. Except for a crucifix behind the Queen's bed the walls are bare. "Even the view is awful. That's hard to find in Venice." Out the dirty window are a few hundred yards of ceramic roof tiles.

The Queen says, "I've seen all I need to see of this world. Views are nothing to me."

The Queen's heavy nose, large black eyes and crimson lips are like exiles in her pallid skin. Her nightgown too looks out of place, a fragile, embroidered silk on her elephant-thick flesh.

Bug wonders if she could've ever stirred anyone. "Could I ever look like this?"

"Do you want this, Betsy?" The Queen hands Betsy a paperback, on whose jacket a nude beauty crawls under a musketeer's whip. "I don't like it. I read it twice."

"No, Serena. I don't read that stuff."

"What else is there? But it's uninteresting. And the story's too complicated."

Betsy tells Bug the Queen isn't up to following anything more complicated than the *Daily Mail.* "She's a second grader in five languages."

"Poor thing."

"She can't go anywhere anymore. They have orders not to let her in."

"Why?"

"She makes scenes. She steals. Her purse is filled with stolen toilet paper."

"Poor Queen."

Abandoned by everyone who counted in her life—royal father dead of a bite from his pet monkey before her birth, royal husband dead from a combination of reality and booze, son publishing articles in *Figaro* about her incapacity, Venetian countesses who, in her presence, used to fall to their knees, turning away from her in the streets—the Queen is as isolated as a blood stain on a ballgown. She writes royal cousins for money. "Dearest Serena," they write, "We understand that you are well provided for."

During World War II, a teenage Balkan princess, Serena crawled in mud under barbed wire to escape partisan guns, hid for days in woods and shepherd's huts, rode in freezing weather across wild rivers, and, after terrible weeks, arrived in London to be nursed back to health by Aunt Elizabeth and Uncle George. Money gone, jewels lost, without brains, beauty or any education but what made her superfluous, she was as forlorn as refugees from the camps. Her aunt and uncle helped her marry Alex, a kingdomless king: she became queen of a country in which she'd never set foot. After the war, she and the little king rocketed through the world's capitals, spending and rioting, smashing champagne bottles on hotel walls, spilling caviar on Persian carpets. Drunk half the nights of their married lives, they sold wedding tiaras, necklaces and silver services to pay the bills. Alex, well-spoken in five languages, got a job as a salesman in Paris, but all he thought of was his lost kingdom and the exiles who rallied round his little body. No wonder he filled it with booze. He felt himself a stamp that no longer franked letters, a bodiless head, helpless with a helpless wife, as useless as a human being could be.

A son was born. English cousins provided nurses, then boarding schools. When Alex died, the Queen moved to her mother's house in Venice, and, when *she* died, lawyers and friends stole her clothes and jewels. (Betsy had seen them for sale in Venetian shops.) The palazzo was sold for a pittance, half of which went to lawyers. Royal cousins put her affairs in the hands of a lawyer who gave her a hundred pounds a day, and kept the rest to pay her bills. The Queen could spend thousands in an hour. Once, she'd bought a ten thousand pound necklace from a woman in the street. Harrod's was a minefield: she couldn't pass it without running up a fortune. The Queen no longer stayed at the *Connaught,* the *Ritz, Hassler's* and the *Gritti.* She declined to the *Dorchester* and the *Europa,* then to the *Bauer* and *Sonesta Arms,* from there to *pensioni* and, finally, to a hot attic apartment in the Palazzo Ticci.

The Queen Seeks a Rebeye

The Queen woke up in the dark. It was terrible, it could be endless, but light was terrible, too. Light meant day, day meant hours, and hours had a terrible weight, the weight of nothing. Nothing was heavier than nothing. Betsy would not see her, Mama was dead, Alex was dead, only Antonella was here, with her hump and stupid tongue.

There was a lipstick to buy at the Farmacia on the Frezzaria. She could find it. The sweetness of an errand. She would wear her gold Valentina suit and the little cloche hat like Mama's.

She would take a bath and do what she could with her face, the face she had never liked seeing. Maybe a thousand years ago when it was fresh, when the eyes were clear and the cheeks unpocked, when it wasn't a face to strike or hate. Alex's mother had struck it. How she'd hated Alex marrying her. "You're too stupid and ugly to be a queen." Alex had hit her, but did not know what he was doing.

The outsider.

She was always outside, even with all the princes and princesses at the weddings and funerals. But they'd had lovely times, Philip was so handsome, she loved him, they all loved him, such a bad boy. At Freddy's wedding he drank two bottles of champagne and standing next to her in church said, "I'm going to be sick," and she'd handed him his top hat, and he was sick in it, and she'd given him some wintergreen, and they'd slipped out and thrown the hat away in the woods behind the palace; but he never kissed her. He would not see her now. Nobody would see her now. Most were dead. The aloneness of it all, the dark of it, the heat of the bones in the skin, the armpit, the knees, the sex, the eyes. One used not to be made of parts. So dark, and no one. No one. To get out. How to get poison. She did not know how much to take, where to get it. Gun. Too terrible. The window. It might not be over, just bones broken and pain.

She had an inspiration: to become a Jew. "Christ was a Jew. Jews suffer. I'll send Antonella to find me a—what do you call it?—a rebeye. Though she's so stupid, she probably thinks there is no such person. I sent her for Carr's No. 3, and she comes back with Ritz Crackers."

In her golden Valentina suit, the Queen started out for the Frezzaria, but ended as usual in Harry's Bar, where she took the best table, against the back wall, and ordered Campari, boiled potatoes and asparagus. *"One* asparagus, no butter, no salt, no pepper, no oil." She sees a vaguely familiar face, and waves it over. It belongs to Van Kelly Tochner, the scion of the Cuddly-Wuddly Shoppes. The Queen is talking as he crosses the room. "I've been looking everywhere for the Frezzaria. I'm so exhausted. Nothing is where it used to be."

Van doesn't understand, but is used to that. Thirty odd years ago, he crawled away from his fears, and since had looked at the world from under the covers of incomprehension. He is the least conspicuous person in any room. Officially six feet tall, he looks whatever size is required. "Good mor, how are, hello your ma."

"They have nothing in Venice anymore. What are you drinking?" Van is carrying a glass.

"Rum." He wears an unpressed white linen suit. "Want?"

"Yes."

Van hands her the glass and sits. For years he's been picked up by one Venetian floater or another. Betsy calls him "The Glove." "He's erect only when someone sticks something in him."

The Queen says, "I'm going to become a Jew." Van nods as if there's nothing more sensible to do on a hot Thursday. "Will you bring me a rebeye?"

Van's eyes, the color of bathtub rings, seem to register this as if he'd actually had a thought. At least something worked its way through him, into his throat. "Rebeye?"

"A Jew priest. Did you think it was a vegetable?" Van's face shows nothing. "Jews suffer, I suffer. So I'm a Jew already. In here." With a besapphired hand she touches her gold-suited chest. "They're picking on the poor Jews, I hear it on the television." The accent was on "vizz." "These Arabs. The Jews should leave them to their own dirt. They'll go right into hell. Bombing, bombing, bombing. Where are those potatoes? Every day they bring me potatoes; you think they'd be prepared. And they don't know how to do them. They don't take off the skin, the poor things can't breathe. Lipstick." The Queen had a vision of herself staggering around to the *farmacia* for lipstick and facial powder, then staggering back in her golden suit to her burning attic, swimming in the filth of battered lipsticks, broken silver cases, powder dripping on the sofas. Oh, to be saved from this world. "I need to be christened. By a rebeye. Or I join Alex in hell. Jews are saved. Are you a Jew?" Van didn't think he was. "You need a rebeye. Greeks hate Jews. My father was Greek. Greeks are always wrong. Alex was not a Jew. Another thing in their favor. Maybe Betsy will find—" She sees another familiar face, which, as she looks, turns away. "Whatsisname," she identifies. "Toony, Moony, Loony. Ceruni. The *Gritti*. Accused me of stealing their toilet paper. I asked him how he expected me to wipe my ass. Screamed at me. 'Out.' It was —*divertente.*"

A waiter asked the Queen if she'd be good enough to follow him.

"Are you a rebeye?"

"Your Majesty?"

"You're not a rebeye. Oh, Sebastian."

The Queen had seen someone whom she not only knows, but, given her limitations, likes. Not "Sebastian," but Sheldon, a forty-year-old drifter living till recently on palimony from Dunker Clift, the Seafruit Tuna Fish heir. In the winter Dunker had suffered a stroke, the palimony stopped, and Sheldon was back up the creek where he'd passed most of his life. Gentle, passive, helpful, he is also—luckily, as the Queen sees it—Jewish. "My Sebastian, precious Jewboy." By some feat of unfathomable scholarship, she calls Sheldon by the names of various martyrs. "If I don't get a rebeye, I'll die. How lucky you are, Sebastian. Tell me how Jews are christened. Will my christening do? No. Nothing's right. Potatoes, Ceruni, Ritz Crackers, nothing. They're making wars on the Jews, I see it in the *Mail.*"

Sheldon is almost as ignorant as the Queen. He reads nothing, spends his days cadging meals. He likes the Queen, is not even sure if she's a real one, or if Queen is a name she has or uses.

He sits with them. The Queen raves about Venetians double-charging Jews for potatoes. "God wants His people to have His *pommes de terre.*"

The waiter says, "Your Majesty is wanted in the office."

"Wanted? Sounds delicious. But I'm concerned with what I want, which is a rebeye. I'm sure you're not one. Stefano," she says to Sheldon, "Find me one of your priests."

"Serena, dear, I've not been near a synagogue since I was barmitzvahed, twenty years ago. I haven't kept up at all, my dear. It's enough of a struggle keeping body and soul to-gether. I wouldn't know how to act anymore, wouldn't know what to wear."

"You're in danger of being, oh, what's the word, expelled, deconsecrated, exiled. You won't be saved. That's true for all of you," the Queen says loudly, sharing her wisdom with a dozen tables. "We're in danger."

The waiter said, "I must ask Your Majesty—"

"Yes, come with us, Serena. We'll see if they have what you want in the office. Luigi has everything."

The Queen turned back, addressing Tochner, who regarded her and his glass equably.

"Did you hear they bombed the Jews' pavilion at the biennale? Enemies everywhere. Who are all these people?" Eaters, drinkers and talkers stopped eating, drinking, talking. "I don't like their looks."

"Come, Serena." Sheldon touched the Queen's wrist. She looked at it with disbelief. "Let's go see Luigi."

"This way, Your Majesty."

Even Tochner rose and became a part of what swept the Queen to the second floor office. Luigi, the assistant manager, had called for a motorboat ambulance. With the help of Sheldon and the waiter, its two attendants got the Queen into the boat, and she was taken again to the hospital.

Del Plunko Performs

Pablo del Plunko.

George and Bug's second week here, he'd come up to their table, passing out flyers for his performance, a small, hairy man in a Tirolian blouse ripped at hair-haloed nipples. Golden knickers inadequately covered his southern zone. Discolored gouts of rear end appeared in the interstice between pants and blouse. Sandals exposed his knobby feet. He was preceded by, stayed with, and left behind a puissant odor. "Week-old fish and stale brick" was Share's analysis.

Examining their pasta, he announced, "I enact poems." Bug invited him to join them. In the next half hour forty thousand lira worth of pasta, fish, *fegato veneziano*, fruit, cheese and tart were shoveled past his carious teeth; several thousand were sprayed over the table. When the check arrived, he reached into his knickers and came up with a thousand lira note which he presented to Share as if endowing an institute. "This should cover mine."

When George paid the check, del Plunko objected. "Tip like a *signore*, not an American cheapo." He reached into George's billfold, extracted a ten thousand lira note and tucked it into the pocket of Alvise, the waiter.

So when George saw del Plunko heading their way across the campo, he looked away toward Bug, Betsy and the Queen. No go. The rotten fish and stale brick sailed up to the table. "Hello, friends. Eating alone?"

"We're not alone," said George.

"Good foods?"

"We're almost finished."

"*La condition humaine*. Art alone makes it bearable." From a pocket of his golden outfit del Plunko unfolded a flyer which read "*Recitazione*: Pablo del Plunko." "Tomorrow," he said.

"Tomorrow?" said the Queen.

"Campo San Stefano. By the *Caca Libri* statue. Del Plunko will recite Trakl, Huidobro, Montale, Ibsen. In original. Del Plunko's Norwegian is perfection. Huidobro he does with Santiago dialection. A marvel of art." He looked for the waiter, snapped his fingers. "Alvise. *Subito*." He plopped down between Bug and Betsy. Alvise, a scowler, looked interrogatively at Share, who shrugged surrender. Del Plunko ordered, "*Zuppa e fettucini bolognese. Poi, vediamo*."

"We will have to leave you," said Share.

Uselessly; del Plunko addressed the ladies. "In Amsterdam del Plunko brought five hundred spectators to ecstasy. In Brussels he was not permitted to stop. Euro-TV is on its knees for a del Plunko Hour. *Rifutato*. Del Plunko does not transmit *electronicamente*. He must be listened to in the flesh. Media is zero for del Plunko. Del Plunko is his own media."

Betsy had told them that del Plunko was in the *Gazzetino* office every day bombarding them with publicity handouts, furious that they had neither advertised nor reviewed his recitals. His only appearance in the paper came after a performance Frothingham the painter had reported to her. "People opened windows and yelled, 'Shut up,' and 'Drop dead.' One man said if he showed up again he'd put cement in his mouth. Finally, someone felled him with a dead rat."

Share said, "We're busy tomorrow."

"Your business is not good for my business," said del Plunko.

"I am free," said the Queen.

"I too," said del Plunko. "*Gratuit*. No charge. I know that is important for Americans."

"I am not American," said the Queen.

"That is something for you," said del Plunko. "Ah. *Zuppa*." Alvise left a deep bowl of soup which del Plunko tipped into his throat. Some of it gullied down his chin and spilled into his chest hair. "Del Plunko exists on the contributions of patrons. *Ammiratori*."

"Maybe we can make it, George," said Bug. "We're poetry lovers. Do you recite American poets, Mr. del Plunko? Wallace Stevens? Sylvia Plath?"

"No women," said del Plunko. "Women do not transmit."

"Pound? Hecht? Justice? Ashbery?"

"English is poor for poetry. Ugly consonants, long vowels. The language is wrong, top and bottom. No reflexivities, no '*ne*,' no '*en*,' no '*se*.' Where is the '*darum*'? No inturning. That's why there are no English poets. Spanish, a wonderful garden. Gongora, Lope, Jimenez. Italian, an orchard. Marino, Zanzotto, Montale, Carducci. Bulgarian. Ah, Bulgarian. That's language for poetry. Ukrainian, Albanian, Montenegrin, Dutch. Even French has some poets. Hugo, Sully-Prudhomme, Adolf Montégut. English is poetic cemetery. I know the literature to perfection. I have performed it. John Gower, Erasmus Darwin, Oren Metzenbaum. I illustrate for you." He crooked his right arm into a hairy bar in front of his chest, threw back his starved child's head and began intoning, moaning. Forks clattered, diners looked up in shock. Words broke out of the bardic moan, some surely English: "Boil . . . fowl . . . sky . . . tea time." Del Plunko stood, head turned toward the dark campo. The words rumbled, roared. In the campo, playing children stopped playing, walkers became gawkers; from the bars, drinkers carried glasses toward the *trattoria*. Del Plunko threw out his arms, then, bending back, clutched his throat, pounded his chest, twisted his body. His gold-trimmed buttocks shook. His feet, purple-knobbed, hairy, callous-tortured, left his sandals and pointed here and there in pedal emphasis. He stood where the moon was brightest, enraptured.

For eighty or ninety seconds, Campo San Margherita wrapped itself around him. Then there was a hoarse cry, "*Basta!*" It came from Alvise, who marched to the troubadour, gripped his blouse and knickers, and threw him ten yards into the campo. Del Plunko stiffened and extended his arms cruciform. Once again he was hurled and this time fell, belly-down, knickered buttocks to the moon. "*Filisteo,*" he cried. Alvise drove his foot into the knickers. Spectators cheered. Kids hooted. A forkful of pasta landed in del Plunko's black hair. Alvise's foot worked the bard's ribs.

Out ran the Queen. She pushed Alvise away. "Stop," she commanded. "Off." She and Bug took the poet under his shoulders and lifted him. "Poor boy," she said. "Come with Serena."

A crooked halo descended on del Plunko's head: the gnats had arrived.

Frothingham and Sommerstenes

The "Sommerstenes of West Hartford" asked Betsy if it was really true that there were good paintings to be seen in Venice.

"Yes," answered not Betsy, but Frothingham, who came up swinging his hairy arms in a burlesque of athletic menace. "Old and new ones. How are you?" he said to the Sommerstenes, who gave him their hands and what passed with them for smiles. "I'm Jack Frothingham, Prissy Stubblefield's ex."

"We're the West Hartford Sommerstenes," said the male.

"Tell them about my work, Betsy."

"Tell them what?"

"About my painting. Tell this man, too—I've seen you. I'm Frothingham."

"I remember," said George. "For the last five years I've failed to acquire one."

"My lot." Frothingham held a hairy wrist under the astonished faces of the Sommerstenes. "It was so hot this morning, I decided to cut it." Bug saw in the blond hair a still-pink cut. "Then I said, 'What the hell. Maybe I'll sell a painting.' Never know when you're going to run into someone with an eye for good stuff. How about picking one out? I've got a couple with me, wait a mo'." From his Woolworth briefcase, he took out a watercolor daub of the Piazza. "Like it?"

"We've just come," said Sommerstene. "From West Hartford. We have paintings. Weren't looking to buy any."

"I've got others you'll like more." Out came a watercolor of a grimy *calle*, some flowerish thing squashed on its brick wall. "Did it last week. *Backstreet, Venice. 4:20 P.M. on a Summer Wednesday*. I can shorten the title for you."

All stared at the repellent daub. "I'll shorten the picture, if you like. Take an inch or two off the sides. It'll fit in nicely anywhere."

Mrs. Sommerstene ventured to say that it was pretty.

"A thousand dollars and you take it home." He passed it to her.

She held up her hands, trembled and shook her head. Her husband said, "Purchases take time. Especially paintings. You have them for life."

"How long can you live?" asked Frothingham. "People get killed every day. A bomb went off at an art gallery last night. You could have been in there, buying one of their pictures." There was sweat on his brow, a grimace in his small-jawed, not unhandsome face. "What the hell is a thousand dollars? Make it seven hundred. I'm broke. I want to go to Milan, I've got prospects there. Five hundred. I'll wrap it myself."

"Let you know tomorrow," said Sommerstene.

"All right. I'll put off Milan."

"Please don't do that," said Mrs. S.

"Why not?"

"Will you take four-fifty?" said Mr. S.

"Four seventy-five."

"You'll have the money in the morning."

"Done." Frothingham put the daub in Mrs. S.'s trembling hands. "You've bought yourself an instant classic. Congratulations."

"To you too, Francis," said Betsy.

"See you here tomorrow morning," said Frothingham.

That night the Sommerstenes left Venice forever. The painting was left at the Cipriani reception desk with a note for Frothingham.

Dear Sir,
    In view of previous artistic commitments, we regret that our acquisition quota is exhausted.
    Sincerely,
    L. P. and W. Sommerstene
    (West Hartford, Connecticut)
Enclosed: Painting (unpurchased)

The Beautiful Widow and the Bakery Girl

Venice was in a stew, at least the Venice of the rich and pretend-rich who spent hundreds of hours finding out who'd be coming to town, what parties they'd be coming to, getting invited to them. The exciting visitant now was not a head of state—just as well, the summit conference of '78 had been a social disaster—not a great actor or beautiful actress, not a literary, musical or pictorial genius, but one of the fifteen or twenty super-super celebrities of the world, *La Bella Vedova,* no longer quite so beautiful—indeed, had she ever been?—but still mysteriously recessive, sexually piquant, and high-lit with the beauty derived from the luminaries who'd paid her court when she'd been mistress of the Great American Court.

Betsy, a sucker for the rich and powerful, was enormously excited. The American prince whose violent death had turned the young beauty into the Beautiful Widow was one of the lights of her pantheon. She'd made a lifesize bronze of his head and sent it, unsolicited, to his grieving parents. (It was not acknowledged.) She was in love with the Beautiful Widow, at least with the images of her grief and bravery, her artistic consolations, her temporary exile from the country which killed the Prince and which, she believed, wanted to kill, break or humiliate their children. In exile the Widow had become a widow twice more, marrying first an official prince—one of the few who had survived the great wars with a part of his family's fortune—and then an industrial prince, a charming international gutter rat whose unscrupulous persistence led to his becoming one of the richest men in history. The Widow was not rich, in fact for years had thought of herself as a pauper. Her marriages had risen from and declined upon mountains of legal paper. She said to a friend whose tongue was the source of much of what the world knew about her, "The mountains labored and brought forth church-poor me." What had these husbands, or their families, spotted in her that they had, independently of each other, willed their money out of her hands, leaving her with funds that would barely pay for her clothes and jewels? Poverty—the poverty of insufficiency—was a family curse. Her father had drunk, gambled and gestured away his small fortune, had died in the Hotel Pierre's slummiest room, barely large enough for his three suits and hundred empty bottles. What the Beautiful Widow had was the radiance of celebrity that had for decades thrilled people as celebrated as she. She was a class of one, and like Wallace Stevens's jar, drew the eyes of everyone in the social landscape as if she were its only significant creation.

Some rumors had it that she was a dear person, an adoring mother, a loyal friend, brave in the face of assaults on her privacy and person. Others had it that she was avaricious to the point of mania. Some claimed she was brilliant, immensely learned, polylingual and soaked in the poetry and culture of a dozen countries. There were counter-stories of her naiveté, stupidity, laziness, callous disregard of suffering, inequity and anything but the happiness of those closest to her. Stories piled around her as they had about the Holy Grail. (She was pursued almost as religiously as that old receptacle of narrative surplus.) Years after the last of her husbands left her, she remained one of the icons of Western celebrity.

No wonder Venice couldn't contain its excitement. There were fifty stories about the time of her arrival. Where was she staying—Grand Canal? the Lido? Torcello? a villa on the Brenta? Surely she wouldn't stay at the Danieli or the Gritti.

Was she coming incognita? Was she already here? Every well-dressed woman between thirty and sixty was inspected.

"She'll be at the Mulligans' party," Betsy told George.

That afternoon, George had gone with Betsy to a bakery in the Calle degli Fabri. Betsy loved their almond cakes and dark spiral rolls. She also wanted to show George the girl behind the counter, one of those beauties that look as if they've fallen out of a Renaissance canvas onto Venetian streets. Behind the counter was—my God, the Beautiful Widow. Or so, for a second, it seemed. No, this girl was more solid, a Veronese girl, her colors red and gold. The redness had oven heat in it, the gold was pocked with carbon. A working girl, with marvelous solid arms and powerful wrists, her white uniform sported workstains at armpit, breast and belly; her hands were rough, the fingernails short; her nose was blunt, the eyes dark with green glints, her complexion extraordinary, something off a mosaic. Dark gold hair looped in chains around her head.

What, she asked, did the *signore* desire? George Share could not speak, could hardly breathe. The bakery, full of hot bread smell, dizzied him. He inhaled as if the warm smell rose from the girl's pudenda. Finally he managed to point to a spiral roll. "*Questo.*"

"*Quanto?*"

He held up both hands.

"*Dieci?*"

He nodded.

"*Cinque mille, trecento-cinquanta.*"

He handed over a five thousand lira note.

"*E trecento-cinquanta.*"

He handed over another five thousand lira note.

When he took the change from her fingers, their roughness made his heart skip. "She knows," he thought. "She's used to what she does to men. "*Grazie, signorina.*"

"*Grazie lei. Buon giorno.*"

"See what I mean?" said Betsy.

"Do I."

He walked Betsy back to Santa Maria del Giglio, went through Campo San Stefano, crossed the Accademia Bridge and made his way through winding *calles* to the apartment, his head and body full of the girl. She would be through at three, would walk home, at four she'd be in her bath. Lucky tub. If Fellini had come into the bakery, he would have spotted her power instantly. Who could escape it? Though there were a thousand beautiful Venetian girls, maybe more, and thousands of visiting beauties, he'd seen del Plunko talking with a black-haired beauty in a red dress at a table in the artists' café in San Barnaba. How could that be? (Del Plunko had seen and ignored him.) A minute later, he saw a blond girl in a short blue dress, bare-legged. George watched her bare legs till they disappeared. Would he see her again? Would he see the girl in the red dress, the bakery girl?

At Mulligan's party the bakery girl stood in the center of an admiring crowd. Astonishing. Who'd had the inspiration, the social guts to bring this Venetian Liza Doolittle? God bless Venice. God bless the democracy of beauty. In a dress that looked like one of Colonel Quadaffi's gaudier outfits—a kind of sand-colored tent, with all kinds of sleeves, real and phony, and a long skirt—the girl made theatrical gestures and spoke like a child who'd swallowed a bassoon. What a voice, an innocent, burping buzz, but it was accentless American.

Not the bakery girl then, but the Beautiful Widow.

THE DEPUTY'S VISITORS

— 1 —

Ambassador Gupta was both eccentric and able. The ability to get what he wanted, what, that is, his government wanted, was tied up with the eccentricity. The negotiation itself was fairly simple: the US wanted to use one of the islands in the Indian Ocean as a fueling station.

India's interest was to make anything that could be called a present expensive. "We were thinking of one year, Mr. Secretary. At most, two. Then, we would see what we would see. As you know, it's important for us not to be seen as your forepaw."

"Self-evident. You're not, and never have been. Many of us feel that if anyone's anyone's forepaw, it's we who are yours."

Gupta's features were modestly tucked away between great cheeks and a massive forehead which ended in a thicket of black hair. His suit was Savile Row, but the tailor's ingenuity had been beaten by the bulges of the youngish fellow's neck, chest, belly and thighs. Put a string on him and it looked as if he could float down Central Park in the Macy's parade. No comic figure though, not with those eyes, jewels of melancholy shrewdness. "Do you know an old text, the *Kama Sutra* of Vatsayana, Mr. Secretary?"

"Can't say that I do, Mr. Ambassador." Share was going to be treated to a diplomatic excursion and he put up his feet on the golden hassock near the fireplace. Perhaps a mistake, for he noted a twinge of scorn, or it might be amusement—and, what would have been a mistake—superiority in the dark face.

"An erotic manual from the fourth century given to brides. You know how traditional we are."

"One of the sources of our great admiration for you," said Share, a bit dreamily, but gathering strength, because in fifty minutes he had what was going to be a difficult meeting with the NSC. He was sitting in for the Secretary.

"You'd be amused by it, I know. I bring it up because it has, like so many of our wisdom books, classifications that are still useful. Men are divided into three classes, according to the size of their *lingham,* hare-man, bull-man, and horse-man. Women are divided by the depth of their *yoni* into deer, mares and female elephants. The *Sutra* talks about various sorts of congress between these varied classes. My point is that our country is a deer-woman, and yours a bull-man. The *Sutra* instructs us that the deer-woman has three ways of lying down, the widely open position, which consists of lowering the head and raising the middle parts, the yawning position, when the thighs are raised and kept apart, and the position of *indrani,* when the legs are doubled back against the sides. And Mr. Secretary, our country is delighted and thrilled to have congress with your own, but as you can imagine, there is a certain amount of pain and difficulty associated with it. The *Sutra* recommends the lavish use of unguents, even for the most receptive, if painful, position of *indrani,* which is a position we dare not assume in this case because of world opinion. The US is a giant male country but it is not the equivalent of the great god Indra. We do not wish to look as if we were thrilled at being buggered by deity. We're interested in a more modest, hole-in-the-corner congress, one eased by enough unguent so that the minimum of noise will be made. You are, sir, fetching my meaning?"

"I'm certainly being educated," said Share, taking his feet off the hassock. "And if I understand you correctly—and as I grew up in Iowa farm country I know something about it—I believe we've been quite straightforward and generous—no, excuse me, that's the wrong word—so that our understanding of your needs should match your understanding of ours. Ambassador Charad in Islamabad is awaiting instructions to talk to Prime Minister Zia about the levelling and then the trailing off of the air supplies, though as you know, because of his enormous assistance to us, this will require at least as much unguent as your lady requires for her pleasures."

"Well, that is of course an indispensable negative, Mr. Secretary. But I have been instructed to pursue the positive as well."

"It is a time of special stringency for us, Mr. Ambassador. But we're not totally unprepared for a modest increase in the figure we mentioned."

"The bull's modesty may be the deer's terror, Mr. Secretary. We are both, after all, interested in each other's joy." Share was getting weary, especially when he saw those signs he'd long been expert at spotting, the swelling eagerness in protracted conversation that certain diplomats—not all, by any means, from Southeast Asia—experienced in this long golden room with the marble fireplace, Chinese vases, and serene canvases of the Hudson River school.

Gupta was just swinging into this second gear when the phone rang. "Yes," said Share into it, "I need a couple of minutes, yes. I will be there. Oh," which came out of him when he heard Miss Fisher telling him, not that the car was waiting, but that his son had just phoned from downstairs and was asking to see him. "Have you a clue? I mean, did he say—No? Well, he'd better come up. Right. Be right there."

The Ambassador was up. He was not an ambassador for nothing. Share walked him down the hall and through the beautiful anterooms, shook his hand at the guards' desk and said it would all work out, he would make the proper consultations, they would be in touch within the week.

He went back to his inner office, pipes, and books, leather chairs, family pictures and autographed ones of the great. He lit up a protective Jamaican cigar, called Miss Fisher, and asked if Reg was there. "All right then, I'll be right out." He had less than fifteen minutes. He was chairing the meeting, there was no way he could be late. He went out, there was Reg, the boy-man, in polo coat, sweater and slacks, no tie, and white sneakers, carrying the fat, orange down-vest which had insulated him for the last six or eight years and looked it.

"Good to see you, Reg."

"Hello," said Reg, omitting both the word Dad and a handshake. "Pretty nice digs. Might've known."

"The government does all right by its old faithfuls. Even deputies."

"Meaning 'I've got the right to perks and you, you shiftless bastard, don't?' "

So, thought Robert Share, I'm in for it. Ten minutes of this would ruin the day. "Come off it, Reg. You didn't make what for you is a long trip just to be nasty to me, did you? There's not much time now, but why don't you sit down. We'll talk a while and arrange to really talk later on. It's been too long since we've been in the same room." His son's eyes were the color of Eileen's beautiful ones, but his were not beautiful. They were small and set too far back. They didn't have Eileen's clarity. So much of what Reg got had gone wrong. Years ago he'd told him that he should try looking people in the eye. Since then, Reg had become a great starer. This, too, he didn't do right. You felt the strain and falsity of the stare. It was not trying to look, but to be looked at.

He had to stop this. He was doing what Reg accused him of doing, indicting him. He had to keep in mind the decency, sweetness and charm, even intelligent charm, that was also his son.

'We haven't done too well that way," said Reg. "Or any other way. This is a big risk for me."

"What does that mean?"

"I don't want to get so angry at you I'll regret it. Cause some kind of national scandal."

"People around here are pretty discreet."

"Please don't top everything I say, Dad."

So much anger, thought Share. Was there anything but that? He had plenty of it himself, but why dig it up? What was the point? His life's work was to transform anger, redirect it, or bury it long enough so that nations could get on to doing something useful. There was no reason—as far as he was concerned—why that shouldn't happen in a family. "I think we've expressed enough hostility to last me a lifetime. It'd be a shorter one if I have to take or express much more of it. Even if that's what you really want—"

"That's not fair."

"Okay, but your tune is that I'm blind to this fury in myself. Even if it's there, is it really necessary that you and I be—

be . . ." He couldn't bring himself to use a word like "enemies" with his son. The absurd session with Gupta had temporarily exhausted whatever pleasure he took in language skirmishes. ". . . unloving to each other?"

Reg, sitting too near the edge of the leather chair across from his own, as if refusing comfort, said, "Why didn't you think of that thirty-five years ago?"

The Secretary felt the air go out of him. He let himself sink into the upholstery and draw from its leathery indifference some of that calm about which newspapers wrote. How to deal with this filial turbulence? There wasn't time. "Reg, you and I have more to work out than the people in this building have with whole countries. Let me tell you where I stand now. The Secretary's in Brussels. I have to take his place at a meeting. If it weren't important, I'd beg off. I can't even be late. I'm a link in a complicated system, and I have no right to cause its breakdown. The car's downstairs. After it drops me off at the E.O.B., it can take you to the house. You can relax there, have a drink, something to eat, talk to mother, read— whatever you like. Or it will take you wherever you want to go, and I can pick you up after the meeting, which should last ninety minutes, if we're lucky. I'll have to do a little dictation in the car, then things are relatively clear. You and I can have a good dinner, any place you like. Home, or if you think mother'll be in the way, in a restaurant. And we'll really talk. How does that strike you?"

"Listen to the verb you just used, Dad. You can't conceal the aggressiveness."

Share supposed he'd meant "strike." He didn't bother to deal with this absurdity. Why should his son be verbally saner than Ambassador Gupta? "Okay, that's what we'll talk about. I want to change as much as I can, vocabulary on down. You can guide me."

"It's too late. For both of us."

"But you're here, Reg. You haven't been in an office of mine in years. You came all the way down to Washington to see me."

"I came to do you in," said Reg, with a smile that could be taken for amusement. "I didn't bring any lethal weapon be- cause I know they search you."

"That's not a good thing to say, Reg. I don't think that's in the realm of permissible things to say. It isn't a good joke, and if it seems like frankness to you, I think it's the sort which can harm both of us."

"Did it ever occur to you that saying something like that makes me feel good? That it's even good for me? Don't you know I've always been terrified to say anything to you? That my life's dominated by fear of you?"

"All right, that's what we can talk about," said Share. "It's surprising to me. That doesn't make it untrue. I'm not exactly famous as an intimidator."

"Everybody in the family feels the same. Mother, Obie, Uncle George."

"That's not true."

"Ask them. I mean," he said, "ask Obie and George."

"They don't deal with me like people who are intimidated. What you say feels absolutely wrong to me. George would laugh at it. He's fashioned a life—and I'd better say right away it's a fine one before you declare I demean it and him—in contrast to mine. As brothers go, we're as good a pair as any I know."

"Don't you see the reason for that? He's afraid to argue with you. You make situations intolerable for those around you, and then you rave about how wonderful they are for everyone." This was more exhausting than hours of negotiation. Share felt his insides lit, he wanted ignition, explosion, but enough of his diplomatic and parental self was there to tell him what was happening. Reg was doing what every expert disputant did, saying that his opponent was incapable of understanding his position.

"I can't see it your way, Reg. I think you're wrong, you think I am. We probably have equal shares of blame."

"We're unequal Shares, and have unequal shares. Of nothing. Stop playing the moderate. It's another way of topping me." Robert Share dug his nails into his fists, telling himself, "*Calme, du calme. Sois sage.*" "At least I've had some therapy. I know some of the tricks I play on myself. You don't. And by now your tricks are so thick it'd take an A-bomb to blow the crust off. Uncle George has talked to me for years, as he can't talk to you."

"I'm glad for both of you, but I don't feel you're right. Which means we've got plenty to talk about. It'll take a lot to make me think George and I aren't equals and good brothers, that he feels the resentment you feel. He's made a life, and a world of his own, which is—"

"What you always want for me. Sure. Don't you think I want it? Don't you think I'd have it, if I weren't in so deep?"

"Yes to both, Reg. And now, please don't resent me for it— I want to continue this, but I'm not my own man. I have to go. We can talk a bit in the limo."

"I'm not going to ride in your limo."

"Then let me give you taxi fare and have Miss Fisher call you one."

"Oh that's beautiful. No wonder you're such a great diplomat."

"How dare you?" Robert Share did not say, nor did he take his son over his knee. He shook his head, and inside shook more, but didn't say anything. It would do no good. His son wanted to enrage him, to see him enraged. But even if it would cure him, there and then, he wasn't going to put on that kind of show. And he had to leave. "I won't bite on that, Reg. Please come to the house."

Reg got up and for a half-second, Robert Share envisioned self-defense. Imagine the security guard coming in, grabbing his son. What a story that would be. No, his son wasn't this crude, or stupid, or infuriated. (Was he?) He did not look furious. As Share shrugged a defeated farewell his way, Reg went ahead of him, out of the office, past the small audience of Miss Fisher and the assistants in the anteroom. It's as if he were telling them, "See how your brilliant boss handles what's supposed to count most to him, what a mess he's made? Just imagine what a mess he makes of the world."

Robert Share looked at Daphne Fisher looking at him with a conspiratorial look of a sort that had almost never been on her face. He accepted it, and let it help him compose himself. Reg stood by the Deputy Secretary's elevator. "That's the button, Reg. I have to do something in here for a second, but if you want to wait for me, just hold the elevator." He went back in the anteroom and fussed with the paper. Giving Reg the time he knew he wanted to go down himself. A relief, for he knew the few seconds alone with his son in that small enclosure would be an excruciation.

—— 2 ——

Reg wasn't at home, but his letter was. The NSC meeting hadn't been taxing. Defense had come in with a weak paper, it took about ten minutes to let it trip over itself. Three of the four tigers weren't there, the fourth was muzzled by the paper. It only took ninety minutes. In the car he dictated the memorandum, then relaxed in the leathered corner.

In the woods along the river, then northeast over the soft hills tiaraed with beautiful estates, Rock Creek Park was lovely with young green. On his own lawn he looked at the new shoots swelling with innocence. He gave himself a good minute here, looking at violets, daffodil buds. At the door, Lali, the somber Ethiopian cook they'd had five years said, "Mr. Reg just leave dis for you, Mr. Share."

"Just?" He opened the door and looked left, right, but there were only trees and bushes.

The letter was written on Department stationery. Reg must have picked it up from Miss Fisher's desk. Share wondered how much more of it he had. No, she wouldn't have let him have more than a sheet. ("Awfully sorry, Reg. Department rules. Even your father doesn't use it at home.")

His title and first name had been crossed out. Reg's tiny, fearful handwriting filled a third of the page.

Dad—No advice, no taxi fare. That's getting off too easy. If you're really serious, I can use $5,000. No questions. I'm not expecting it—you've never exactly disgorged your dough. (George told me you wouldn't lend him the money for his store.) Still, you claim you're changing, or want to. Let's see. I don't think there's much point in another one of our talks until something is changed. Anyway, thanks for inviting me home. But why should I darken your house?

No signature.

Five thousand? What could that mean? Trouble, surely. Or was it a test. In any case, at least he knew why Reg had coughed up fifty or sixty dollars to come to Washington.

REG IN VENICE

— 1 —

Reg was amused at the arbitrariness of Venice. "It's like water," he said. "The least obstruction and there's another eddy. All these spirals, these snail shells. Like that crazy staircase we saw." This was the one called *Il Bovolo,* in the cylindrical entrance of the Palazzo Contarini. After seeing it, they'd run into Frothingham going into his favorite bar in the Calle degli Assassini. Besatcheled daubs on his back, short, hairy arms swinging a space for himself, he straightened the right one in a *Sieg Heil* salute.

"Hey there, pretty one. Dumped the old gent, have you?"

"Hi," said Bug, coldly. "This is Reg Share, George's nephew."

"Practically a contemporary," said Frothingham, shaking hands. "Do you like paintings?"

"No," said Reg.

"All right, buy me a *grappa* and I'll tell you about Venice."

Bug said, "We have to—"

"Shall do," said Reg, and they had half an hour on stools over a high wooden table, beating off Frothingham's direct and indirect appeals for subsidies, purchases, installments, loans, joint enterprises.

Mostly Bug and Reg ran into no one. Their only aim was to stay away from the Piazza and the Rialto for most of the day. "The place is like my mind," said Reg. "There's method somewhere, but you never quite get anywhere. Or if you do, you don't know where you are, and it doesn't matter. It's like a philosophical argument about free will. The stone thinks it's choosing to fall to earth. You read philosophy?"

"One survey course."

"It takes you out of yourself, then poof. The way we go about Venice is like Descartes' notion of the arbitrary: a little urge uncontrolled by reason. He said it did violence to the mind, the mind was victimized by it. You're only really free in the necessary. I feel wonderfully free wandering around like this." They were standing by a carved wellhead in a tiny *campiello*. "We don't know where we are. We have no map, but we're not lost because we don't care. If we want to get somewhere, we can ask anybody how to get to the Piazza, and eventually we'll get there. New York is bigger, but this place feels infinite."

"To me it's cozy."

"Cozily infinite, infinitely cozy. Unconditional. 'The unconditional is what can't be made into a thing.' That's Schelling. Aren't the Germans wonderful? All the philosophers, and all the music. The one I prefer is Schopenhauer."

"The misogynist?"

"He despised and lusted after women. He finished his big book, six years younger than I am, came down here to Venice with a letter of introduction to Lord Byron from Goethe, and picked up a girl on its strength. The next day they saw Byron riding his horse along the shore, the girl started babbling she was seeing a god. Schopenhauer didn't use the letter."

"You know lots, Reg."

"I know trivia. Let's take the *circolare*."

Trust Reg to find this most inexpensive of protracted boat rides. They usually took it when they were tired of curling in and out of the *calles*, *rios*, *rivas*, *campi*. They caught it in five or ten minutes of wherever they were, and, if there wasn't too much spray or sun, sat on the open back bench. They circled the main islands, getting off at a different stop each time.

For her, the feel, look, sound and smell of Venice shifted from strangeness and surprise to possession and affection. Reg was a fellow crewman in this shift, partly because she was discovering him as well. He shifted from observation to confession, from trivia to his problems. For much of his life, he'd been running in place, exhausting himself. "Never get-

ting anywhere. Daydreams. That's been the big thing for me."
He told her about a scene in a Malraux novel. "A gas attack
in World War I, these giants staggering out of the clouds of
gas. They're really two men, one sitting on the other's shoulders. So I've had a gigantic figure in my life, and it's taken me
years of shrinkwork to let me see that the giant's not only an
ordinary man, but that it's I, on his shoulders, who made him
gigantic."

"Your father."

"My version of him, protector and threat. It's awful what
happens. Love becomes resentment, admiration envy. I can't
get rid of it. It's like someone with stomach cramps. They
make him thirsty, but if he drinks, the cramps get worse. Yet
he's got to drink. Even if it kills him. I'm sorry, Bug. It's
monomania. I know it, but can't get free of it. It isn't free for
him either. Five thousand bucks."

"So that's how *you* got here."

"The Share Foundation."

"I know a little about that."

—— 2 ——

They took the boat to Torcello, brought a wicker basket with
prosciutto and goat cheese sandwiches, a bottle of George's
wine, a blanket. No bathing suits. That would have suggested
something else to George. It was necessary to see this reedy,
straggly, pond-freckled island where refugees had first made
themselves a city and which now had little more than a few
farms, expensive retreats, a great restaurant, a couple of
cafés and bars, and the church with the black, Byzantine
Madonna, a long warning finger in the hollow of a gold dome.

They separated from the fifteen other visitors at the *vapor-
etto* stop, then made their way up the main dirt road past
fields, trellises, vegetable rows, a few horses, a farmer, fruit
trees, a wooden cart, a hay wagon. The air was touched with
hay odor and the water-and-fish fragrance of the lagoon. In
the church, Reg gave the huge, severe Madonna the once-
over. "The great maternal rebuke. It's too much. Let's picnic."
They walked past farmhouses and barns, Reg a step behind,
looking at her strong legs in the denim walking shorts and
white sandals. Between the shorts and a green shirt tied at

the waist was a band of tan flesh. More than anything, this drove him through resistance and restraint. He'd worked up anger at his uncle's erotic empire, its bribing seduction. Why should Bug have to crawl into the sack with the old guy? Disgust annihilated his old affection for George. Reg was a surgeon of scruples which, at other times, advertised his superiority. Rational human beings shouldn't be chained by scruples devised by the weak to shackle them. Expert in slaking his own desires, indulging himself the quickest, cheapest, easiest way, Reg felt here a new health, a new expertise. The calves, thighs, knee-joints, the firm, denimed rear, the heart-thumping band of flesh, the collar-bone and tan neck coming out of the green shirt toward the yellow hair, the mysterious excitement of the rest of Bug, screwed into a hard need. Crazy to think of anything else. A few minutes of huffing and friction, gyrating and plunging, and that would be that. A no-loser deal. A big easy. A plus in the world. A rebuke to those antique rebukers, old-world proprietors who made copulation a stage of economic warfare. He touched Bug's arm and when she turned around, he pointed toward a patch of ground near a stand of locust trees.

The warmth, the fragrance of the fields, the distant voices, their solitude on this island, intensified Bug's awareness of Reg. George had pushed them together, had assigned her to take care of him. This was the outcome of it. What was the difference after all, touching instead of talking, a different use for the mouth, no, she didn't want to think this way, just let things happen in the isolated field out here in the lagoon.

VENICE BY AIR

— 1 —

The idea was balloons. The second idea—which came from Frothingham, one of Reg's partners—was Van Kelly Tochner, who was talked into putting up money. Reg had heard about balloon flights from Teddy French, a New Zealand pilot who ran them for the Block hotel chain in Nairobi six months a year. Reg knew at once they'd be great for Venice. He found out at the Municipio that the city didn't allow small plane or helicopter flights over it—too noisy. Silent balloons were different. Made by the Royal Society for the Blind, they were as high as a seven story building, and operated by valves on methane cylinders. Their wicker gondolas held six people, including the pilot. Ten thousand dollars could buy permission for four early morning low-wind flights taking off from Torcello. At five hundred dollars a ticket, you'd pay back the permission fees in five flights. It would take two weeks to pay off the balloon, one to pay Teddy, another to cover other expenses: insurance; the balloon assemblage and recovery crew; a motorboat to follow the balloon and pick up the passengers; champagne, chicken and croissants to welcome them back on *terra firma*. "I'm gonna use the Queen as a come-on. People will pay triple to go up with her. I'll pay her. It'll give her something to look forward to."

"You'll be the Disney of Venice," said George.

"Today Venice, tomorrow Vicenza. Who knows, we might even have a Venice-Dubrovnik crossing."

"You're really cooking, Reg."

Reg was interviewed by the *Gazzetino*. He was full of the history of balloon flight. A seventeenth century bishop named John Wilkins claimed that there'd been balloon flights from Venice; his contemporary, Cyrano de Bergerac, described journeys to the moon and sun in which travellers flew by fastening thin flasks filled with dew which was heated by the sun. "You sank," said Reg, "by breaking flasks." He briefed reporters on the linen globe of the Montgolfier brothers, the physicist Charles's silk balloon filled with hydrogen, Cavendish, Rittenhouse, Hopkinson, Count Zambecarri, Lunardi, Blanchard—"the first to cross the channel"—Reg knew them all. They were a preface to his vision of the palaces, bell towers and islands of the lagoon seen from a thousand, two thousand, three thousand feet. " *'It will be one of the great sights of the world.' said the American. 'The water city seen from the air.'* "

— 2 —

The first flight took off from Torcello. The *Gazzetino* had a reporter there, though neither the Cardinal nor the Mayor had accepted Reg's invitation to attend. Still, it was a great event. Reg had the business instincts he scorned in others. He'd made arrangements with the hotels, Cipriani's, the Gritti, the Danieli, the Bauer. They'd signed up enough people to fill ten balloons, at five hundred dollars a ride. Now there was only one balloon, but, Reg told George, two others were ordered. "What diamonds were to Rhodes and oil to Rockefellers, railroads to Harriman, jeans to Levi Strauss, hot air is to Reg Share. Not a bad slogan, Uncle George, eh? 'Reg Share's Venetian Hot Air.' "

Teddy French brought in a second pilot, an Australian colleague from Nairobi. Van Kelly Tochner was talked into putting up more money. (Reg regarded money as a smallish detail.) "Business is built on nothing. On hot air. People are dying to give you money."

"What if there's an accident, Reg?"

"Insurance. I've got everything covered. What can happen in Venice? The jerks get soaked. Which they do anyway."

A hundred publicists, tourists, friends and locals assembled to watch the first launch. The huge mat of poly-colored nylon swelled, then straightened with heated gas. The first five passengers climbed into the wicker gondola, where Teddy, in a spiffy blue safari vest with gold lion insignia, ignited the gas spouts and issued release orders to the crew. Up went the beautiful, crazy bulb, while people applauded and took pictures.

Venice by Air.

George and Bug were invited to go aloft. "No charge." It was terrific, although the wind came in over the Lido and they didn't fly over the Grand Canal or San Marco, but over Cannareggio, the railroad tracks and the automotive mess of Piazzale Roma. Still, they were up there with and beyond the bell towers as if one of the domes of the cathedral had been inspired to take off by itself and float like a king over the Queen of the Adriatic. They set down in the *ghetto nuovo*.

The motorboat followed them, streaking through the canals. The crew jumped out with weights and stakes, tied up the balloon and helped out the passengers. A hundred amazed Venetians applauded.

—— 3 ——

Within ten days, Reg's balloons had been featured in newspapers and magazines around the world. His long, clever face was better-known than his father's.

More than his face. Interviewers discovered that this son of an American diplomat was a prince of antidiplomacy, indiscreet, fluent and as full of quotable lines as a fig of meat. A week before he left Venice, George caught up with him on the fly. "Do you need to say all those things about statesmen, Reg? People may get the wrong idea. 'A statesman's a fool if he doesn't let a country pay for his personal pleasures.' That's not going to help your Dad."

"It's from the Marquis de Sade. The ignoramuses left out the quote marks. The cretins did the same thing with my King Lear quotes: 'A dog's obeyed in office'; 'Robes and furred gowns hide all'; 'Plate sin with gold, the strong lance of justice hurtless breaks.' You'd think they couldn't miss those. I can't take the blame." They were at Quadri's in the Piazza. It had become Reg's office. In the morning, when the sun hit it before noon, he went across the street to Florian's. Now he didn't breakfast with the ballooners. He had assistants for everything. His breakfast Virgil was Del Plunko, but a Del Plunko commanded into semicivility. Said Reg, "He shaves twice a day, wears white flannels, blue blazer and commander's cap. If he utters one line of poetry, he's had it. He's a natural host. It's all he wanted, a bunch of suckers listening to him."

"Maybe they garbled the quotes, but you picked them out. Just listen to them. You're plucking one string."

"Not so, George. You're picking them out. Anyway, Dad's proud of me. Obie wrote me. He's going to take a ride in the balloon when he comes over for the Rome meetings next month. He better do it then, because it's the end of the season."

"Then what are you going to do?"

"I have an idea for a religious Deer Park."

"What are you talking about?"

"You watch these TV preachers, you know, sex and fear are ninety percent of what they sell. So instead of that Disneyland park the Bakkers started, we'll work out something authentic, along the lines of Louis Quinze's Deer Park. The girls will all be spiritual. As they strip, they'll say psalms. There'll be real laying on of hands. Throw in food, you've got a Las Vegas of Salvation and Cunt. I'll make Trump look like the nothing he is. It's easy, George. I get ideas like this five times a night. I've always had them, I just never did anything about it."

—— 4 ——

Reg heard about it on the *Accademia* bridge. Sheldon called to him. "J'hear, j'hear? S'awful, s'awful. Serena. Froth. Betsy." Old ladies, children, delivery men with carts, polylingual tourists, Venetians of every stripe and shade passed them up and down the hump of the bridge. *Vaporetti* honked, gondoliers and draymen cried out. "I was at Cipriani's—my swim. I did my laps—saw Toch—collapsed. I thought he was reciting a poem: 'Balloon . . . lagoon . . . Queen . . . Seren' . . .' "

With which Reg, somehow knowing everything, was off.

—— 5 ——

His empathizing gift, the most precious and scary one he had, woke every now and then by itself, leaving him in a kind of no-space space, free of his daily self as if that had been nothing but a prop. Once, early in the summer, it had come to him in Campo San Margherita while he was licking a blackberry cone at the café. He had felt what it was like to be Bug. A wonderful, surprising feeling, full of warm, wavy drift, tranquility, acceptance. He'd felt himself shopping in the *campo* for fish, delighted at the silvery shapes.

The second time in Venice the gift woke in him, he'd entered Frothingham. This came after the catastrophe.

As it was, the flight was irregular. There were three nonpaying passengers: the Queen, Betsy and Frothingham himself. Reg didn't know about it. The flights had been going so smoothly he'd stopped showing up for them, only arriving at the end of the morning to bank the lira. Del Plunko, Frothingham and Teddy managed everything: transport from the hotels, tickets, publicity, the crew, purchase of the champagne, croissants, chicken and scampi.

Two days later, out of his head with fury, fear, worry and pity, he was wandering the back streets. Thoughts bombarded him: the deaths, the ruin, the money, the reporters, the telegrams, the fear of arrest, the questions from and about his father. Headlines zoomed in his head. Streams of print and faces, legs, arms, heads, fiery fragments of cloth, burning rainbows, falling, breaking, the poor Queen in parts, that terrible, crazy, pathetic, stupid Frothingham. Betsy. Teddy. Bits of them falling into the lagoon. Terrible. And then, like that, he was inside Frothingham: terrified, dense with hatred, the scheme coming like inspiration. Reg understood Frothingham's daubs, the expressionless faces and stick bodies, precise and mindless. Anything to divert him from the burning crookedness inside. Reg could feel Frothingham walking lumpishly with phony linebaker's swinging heaviness, briefcase in hand, inside not his daubs, but the detonator. The target of destruction—Reg felt it—was Reg, all the triumphant Reg's of the world. They'd be left holding the ruptured sack. Reg felt in Frothingham life as rage, life lived not in itself, but in an endless boil of comparison. Murder and suicide were all that could ease it.

—— 6 ——

Before they pinned it on Frothingham, everyone and everything came in for blame, Reg, the pilot, the Queen, the passengers who'd insisted on going up despite the exceptionally strong wind, the greedy Commissioners who allowed the flight in the first place. Catastrophe's hundred fathers.

The Queen had been late for this, her first flight. Frothingham had been sent to pick her up. He was late too, stopping for Dutch courage in the bar in the Calle degli Assassini. When they arrived at the Torcello launch site, the sun was doing its fierce work. Teddy, the pilot, said they'd have to postpone the flight. The passengers, who'd motor-boated over from the Danieli and the Gritti at six A.M., made a fuss. Frothingham told Teddy, "It'll be a disaster if we cancel. Cut it down to twenty minutes. There'll be an extra two hundred in it for you."

The Queen was nervous about getting into the gondola. Betsy lifted her in bodily; Frothingham pacified her. One of the passengers, a Brazilian shoe manufacturer, had a hundred pounds of video equipment. An argument about that, won by the man, augmented the Queen's uneasiness.

At last, to the cheers of the gawking locals, the gold and purple pear took off and hung in the sky. At two thousand feet it caught a breeze and sped over the lagoon to the main island. Teddy brought it down within ten yards of the Colleoni statue, then up again over San Stefano, rousing cheers and terrors in the campo. Later, some said they could hear the Queen squalling, but whether with ecstasy or terror they didn't know.

A breeze took them right over the *piazza*. Luckily, there were only a couple of hundred tourists feeding sacks of corn kernels to the pigeons. The balloon came close enough so that people reported hearing a woman's voice screaming in English, "I want to get out." Some reported seeing a struggle. "The little basket was shaking." The pilot shot flames out of the cylinders to heat the gas, and the balloon rose along the Campanile. For seconds, it seemed suspended on top of it. Then it happened.

At first it was thought that the hot copper of the angel Gabriel burned the fabric. When George and Bug first heard about it in Willsville, that was the supposition. It was also thought that the Queen had gotten hysterical and diverted Teddy long enough to cause a miscalculation. Whatever, there was a terrible bang, a terrible hissing sound and a terrible descent. The Piazza swirled in panic. Tourists, shopkeepers from the arcades, pigeons, waiters, musicians became a vortex of terror around the burning gondola. The shoe manufacturer survived long enough to supply the headline for the *New York Daily News*'s coverage: THAT GODDAMN QUEEN.

A SHARE OF THE PACIFIC

—— 1 ——

Reg discovered Moorea. Not like Captain Cook or Sieur de Bougainville, but as he discovered many things, browsing through New York bookstores. It was in a biography of Herman Melville. Melville had been arrested in Tahiti for jumping ship and was assigned to build what was still its main road, and then transferred to a plantation on Moorea, the island twelve miles northwest (then known as Eimao). What attracted Reg to Melville was that he'd been a wastrel. "He'd failed as schoolteacher, clerk, bank teller." (Reg didn't add that this happened before Melville was twenty-one.) "He had even less to brag about than I."

Thought Bug, "If only men could stop thinking about their failures and we our looks." She said, "You had a wonderful idea. It wasn't your fault it went up in smoke."

"I picked the creep. Like Bush picked Quayle. I thought I'd do what Castro did in Cuba, cure the crooks by making them policemen."

In Moorea, Reg slept ten hours, ate the hotel's boring food, looked at the ocean, went for one dip at sunset and read the paper over coffee at Mlle. Sylesie's Café.

He'd recovered from the catatonia to which he'd retreated after Venice, but was not up to opposition. For two years, his triumph was staying alive. Sometimes in dreams or daytime seizures, the sight of the falling balloon gripped him roughly. "I deserve it. I deserve it."

For a while, he was grateful to his father: whatever levers he pressed, had been the right ones. Back in Washington for consolation and recovery, Reg regained his equilibrium.

—— 2 ——

There'd been three stories about the disaster in the *Washington Post,* but Bobby, one of the administration's noblemen, came off all right. (The levers had been concealed.) Buchwald did a column; that was the worst of the publicity.

The departmental reaction was subtler. There were always reasons to oppose anyone; no weapon was neglected. Jokes were made, words like "ballooned" and "burst," phrases like "fiery descent" and "merchant of Venice" were heard more frequently than would have been the case had nothing happened to the deputy's son.

When Eileen got pneumonia, the first of the illnesses which marked her decline, Bobby resigned and became assistant general counsel to the Chemical Bank.

—— 3 ——

At night, Reg and Bug lit coils of citronella and incense that drove off mosquitoes. After their rapid and detached love sessions, Bug would wrap the green and gold *pareo* she'd bought in Papeete around her hips and legs and sit barebreasted on the porch. Lights blinked from an occasional boat. The only noise was the sea shushing the rocks. Occasionally she walked into the mild water, swam fifty or sixty yards out and floated under a new moon.

She did not sunbathe nude. Reg, excited by naked breasts and rears, plopped down in view of them. Bug watched him watch a heavy-breasted bleach-blond German reading a book called *Kassandra.* "That's probably whom he really made love with last night." Her body had no surprises for him, a far cry from Torcello.

Back in New York, they would not be together. (She had her catering business; he had himself.) Which gave their time here some piquancy. " 'The eternal bars and bolts of the ocean,' " Reg said that morning, looking up from his book. "*Robinson Crusoe.* It's the same life as New York: coffee, newspapers, walks, books, dinner, Polynesians instead of crazies. Souvenir hunting instead of the tube."

Said Bug, "So my six thousand dollars goes for nothing?"
"Finding that out is worth it."

—— 4 ——

Bug's climbing. She pushes through elephant-ear ferns like a breast-stroker, jumps from rock to rock. It's the first time here that she feels what she'd come to feel. The every-which-way of branch, twig, fern and creeper resembles her mind, a confusion of clarities. Except for the shivery scoot of lizards in the leaves, it's still. If she could only yield all the way, it might be sublime, but she's scared of being lost. Still there's intimacy here, a cousinship of sorts with other life, other things, the black brook, the ferns.

On one of the coral islets, Reg is having a picnic with the waiters. "A coup for me," he said. "I offer them Tiparillos and they invite me."

"Maybe I'll take the historic tour of the island," she said.

"They don't have history here."

"They have troubles like other people. Why not history?"

But she climbed instead, following the dirt road past the Rupe-Rupe ranch, up the conical mountain, breast-stroking and jumping. She used Reg's switchblade to cut herself a bouquet of scarlet flowers and arranged them like an offering in a clearing by a rock almost her size. It was actually three blocks piled to make a rough figure. "A *tiki*," she thought. "Or maybe it wasn't godlike enough for that." It was god enough for her.

A frigate bird glided by. "Soar, my heart," said Bug. She'd come ten thousand expensive miles to a tropical dot in the middle of the Pacific, climbed a few hundred feet through thoughtless shrubs, bumped into an almost-shrine, and tried to guru up release on a bird's wing. She put her arms around the maybe-god. "Give me a break," she said. "Earn your keep."

—— 5 ——

"How was your walk?" asked Reg.
"Climb."
"Your climb?"
"Something to remember."

"Memorable, then."

"Depends."

"On?"

"I'm hungry. You ready?"

"On?"

"Like everything else, me."

On the porch, they watched the sun plunge into the sea. There were lots of colors tonight, then the green flash, the final color. The eight other guests exhaled appreciation for the quotidian show.

Said Reg, "I was talking with the blond guy at reception. He's married to a local woman. He's been here six years and thinks I could get a job here. Could you stand it here?"

"I? Why I? No, I couldn't."

"I, on the other hand, could. I feel a George-like desire to start something again. An entrepreneurial twitch. On the ground this time."

"You're cashing in the return?"

"Thinking of it."

Bug started to say something, then held back, as, all her life, in the interests of harmony, she'd held back. Reg saw her hold and said, "I regard it as a loan, Bug. A wonderful generosity, but a loan. One of the things I'd live for would be to pay you back."

"I don't need it. I don't want it. But I appreciate it." It was nice of him. Decency was nice. More than nice. Beautiful. "Let's have coffee at Mlle. Sylesie's."

"My treat," said Reg.

PART·IV

TWO
STORIES

THE ANAXIMANDER FRAGMENT

—— 1 ——

Nibbenour arrived the day after Thanksgiving. Five of us, sitting in the shade of the tent, hear this rough purr and see a six-wheel wombat coming out of the Great Nothing, pulling up to our twelve puffs of grass. Out come four helmets; one's removed, and there's a mess of brown curls. "Nibbenour," she says. "You guys wanna see the C-I-C's autograph?"

Dubbda: "General Blackhead's?"

"*The* C-I-C, dummy." Dubbda has a pharmacist's degree from Georgia State. "Your President. We ate Thanksgiving with'm."

Dubbda: "Old Bird-in-the-Hand himself?"

She hands over polaroids, one of her and President B. stuffing their faces, the other him autographing the wombat's rear end.

We went over—not Vlach, he's reading—and there it was, a purple scrawl.

Pelz: "What's he like?"

Nibbenour: "Big. And built, for an old guy. Laughs. A lot."

Dubbda: "You thank him for sending us to the resort?"

"Right place, right time, and the right butt-kickers is what I told'm."

Dubbda: "A news-bite."

Nibbenour: "Wanna see The Fox?"

Nothing was playing at the movies, we took the tour: amphibious, six tires, back two silicon, suck up what they ride on, heat it five hundred degrees Fahrenheit, analyze it for nerve agents, radiation, mustard gas, then crap weighted warning markers. "Nice?" Nibbenour's got grey eyes, rimless librarian specs, is built low like The Fox.

Pelz: "I prefer the M-9." The M-9 knocks holes in the big sand berms.

Dubbda: "The M-60 for me." The M-60 rolls out a sixty-foot bridge for ditches, wadis.

Vlach's reading. Nibbenour calls over, "What's with you, soldier? Got something up it for the C-I-C?" Vlach has black eyes and a rug of black hair slapped down like an after-thought. "Excuse me?"

"The President. Chief Medicine Man. You American?"

"North American."

"Christ. Pawnee? Cheyenne? Navaho?" Vlach's dark-com-plected, has a big, straight nose, could be Indian.

"Excuse me?"

"Forget it." Sticks out a little mitt. "Nibbenour."

Vlach went over and shook it. "Vlach."

"Where you from, Flak?"

I could see him taking that question in, *thinking* about it. I'm next to him in the tent, know his ways. She was about to throw in the conversational towel. "*To apeiron*," he said.

"Wherezat? Carolina?"

I stepped in for him. "Georgia. He's a professor in Savan-nah."

"Well, well, you and I are going to have lots to talk about. Whaddya profess?"

Vlach tossed that around about twenty seconds. "Skepti-cism."

Nibbenour: "That's a course?"

I: "He teaches Humanities. At Armstrong."

Nibbenour: "You his translator?"

Vlach looks at us as if we're in an aquarium.

I: "He bunks next to me."

Nibbenour: "I'll bet. On, over and between."

—— 2 ——

We're activated reserves out of Ft. Stewart, Georgia. Nib-benour's RA, stationed in Bad Nauheim. No dummy, a soil technican. Mail call, she gets subscriptions, *Newsweek, Army Times, Scientific American,* three or four others I don't know.

Waiting for the war, she took on everyone. It'd be late afternoon, the sun sliding off the desert, full of color instead of bricks of glare, and here comes Nibbenour with her MRE (our plastic food), boots, camo-pants, gas mask at the belt, a red T-shirt with SO ARE YOU over what's there. "What you Einsteins think of—?" It could be anything, Bush, Baker, Baghdad Charlie, Arabs, Madonna, newspapers, Picasso, alternative fuels, satellite grids, the superiority—her favorite— of women to men in or out of combat. Somebody would answer, she'd top him, he'd agree or he'd top her and get challenged: "Dummy." "Paper face." "Pig balls." The mitts would fist, she'd spread her legs, toss up her chin. "You looking for a guided tour of your asshole?"

Most of us got out of her way. Which left Vlach, who had no evasion skills. Somehow they talked, they walked—usually into the old lava bed, the *harra*, or behind the pile of rocks Nibbenour said was a Crusader castle.

She told Pelz, "Vlach and me're on another plane of discussion."

—— 3 ——

Vlach did what we all did. Up at ten, gear, rifle, mask, then crawling, sand in our mouths, noses, boots. We lay down smoke, fire beehives—pellets—flares, follow The Fox, the earth movers, cross ditches on fascines—plastic tubes dropped from tanks—back at four or five, the blue tent like Buckingham Palace, sleep the best thing on earth.

Vlach wasn't strong, but he made it, night after night after night.

Bunk four feet from a guy, he becomes part of you: his noises, smells, habits are like the hard ground and the cold, part of your life.

Wake to drink or piss, he's reading with a pencil light. He had four books. When I finished my three, I asked did he want to exchange. He hands one over: *Heidegger and the Anaximander Fragment.*

"A mystery?" Surprised, I'd figured him for *Crime and Punishment* or *Rabbit Something.*

"Unfortunately."

"Thought you'd be going for better-class stuff. Hemingway. Elmore Leonard."

"Don't know them."

He handed over the book. I turned pages, read words; a blind man at the silent movie. "I don't get it. Not a sentence."

"People study it for years they don't get it."

"So what's going on?"

He shook his head.

"You don't know?"

"I don't know if I know."

"I like to know things. Tell me what you know."

So he went on about Greek philosophers before Plato— who we read in Hum II—how there were only fragments of them quoted in other fragments. "I'm studying two sentences by Anaximander. Five hundred B.C."

"What are they? In plain English."

"It's not plain."

"Maybe you should switch sentences."

"Too late."

"Gimme a general idea, just the subject matter."

"Where things come from, what happens to them when they're here."

"Physics."

"Metaphysics was physics."

"And the words. The real words. I don't mean the Greek."

"I don't know Greek."

What does he know? Spending years figuring out a few words, he doesn't even know the right words.

He turned pages, pointed. There were two sentences in italics. I got out the tablet I write home on and copied them down.

The first wasn't bad. *"The beginning and origin of existing things is the unlimited (to apeiron)."*

"That's not bad," I said. "It's like Genesis."

"Yes."

"To apeiron. Greek?"

"Greek."

"Why throw it in?"

"It can mean different things. That's one of the problems."

The second sentence was something else: " '*Out of which, however, becoming relates to existing things, even though it also exists in what lies beyond; passing into obligation, for they pay just penalty and retribution to each other for their injustice, according to the disposition of time.*' Something sounds wrong here."

"That's what happens. Things get passed on, mouth to mouth, parchment to parchment, and something drops off. The idea's to recover what the man thought."

"They can't even do that with this thief in Baghdad."

Out of the back of the tent, Dubbda or Oxenhandler, came a "Break it off."

"Outside," I said.

It's cold. A big moon lights the desert, looks like a huge lion. Forty billion stars. If it wasn't for what was going to happen, it wouldn't be bad. It was a place to talk about big things. Our brain cells might be doing some of the last work of their life.

Vlach's a little guy, the head fools you. It's good to have a guy like this, thinking of something else than what Mom cooks for dinner. "So whatta you think, Vlach? What did the old Greek mean?"

The big nose tilts out to the *harra*. "It almost makes sense out here." He nods a while. I'm patient, I have no appointments. "Erosion," he says. "Things losing shape, meaning. Just by coming into existence. Existence disturbs the order of things so it has to be punished. Like this desert's the punishment for the green that used to be here. Or death. Our punishment."

"Not for a while, though, right?"

"War's speeded up punishment."

"That sounds like Jimmy Swaggart."

That he doesn't get either.

—— 4 ——

I'm mixed about fleshy women. I appreciate a lot of flesh, if it isn't jouncing around. (Joke: He: "Is this it?" She: "No, that's a fold.") Fleshiness can mean a woman believes in herself, isn't tuning in to what other people want. Or it can mean she's out of touch, selfish, greedy, you're just another mouthful to her. Nibbenour? I'm not sure. If you like the person, you like the looks. I got used to her. She came on strong, no apology. (Why should there be?)

We didn't see that much of her. The Fox takes off an hour before we do. At base, the crew work it over, study the readouts, check its parts, treat it like you treat a new car. Still, every two or three late afternoons she was over, sometimes with Shirlee, who started walking around with Pelz, while Nibbenour ate and walked off with Vlach. You could see them talking, arguing, getting into things. Vlach watched her, hard, like he read his fragment. Nibbenour changed too: this down-to-earth, charged-up, tough-mouthed person with the strong arms out of her T-shirt, her good bottom and good top, became sort of airy, made little flutter gestures, didn't bark so much. If you were looking at her when Vlach talked, her eyes goggled; she'd taken off her specs.

Fear shows in the gut, jealousy in the stomach. Maybe jealousy's not the right word. I had no right to be jealous, not of Vlach. Maybe it was that out there, everybody else ten thousand miles away from those he cared about, these two had found each other.

—— 5 ——

"What do you two talk about?"

Vlach wouldn't say, "It's none of your business." He just buttoned up.

"Sorry," I said. "None of my business."

"Philosophy," he said. "She has an aptitude."

"You like her!"

"I like talking to her."

"You like looking at her?"

We're outside the tent, in the dark. "When I see her, it's pleasing."

What a person, I thought. Here we are in the middle of nothing, and this odd ghoul is making it. "You like to touch her?"

Nothing.

"So something's cooking?" Silence. "You and Nibbenour." I felt him thinking. "You and she take your little walks behind the tower." Nothing. "You been together? You made it?" Zero. "You made love? You know, fucked?"

"Twice."

___ 6 ___

Christmas we had something like a meal—turkey, cranberry slabs, stuffing that didn't taste like pillow-filling. There was a plastic tree, toilet paper ribbons, pop-can rings, and underneath, packages from the States, half from strangers, candy, books, games, cards ("How we love you!"). Some liked all that.

Vlach opened neither letters nor packages. He never got personal mail.

"Your folks don't write?"

"Dead. No wife."

Naturally. I take this cactus as my lawful wedded husband. "Free as a bird, eh?"

"Freer." Then, not to explain, just thinking aloud. "It's not easy to be."

"Free?"

"Yes. And alone."

"That's what you like?"

"It's what I use." The beak tilted—to the *harra*, the dunes, the sky. "Thought comes from this."

"There's nothing else to think about. But no Platos, right?"

"Maybe they kept what they found to themselves."

He walked off. And ran into Nibbenour, decked out: bead necklace, silvery earrings, red T-shirt with the SO ARE YOU. Carrying a Christmas box with a yellow ribbon. "Merry Christmas, Walter." She handed it to him.

He didn't take it. She untied the ribbon, took out a Jack-in-the-box (some kid from Kansas sacrificing his present?), wound it up to "Hickory Dickory Doc," and whammo, out pops a red-nosed clown.

Vlach: "What's this mean?"

Nibbenour: "It's all I have for you."

Vlach: "It's more than all you have. And less than nothing. Save it for your children."

I watched Nibbenour's lights dim. Not pretty. Seeing me see it, she handed the box to me. "Merry X, Potts."

—— 7 ——

Pelz, out with Shirlee, saw them. "Thought it was a mirage. 'They dancing?' Shirlee asks. 'Or doing a Chinese exercise?' Then we realize. Crazy. They're hitting each other, slugging, kicking. Vlach and Nibbenour. Claws. You seen him yet? She did him good."

He's in the tent, doubled over, bloody, right eye closed, big-lipped, cheek swollen, rubbing his side, groaning. I could just make out "Kidneys. Get a medic. She kicked me."

—— 8 ——

The next day, they helicopter him to Dhahran. Nobody said anything about Nibbenour. He'd asked for what he got. I saw him just before, in the medic's tent, blanketed to the chin, face purple, eye swollen shut. (The other looked at peace.) "You lucky bastard," I say. "You're gettin' out of here." (Though of all the Americans in Arabia, Vlach was probably most at home.) "How are you?" He had an arm outside the blanket. He points it to his face, meaning "See for yourself." But there's a little smile on it, another little message: "I'm fine."

"What in hell was it all about?"

He made some sounds. I wouldn't have understood if he hadn't given me the Anaximander poop. "Punishment . . . penalty . . . retribution."

"She was angry at you for ignoring her, refusing her?"

"I provoked her."

"I saw you. Wasn't like you. Why?"

He went on a while. What I made out was something like this: "Something came into existence between us. We disturbed the order of things; we had to pay the penalty."

The crazy coot's fragment had gone to his head; like nerve gas. He'd taken that Greek fog literally. He fought over it, fought on principle. Or so he thought.

Anyway, he does something then that surprises me, stretches out his hand and looks at mine until it shakes his, then, "Hope you make it out okay, Hugo." I didn't know he cared enough for anything human to say that.

—— 9 ——

The third week of February, we took off, like a line of steel bats, in a big loop west. Twenty-five hours over sand, the only breaks planes cracking the glare and a few guys driving shaggy goats. They hardly looked at what must have been quite a sight. Maybe they'd seen the desert swallow up everything, why not us?

Looping east, we run into berms, ditches, wire, antennas, coming out of the sand. We tank through, bridge ditches, blow explosives. We take no fire, just prisoners, starved-looking guys materializing out of lids in the sand, waving undershirts, yelling, sometimes English—"Peace, us want, hello, thank you"—raising their arms, falling on their knees. We give them water, feed them.

Then the news, it's over. We haven't lost a man. We haven't taken fire. It's done, the air did it. It was crazy, wonderful, we'd be home before spring.

We drive south on what Dubbda calls "death row." A river of busted steel: tanks, every kind of armor, broken, smashed, charred, or just turned over, just left. Men in some of them, parts of men, and stuff: carpets, TV's, dresses, piles of new shirts in cellophane, hair dryers, calculators, neckties, a carton of lipsticks, digital watches, gold necklaces, electric fryers, tires, boxes of pills.

Sights: a pair of arms hugging an air conditioner, no body; a uniformed arm on a window sill, no body; a shoulder, nothing else; a head of hair on half a face in the sand, nothing else; bodies swelled triple size; two guys in the front seat of a jeep, carbonized like marshmallows; a mustached guy, an officer, his hands on a wheel, and in back of his face and chest, nothing, gunk.

Some motors were running, radios playing.

The smell: take a vinegar factory, a thousand rotten eggs, a million gallons of wolf piss, age in hatred and inject it through your nostrils into your brain.

Near the border, hundred-foot spools of black smoke, the sky like a thunderstorm.

Dubbda and I walked off the road and heard "The Blue Danube." It's coming from a dead kid, seventeen, maybe less, in uniform. In his hand's a music box. "Take it for a souvenir," said Dubbda.

I didn't; neither did he.

All this built in me, I don't know what. The night before we took off from Dhahran, I let some of it out writing the longest letter I ever wrote. Odd thing is I sent it not to my folks—my mom doesn't take to bad things, won't listen, shuts her eyes—but to Vlach, care of the Philosophy Department, Armstrong College, Savannah.

—— 10 ——

We got back March sixteenth. The folks drove down to Ft. Stewart, so there was a big show. Turns you into what you're not, which once in a while is all right. Ten days later, things are back where they'd been, I'm doing accounts at Jordan's. Fine with me, numbers are my thing.

I take up where I'd left off looking for my own place and someone to live there with. I tell my war stories. They don't go over right; not enough blood, maybe.

I meant to call Vlach when I was in Savannah, thought of it a few times when I was home, figured I'd drive down some weekend; but there'd been no answer to my letter, I figured he wasn't interested. He had his own numbers. Then, too, he might not've wanted to be reminded of his little Desert Storm.

I watch the evening news. The minute we left, the Iraqis started banging each other around. After the first week or two, Mustache looked firm in the saddle. End of April, the news showed him on his birthday, walking through a room in a white suit, little girls kissing his cheeks, and what the reporter said was the Iraq Symphony Orchestra—nine gee-zers in white blouses—playing "I Did It My Way." That broke it for me.

Mama said, "*What* is humorous, Hugo? Ah didn't see anything humorous."

"I wish I'd thought to send him a present." I should have kept Nibbenour's jack-in-the-box. It would have been worth twenty bucks to send it to him, the mother of all jack-in-the-boxes.

—— 11 ——

May first, a Wednesday, a letter from Vlach. It had gone through APO to Dhahran and followed me back. Green ink on an Armstrong College memo pad sheet. No "Dear Potts," let alone "Dear Hugo." Just

Glad you and the others came through.

I hope you won't have to pay for not having paid enough. Looks like the unit's only casualty was yours truly. Your account of those human fragments wiped mine out. I'm thinking of another one. By Heraclitus. Immortal mortals (athánatoi thanetoi), mortal immortals, living their death, dying their life.

If you have any ideas about it, write me, same address. He did sign off—it made me feel good—Your friend, W. Vlach.

IN A WORD, TROWBRIDGE

Her name, a famous name for—as she saw and felt it—a nonentity, was what the policeman who called the ambulance heard her saying: "Trowbridge." The name that made her something before she was anything was what she said when she could say nothing else. The mugger had clubbed her behind the right ear. The two syllables full of rectitude and connectedness, were, apparently, what sustained her. Her identity, her stake in the world. What her mother claimed she took too lightly. (Though she'd kept the name *she'd* grown with, she'd married in part for that name. Her own fame was underwritten by it, as a great corporation looms behind its subsidiaries.)

That Charlotte had been born with the name provoked her mother. That she could "drag it into the mud" was a disgrace. Her "slovenliness, imprecision, ignorance and carelessness," bad in themselves, were monstrous because she was a Trowbridge. Once, an unforgettable once, the maternal indictment was "ugliness." Torrents of babble about cuteness, prettiness, even beauty did not annul that. Her long Trowbridge jaw and nostrils, her hyperthyroid eyes confirmed it. The sense of ugliness lit her victimage, spotlit her head for muggers.

She was the Trowbridge who served as a subject of parental anecdotes, parental pride in the fact of parentage.

Charlotte Trowbridge.

A monicker out of nineteenth-century arrogance. Nineteen

letters, enough for three names; French topping of Anglo-Saxon assertiveness; a scoop of New England pride in plain-ness. "Family,", it proclaimed. "Old American stock."

Part of what sustained her father in the fugal wildness of his life: monumental idleness and monumental frenzy. The Great American Painter of His Time. His gallantry, foolishness, pu-rity, jokes, his proclamations and marching for causes; his famous refusals. "I prefer not to." The Great Novelist said he "was carted around like a piece of the true cross." All that uprightness and, on the nightside of his life, the careening on the razor's edge, fights, binges, arrests, outrages of every sort; his public abandonment of Mother; marriage to the French actress; fathering the doomed twins; leaving them all for the Swedish premier's wife; getting arrested with the Los Angeles drug gang whom he painted into his Last Judgment as angels, while his wives and children struggled in loony abstraction between Hell and Purgatory. Finally, the return to Mother and the pathetic death on the 81st Street platform of the Independent Subway station, embracing and sliding down the iron pillar, curled in a great heap, ignored for hours until the old woman—who claimed she heard his last words—called a policeman. " 'Take it,' " she said he'd said. " 'Take it.' " "But the strange thing," wrote the *Times* reporter, "was that nothing appeared to have been taken. Henry Trowbridge died with his watch and wallet. No thief or mugger had touched him."

Take it.

His words. Charlotte's would have been, "You can't take it." Or "I don't have anything to give." Like Mother's. Mother had grown up poor in a house full of sisters who had nothing but each other. Anything received or taken was held on to des-perately. The crime of crimes was theft. Under it lay the fearfulness of starved egos. No prosperity repaired it, no praise, no prizes displaced the sense that others wanted what you had and were. So Mother would do anything to keep whatever she had, money, reputation, power. She served on every committee which distributed memberships or awards. If she could not win prizes herself, she could at least control who got them.

Take it.

Father gave, and gave easily, time, money, self. He'd been given the adoration of a brilliant, resentful mother, was deferred to by a shaky father, relished the large stage of onlychild-dom. Huge, strong, wilful, awkward, he was a bully, a leader, smart, energetic, good-looking, self-confident of his place and power. All this until his system trapped itself. He "paid for" the power with terrifying mental storms. A month of ecstatic ebullience became two of paralysing fatigue. "To tie a shoelace," he told ten-year-old Charlotte, "is as hard as painting the Sistine Chapel." In the Sixties, the Danes came up with the lithium salts which planed off the heights and depths and gave him an extra decade. Meanwhile, his escapades and his talent made him the best-known American painter of his time.

"Take it." Because he'd grown with love at the top of the world, country houses, town houses, classes in everything from carving to the fox trot. After a year at Yale, he declared himself a painter and took off for Paris, Arles, Brittany, the valley towns of Idaho and Montana. He created what made his name count for more than property and family history. And it was then that he began to feel for those whose rights were concealed by all they lacked.

Take it.

He gave to the tyrannised, the insulted, the bedeviled, the wounded, the nameless. He fattened the American myth of the noble democrat. It went back to Saint Francis, to Gautama, up through the patriots of Massachusetts and Virginia to the Roosevelts and the latest, thinnest White House version of it.

What was not so conspicuously American was the erotic give-and-take, the women in and out of his life. When mania charged his system, he took off, emptying bank accounts to buy up the world for these transient enchanters, his muses, his subjects. Painted onto the walls and canvases of contemporary culture, they became her mother's public humiliation. What was worse were his public apologies to her.

No wonder that neither Charlotte nor her mother could have said, "Take it." She could not give *anything,* let alone the most private part of her self. So she was withering into what Mother couldn't bear (though she herself hadn't married till she was thirty-five). For Mother, though, it had been independence and a self-advertised sexual free-for-all. Charlotte was simply a spinster, like her great-great aunts. Not a virgin, not lesbian, neither self-sufficient nor independent, but alone, a large, clumsy, half-pretty offshoot of two famous Americans, one a proclaimed genius, the other an efficient, useful caretaker and servant of the arts.

It wasn't until the huge biography of her father came out that she learned why she'd been destined for spinsterhood. More, why she'd been meant not to exist.

"I won't put this madness into a child," he'd told friends. The biographer said nothing about a mistake, they'd not married because she'd been started; it was two years after their marriage and a dozen before the lithium, so *why was she?*

Welcomed, cheered, a famous baby, alluded to in hundreds of letters—her infantile doings documented like a king's—painted as often as an infanta or the Picasso and Renoir children, by age five, she had a niche in cultural history, was a subject of dissertations.

Not a hint that a girl was less welcome than a boy, somehow she knew that. First destined not to be, then to be an only male child, and finally, an unfruitful woman. Not only the name, but the line of Henry Trowbridge and Vanna Peete would stop with her. Trowbridge cousins could, would and did perpetuate the name that festooned streets, but she would exist only to entitle her parents: *father, mother.* Still, Father would say, "When you have your children." Grandfatherdom appealed to him more than fatherhood, fattened his large, if ironic affection for continuity, transmission, the variation of features. He would have relished seeing refigurations of himself and his parents. (His paintings were full of familial variation. A cover story in *Vanity Fair* called him "The Last Portraitist.")

But his drive to her motherhood was stopped by Mother.

At first, it was the standard mother-daugher cut-down. Her few friends suffered similar cuts and, by adolescence, recognized the sexual rivalry. Here, though, there was intellectual rivalry as well. Not since her father had raved about a kindergarten drawing, which he'd framed and put into his studio, had she known anything but dismissal of any accomplishment, drawn, written, played, thought out. At best, there was laughter or the patronising dismissal of "charm," "amateur ease," "sweet," maybe "moving" or "touching." What counted was the annihilation of whatever gift the child of two artists would more than possibly show. It was a systematic refrigeration which she felt in her whole being.

And there was an erotic complement. Anyone who hugged or kissed her was eyed like a rapist; even Father could be made to blush for a hearty kiss, a second-longer-than-necessary embrace.

"I don't think you have the legs for that dress." "Your shoulders are too defined for décolletage." "You're developing a pubescent paunch." "I don't think boys admire aggressive charm."

Or life-lasting touches, twists, slaps, looks. The clearest messages she ever got.

What she also learned from the biography was Mother's self-advertised bed-hopping. Not only the easiest lay in American Bohemia but the readiest recorder of sexual performance. With—and Charlotte knew this deeply—about as much erotic feeling as the recording typewriter. Mother was the sort of woman who looked as if she'd once been beautiful. Father had met her when they were both thirty-five—no, Mother was two years older, a preserved secret—she'd just started looking pretty, her legs halfway between youthful stems and the soft trunks they were now. She'd also just painted the only good painting of her career and begun writing the art criticism that became the source of her influence. For the ambitious, uncertain, shrewd, troubled, gifted painter, she was an attraction, a catch. Mother's father had walked away from home when she was eight, she had no sense of or need for a man around the house. She'd made it on her own in difficult New York, she was proud and independent, but there were also fears that things would not last; she never trusted the affection of others; besides, if she wanted a child, it was time to have it. Henry was funny, attractive, learned, gifted, he could make money and had some coming to him; and there was that tremendous name that automatically earned what almost no achievement could—since achievement was its contradiction. (Achievement represented present and future, the name the past.) "So, daughter, despite his rough times—I had no idea how rough they were, how rough they'd be—I married him."

Charlotte lived seventy blocks south and four east of the apartment in which she'd grown up. Not all that far by cab or train, but too far for mother and daughter. How often Mother thought of her now she didn't know. Once in a while the phone would ring and be hung up at her "Hello," Mother checking to see if she were alive, not caring to speak to her. She lived on 12th Street west of Broadway, an old brownstone neighborhood publishing companies were just moving into. It felt like the New York her parents knew in the Thirties and Forties. She lived above a Vietnamese Cleaner-Tailor, below a charming, gay retired high school teacher who was writing a novel about eighteenth-century New York. Which she'd agreed to read. (It "revealed" a totally homosexual society, from Washington and Hamilton to pirates and scullery maids. Felix said, "It is completely researched.") In return for the reading, he gave her his sister's dress, the only really beautiful one she'd ever owned.

Wouldn't you know it was the dress she wore the night she'd been clubbed? The taxi had stopped a block from the entrance, a standard precaution. Her young man was up to a verbal grab and suggested another date. She went off with relief toward a warm bath. She walked the block without fear or thought, "Call soon," just off her lips and a touch of lips on them, in mind, the relief which sealed her all-but-technical virginity. (Twenty years before, a Trowbridge cousin had fucked her twice.) In the penumbra of the streetlight, her head was crunched, she was gripped, thrown, kicked and, while out, robbed. Left in a heap like the one Father made in the subway station an ocean away from his official wife and the insane twins who divided the trust with her. She must have lain in her heap about as long as he'd lain in his before the policeman who called the ambulance had been called by the early-waking novelist off for his morning Egg MacMuffin.

Swathed and befogged, a floating zero, a vague pain zone, she lay in a white room at St. Vincent's. "Trowbridge, Trowbridge." (Enough to get Mother down, her blue eyes terrified—at last—with the fear that she might lose what she'd more or less thrown away.) She reclaimed Charlotte who came slowly back into what made her Charlotte. She was visited by Samantha, who'd been at Miss Hewitt's and Brearley with her, by Tiffany who'd roomed with her at Bryn Mawr, by Eliza, who'd worked with her at the Whitney, and Andrea, who'd been her boss at Sotheby's. So life was reassembled, Mother guiding, directing, interpreting.

Then it was time to leave the white room. The beautiful, ripped dress was pushed into the overnight bag in which Mother had brought a schoolgirl's skirt and blouse. She was left off at her own place under Felix and above Le Tho Cleaning and Repair. Her place. After all, she was a Trowbridge, strong enough to either add something to the name or to resist the subtraction willed on it by others. "I'm just the age you were when you married, Mother, when you and Daddy began doing the best work of your life."

Not that she was setting up a rivalry. Success was less important than resolve. Success was transient and problematic, resolve was a way of existing. No point in continuity if it wasn't inspired by that. If you had the confidence of your name, you were even prepared to lose it. That too was not out of the question, so maybe, Mother, you'll dance at my wedding, clumsy at that as you, Daddy and I always were at it; anyway, be prepared. I say that giving you more than you gave me, which doesn't mean I don't care what happens to you. On the contrary, but the terms are altered. It's time for the old to be old, the young to be whatever they are—it passed me by—and us middlers to do whatever it is we can, which, the way I feel now—tossing the bagstrap over her shoulder with the ease of a climber—is plenty.